HYSTERIA

Megan Miranda

BLOOMSBURY
NEW YORK LONDON OXFORD NEW DELHI SYDNEY

First published in the United States of America in February 2013
by Walker Books for Young Readers, an imprint of Bloomsbury Publishing, Inc.
Paperback edition published in January 2014
www.bloomsbury.com

For information about permission to reproduce selections from this book, write to Permissions, Bloomsbury Children's Books, 1385 Broadway, New York, New York 10018
Bloomsbury books may be purchased for business or promotional use. For information on bulk purchases please contact Macmillan Corporate and Premium Sales Department at specialmarkets@macmillan.com

The Library of Congress has cataloged the hardcover edition as follows:
Miranda, Megan.
Hysteria / by Megan Miranda.
p. cm.
Summary: After stabbing and killing her boyfriend, sixteen-year-old Mallory, who has no memory of the event, is sent away to a boarding school to escape the gossip and threats, but someone or something is following her.
ISBN 978-0-8027-2310-9 (hardcover)
[1. Death—Fiction. 2. Memory—Fiction. 3. Boarding schools—Fiction. 4. Schools—Fiction.]
I. Title.
PZ7.M67352Hy 2013 [Fic]—dc23 2012015780

ISBN 978-0-8027-3592-8 (paperback) • ISBN 978-0-8027-2328-4 (e-book)

Book design by Nicole Gastonguay and John Candell
Typeset by Westchester Book Composition
Printed and bound in the U.S.A.
6 8 10 9 7 5

For Luis, who reminded me
of the dream that I had forgotten

CHAPTER 1

My mother hid the knife block.

In hindsight, that was the first sign. And then, two nights ago, she locked her bedroom door. It had to be subconscious, but still, I didn't want to think too hard about what she was secretly thinking. I guess that was the second sign. And now there was a suitcase on my bed. Which wasn't really a sign at all. It was the actual event.

The suitcase was full, bulging at the top, but nothing seemed missing from my closet. Jean skirts. Check. Twenty thousand tank tops. Check. Floor covered with mismatched flip-flops. Check. When I unzipped the top and peered inside, all the hope drained out of me in a single breath. Khaki pants, tags still on. A stack of identical collared shirts. I recognized the emblem from my father's old pictures. Gold crest on red material. Oh, excuse me, not red—*scarlet*.

Those were the colors at Monroe Prep. Gold for victory, scarlet for the bond of blood. They were wrong, though. Scarlet was not the color of blood. And despite what Nathaniel Hawthorne led me to believe, it wasn't the color of shame either.

I should know.

Brian's blood had stained the kitchen tiles a fire-engine red. And as I watched him slide to the floor, the color I felt inside was a deep, deep burgundy.

I closed the suitcase, tiptoed down the wooden steps, and curled my toes on the cold tiled floor. The air conditioner was set too low and the vent rattled above my head. It was Labor Day weekend, humid, practically stifling, but using the air conditioner was a new thing in our house. We were a block from the beach and the cross breeze kept things perfectly cool as long as the windows were open.

But we didn't open the windows anymore.

I walked toward the couch where my parents were busy ignoring me and rubbed at the goose bumps forming on my arms—partially from the artificially cold air, but mostly from the feeling coming from behind me, from the kitchen. Like a high-pitched frequency with no sound. I kept my back to it.

Dad had the newspaper folded open to the crossword puzzle in his lap, and Mom had her feet propped up on the coffee table, painting her toenails a pale pink. But her hands kept shaking, and the pink seeped out from the borders and onto her skin, spreading like blood.

I cleared my throat, and Dad looked up. Mom concentrated on her shaking hand, like she wasn't sure what it would do next.

"You're sending me to Monroe," I said. I phrased it like an accusation, but it still came out sounding like a question.

Mom closed the bottle of polish and frowned at her feet. She wiped her nails with her bare hand. Then she looked at her palm like she was confused about how the color got there, mumbled to herself, and walked into the kitchen. She didn't seem to notice that the kitchen was pulsating.

Dad spoke. "Mallory, we're incredibly fortunate. They usually don't accept applications this late in the process. But given the circumstances, and given my connections, they were willing to make an exception."

"The circumstances?" I asked, but he didn't respond. Must've been an interesting conversation. *We have a bit of a* situation, *being that my daughter killed a boy—specifically, her boyfriend—in our kitchen, and people are really none too pleased about that here, you see.*

He could rearrange the sentence any way he chose. It'd still end with me holding the knife and Brian dying on the floor.

Mom walked back to the couch, drying her hands on a dish towel. "Mom?" I asked. This wasn't the first time Dad had tried to send me to Monroe. As a kid, he had dragged me to reunions and weddings and charity golf tournaments. I guess he just expected I'd eventually go there, like most alumni kids. So two years ago, before the start of freshman year, he had sent in a preliminary application. Mom got the phone call from the school requesting my transcript. It didn't go over well.

"Over my dead body," she had said back then.

Now she still wouldn't look at me. She opened the nail polish, propped her feet up, and started again. "It's a fresh start," she said to her toes.

Apparently, two years ago, my mother had lied. Apparently, any dead body would do.

I ran back upstairs, taking the steps two at a time, and dialed Colleen's number. Someone answered and promptly hung up. I tried her cell phone, but it went straight to voice mail. Still grounded. Colleen was always getting grounded, though it had never lasted this long before.

She typically got a weekend of house arrest for sneaking out at night. She was sentenced to three days for plagiarizing an English paper once, but it was midweek, so that barely even counted. And that one time she lugged her mom's supply of alcohol down to the beach in her guitar case and the cops dragged her home got her two full weeks. I ran when the cops showed.

I always ran.

This punishment was going on six weeks. Six weeks for one lie. Such a waste. No matter what she told the police, I wasn't going to be charged. That's what my lawyer said anyway.

He'd been here the week before, when the knife block was still on the counter and my parents still left their bedroom door unlocked. John Defano or Defarlo or something. He was tanning-bed dark with slicked-back hair, bleached teeth, and a gold chain that was visible if his collar was unbuttoned (which it was)—and he was, unfortunately, as sleazy as he looked.

"Mallory Murphy," he'd said, scanning my tanned legs resting on the coffee table. "Just rolls off the tongue."

"So does Lolita," I mumbled, picking at a nearly invisible speck on the sofa. But then I stopped digging at the couch cushion and stared at him, at his unnaturally white teeth smiling at me.

The lawyer had never spoken to me before. It was always, "Keep her inside," or "Don't let her talk to anyone," with a thumb jutting in my general direction. And now he was talking to me. And smiling. Even my parents could sense it. They leaned forward in their seats, practically salivating for the news.

"It's over," he'd said. Mom jumped up and looked around like she wanted to grab onto someone. Possibly me. Instead she wrapped the lawyer in an awkward hug. Then Dad and the lawyer did this overly enthusiastic handshaking, and Dad smiled so wide I could see his gums. Then they all turned to me, like they were waiting for something to happen. Like maybe I should hug someone or smile or something.

"What happened?" I'd asked, staying on the couch.

The lawyer stretched his arms out to his sides and waved them around the open floorplan of the downstairs, taking in the living room, dining room, and kitchen beyond. "This is your home," he said. "It's yours to defend. Here in New Jersey, you have no duty to attempt to flee the premises unless you are positive you can make it out unharmed." The lawyer's gaze slid down my exposed arms, but this time he wasn't checking me out. He was eyeing the fading pink scars that covered my forearms. "Based on the evidence," he said, pointing at my arms, "the prosecutors are satisfied with your choice."

I glanced at my parents, but they were looking toward the kitchen. No, they were looking *past* it. At the door. "The victim was committing a felony," the lawyer continued. He motioned toward the living room window, still missing a screen. And below it, the display table, now lacking anything to display. "As such, the homicide is justifiable."

Mom kept saying things like "How wonderful" and "Fantastic," but I could tell she wasn't really listening anymore.

I squeezed my eyes shut so I wouldn't sneak a glance at the kitchen. It didn't matter. I still saw it burned on the insides of my eyelids. The granite island in the center of the white tile floor. The stainless steel appliances. The skylight. The knife block, now missing one knife. And the door. Of course, the door.

Homicide.

I could've made it. It's what the lawyer thought. It's what my parents thought. It's what everyone thought. I could tell because they never asked.

I heard Mom rummaging around in the cabinets while Dad walked the lawyer to his car. And that night, when I ran into the kitchen to grab a soda, the entire knife block was missing. Just in case I didn't already know what she thought.

I snuck out the side door—not the one in the kitchen—behind the laundry room, and kept to the sidewalk alley between the backs of the beach houses. I walked, arms folded across my stomach, until I reached the intersection two blocks away. Then I paused, took a deep breath, and ran. I didn't turn my head, but I still saw the pine-green car sitting at the corner, where I knew it would be. Exactly two hundred yards from my front door. Where it had been every day since.

I barely caught a glimpse as I ran, but I knew she saw me. I knew by the way the hairs on the back of my neck stood on end and the way my ears rang and the way my instincts begged me to keep running. I felt his mom's eyes on me. I felt her hate. I didn't have to look to feel it.

I never looked.

I kept running until I reached the back of Colleen's house halfway down the next block. I didn't feel safe until I opened the gate of her high wooden fence, eased my body through the tiny entrance, and latched it silently behind me. I kept off the noisy pebbles by jumping from stepping stone to stepping stone. The house was one level—an older beach home that hadn't been demolished and rebuilt like the rest of ours—and its windows were wide open.

"Coll," I whispered into her bedroom window.

She had her music turned up and face turned away, brown curls bouncing to the beat. Yet somehow she knew I was there. She spun around, glanced at her open bedroom door, and sent me a quick sequence of hand signals. A twist of her first two fingers. A cross of her wrists. A flash of three fingers. Dairy Twist. The one near the Exxon. Three minutes.

Yes, there were two Dairy Twists within walking distance. Yes, we ate at both. I let myself out of her yard and walked the last two blocks to the Dairy Twist. I was slouched against the white vinyl on the side of the building when Colleen strode across the intersection. She sank down beside me on the pavement, like me and nothing like me. She was pale and curvy where I was tan and straight. Curly light-brown hair to my dark straight hair. Blue eyes to my brown.

People still got us confused. Must've been the way we walked, or maybe talked. We'd been inseparable since her family moved to town in the fifth grade. Ever since Carly Preston made fun of the gap between her front teeth and I'd told Carly it was better than walking around with a hideous mouth full of metal. Nobody makes fun of anything about the way Colleen looks anymore, but not because of me.

Colleen laced her fingers with mine and leaned her head back on the wall. "She says I'm grounded for life. What do you think that means in Dabner family talk? Two months? Three? What will you do without me?"

"They're sending me away," I said, my voice wavering.

Colleen released my hand and stood up. "Sending you where? Did the lawyer come back?"

I shook my head and stood. "Not prison. Boarding school."

Colleen sucked in a giant breath and exhaled, "No!"

"Yes. New Hampshire. My dad's old school."

She shook her head, her curls whipping around. "No. No fucking way. This isn't happening."

I started to panic at the way she was panicking—so unlike Colleen. When the cops showed up, she lied through her teeth.

And when she found me later that night under the boardwalk, she didn't freak out. Didn't adamantly shake her head or say things like *no* or *no fucking way* or *this isn't happening*. Instead she'd said, "I'm sorry," which made no sense. And besides, I hated apologies.

And now she was freaking out. "God, I can't *believe* I didn't go home with you that night."

"Cody Parker," I said, forcing a smile. Trying to force *her* to smile. "Who could blame you?"

"Cody fucking Parker," she mumbled. "So not worth it. God, this is one of those things I don't think I'll ever be able to make up to you, you know?"

"Coll, it wasn't your fault," I said, because it wasn't.

And she said, "No, it was Brian's fault. That little prick." Because that was just the sort of thing a best friend should say. She started crying and said, "Shit," as she wiped at the mascara under her eye.

She grabbed me around the middle and cried into my shoulder, and I felt that ache in my throat like I was going to cry too, but nothing came out. I held on tight, reasonably sure that I would never love another human being as much as I loved Colleen Dabner in that moment.

Someone leaned out a car window and whistled. We both shot him the middle finger. And then Colleen's hand tightened around my arm. Because standing on the corner of the street was a group of guys, watching us in a way that made Colleen dig her fingers into my skin.

Joe and Sammy and Cody fucking Parker. And Dylan. Brian's brother, Dylan. I did a double take before I realized it was him. Even though Dylan was three years younger than Brian, sixteen like me, he had his brother's same lanky build, same blond hair, same amber eyes.

Empty now, just like Brian's.

They didn't speak. Dylan stood so still I wondered whether he was breathing at all, until I noticed the fingers on his left hand twitching. Cody stared straight at me, but he wasn't making eye contact. Sammy dropped his hands to his sides, and chocolate milk shake sloshed out the top of his cup, running across his knuckles. And without communicating with each other, they spread out in a semicircle in front of us. I could see it happen, the shift in thinking. Like they were losing individual accountability, becoming part of something more.

"Hey now," Colleen said, putting her hand palm out in front of her.

They shuffled closer, and we backed up against the dirty siding. The only one who seemed to be thinking anything for himself was Dylan, and it didn't look like he was thinking anything good.

"Cody," Colleen said, brushing her hair off her shoulder. Cody jerked his head, registering Colleen for the first time.

Colleen could get guys to do whatever she wanted with a single sway of her hips or a tilt of her head, and this was no exception. Cody stepped to the side, forming a little path.

"Get out of here, Colleen."

"Yeah, I'm gone." She gripped me by the wrist and pulled, like maybe they'd think I was just an extension of her. I brushed Dylan's shoulder as I passed, and all the muscles in his arm went rigid.

I turned my head to say something, but really, there was nothing to say. And Colleen was moving fast. One more step, and we were gone. We sprinted until we reached Colleen's back fence.

"Maybe leaving for just a little while isn't such a bad idea, huh?" Then she squinted, even though there wasn't any glare, and backed into her yard. I heard her feet scrape against the siding as she scrambled back through her bedroom window.

There was pizza on the dining room table, but my parents were eating on the couches in the living room. We didn't eat in the dining room anymore because of the tiny fragments of glass. There weren't any, really, not anymore. But no matter how many times my mother vacuumed the floor, she swore there were pieces left behind. She said it wasn't safe. And the kitchen, well, it looked pretty much the same as always except for the spot on the floor where the cleaning company had used bleach. Even though the tile and the grout were both white, we could still see the outline where they had to scrub out the blood. Whiter than all the rest.

And there was this feeling now. A presence. Not quite a ghost. But *something.*

It was that same something my grandma tried to tell me about before she died, but after she knew she was dying. I'd sat on the side of her bed, looking anywhere but at her, and she snatched my hand and pressed it into her bony chest. "Do you feel that?" she asked. I didn't know whether she was talking about her heart or her soul, but all I felt was knobby bone, riddled with cancer. And then, below that, a weak pulse. "That has consequence."

I glanced to the door, hoping Mom would come in soon. I never knew what to say when the medicine took control of her mouth. She squeezed my hand tighter and said, "Mallory. Pay attention. That's real. It lives on. It *has* to." Then she released me. "It's not the end," she'd said. "This cannot be the end."

She died anyway. All of her. But sometimes when I'd walk by her room, I'd catch a whiff of her perfume, feel a fullness to her room. I'd think about what she told me, and I'd stand at the entrance, staring in. Not sure what was left behind. But it was something. And sometimes I'd turn around and find my mom standing behind me, watching me, watching the room.

But I didn't stand at the entrance of the kitchen contemplating what that *something* was. I didn't really want to know. This one time I was supposed to meet Brian on the boardwalk after lunch, which was infuriating because he wouldn't specify a time. Summer was supposed to be timeless, he'd said, which usually meant I ended up waiting so I wouldn't miss him. I found Colleen hanging out with a group of guys from school and joined her. We were both in the usual dress code for the shore: bathing suit tops and short shorts, and some guy had his hand on my bare back when Brian walked up behind me.

He'd wrapped his arms over my shoulders and said "Hey" into my ear, and I could tell he was smiling. Then he pulled me backward and tightened his arms and said, "Sorry, guys, this one's mine." I smiled and mouthed the word "Bye" to Colleen, and walked with Brian's arms around me, smiling because he had called me his.

But now when I walked in the kitchen, the fullness to the room was suffocating. Like his arms, wrapped around me, squeezing and squeezing until I was short of breath and then out of breath. I felt the word whispered throughout the room, grazing the exposed skin on my arms, my legs, my neck. *Mine*, it whispered. *This one's mine.*

I shivered and grabbed a slice of pizza from the dining room table and took it to my room. I packed a second suitcase. My flip-flops and shorts and frayed jeans. My toothbrush and cell phone charger and sleeping pills. The essentials.

Then I swallowed a sleeping pill and waited. It sucked me down into the mattress, my limbs heavy and sluggish. And as I waited, I stared at the ceiling fan, same as every night. I looked straight upward so I wouldn't catch a glimpse of his shadow beside my closet door, his outline on the curve of my dresser. I kept the comforter pulled up to my chin so I wouldn't feel his breath against my neck. The word "mine" whispered onto my skin.

I heard it coming, same as every night. Far away at first. Downstairs somewhere.

Boom, boom, boom.

Coming closer. Slow and steady, in that place between sleep and wake. Like I was half hearing, half imagining.

I couldn't keep my eyes open any longer. I didn't want to, anyway.

Because it was here.

Boom, boom, boom.

My whole room throbbed with it.

The beating of his hideous heart.

And then there was nothing but the dream. Same as every night. One moment, stretched out to fill the hours. A breath. A blink. Infinity in a heartbeat.

Amber eyes clouding with confusion. A raspy voice pleading, "Mallory, wait." The word "no" dying on his mouth.

The blood on the floor, the blood on my hands.

The door as I pushed through it, staining it red.

The dark. The night.

Even in my dream I ran.

I always ran.

CHAPTER 2

There were voices downstairs. Familiar, but not. It took me a second to place them. The new tightness in my mother's voice, the way she squeezed her words out of her throat. And my father, who spoke too deliberately. Like every line had been rehearsed before he released it for consumption.

I swung my legs out of bed and jerked myself upright, steadying myself against the wall. Then I tiptoed into the hall and waited at the top of the stairs.

"Call the police, Bill."

"And tell them what exactly? We can't prove anything."

"She's supposed to stay two hundred yards away. Two hundred yards. That's what the restraining order is for."

"You don't know it was her."

Her. The word lodged in the base of my skull, sent chills across my shoulders. I gripped the stair rail and ran down the steps, feeling the wood grains bite at my palm. I stood at the kitchen entrance, back door swung wide open. Open, so I could see the outside of the door. The weathered white now stained a mottled purple, tiny globs of flesh clinging to the smears. Near the edges, the smears spread out in distinct lines, like being dragged by fingers.

My parents noticed me hovering in the entranceway, and Dad moved his body in front of the door so I couldn't see.

"Don't worry, Mallory," Dad said. "It's not what you think. It's not blood."

But I already knew that. It looked nothing like blood. It looked like blueberries. Which was how I knew it was her.

I'd met Brian's mom before. Just once. She didn't really like me. Well, she liked me at first, and then she didn't. I'd met Brian at sunrise that June morning so he could teach me to surf. That's where I met his friends Joe and Sammy for the first time. They liked me at first too. More than his mom. They liked me all the way up until the day I killed him.

So we surfed. Or they did, anyway. Turned out Brian didn't really want to teach me. He wanted me to watch him surf. And then he wanted me to lie on his board while he floated next to me, tracing circles on my back.

"New Girl coming to breakfast?" Joe asked when we were all back on the sand. Joe and Sammy both had this dark hair that got impossibly darker in the water. They were twins, but easy to tell apart. Joe was bigger and his nose was crooked from a fight.

"We'll meet you there," Brian said, snaking an arm around my waist. "Gotta swing by home to get my wallet."

"I hope New Girl likes grease," Sammy said. "New Girl doesn't look like she eats bacon."

"New Girl loves bacon," I said. As long as it was chopped into microscopic pieces and sprinkled on a salad. Except for today. Today, I'd eat it, swallowing my nausea along with the grease.

And with that, Brian led me to his home. At the time I thought maybe it meant something. But it probably only meant he needed his wallet.

Brian's house was more like mine than Colleen's. Big, open, airy. White. Everything echoed. The grinding blender echoed through the hallway, then wound down to silence. "Who's there?" someone called from down the hall.

"Just me, Mom."

He walked toward the kitchen, pulling me behind. Brian's mom was scooping blueberries into the top of the blender. She was blond and kind of stocky, and she'd probably been pretty when she was younger. But now she poofed her hair too much and slathered foundation on too thick, which settled into the lines in her face. She reached out to hug Brian but kept her hands out to the sides. "Careful," she said, "it'll stain."

Her palms were a mix of purple and blue swirls. "And who's this?"

"Mallory," I said.

"Mallory. I'm Paula. Nice to meet you. Would you like a smoothie?"

I started to decline but Brian spoke for me. "Going out for breakfast."

Brian reached into the strainer in the sink and pulled out a handful of blueberries, popping them into his mouth. His fingertips were purple. His mom—Paula—shook her head. "Don't let him touch your white shirt with that hand." Shirt was kind of an overstatement. It was a tank top, tight, nearly transparent, so anyone could see the detailing on the top of my pink bikini. I folded my arms across my stomach.

Brian grinned, reached his fist into the colander again, and squeezed a handful of berries. His hand came out coated in purple. He walked toward me, smiling. I backed up against the wall, looking from him to his mother. "Brian, leave the poor girl alone."

But he didn't. He leaned into the wall, blocking me in, which was way too intimate for his mother to see, and apparently she agreed because she looked away. He whispered, "Won't hurt a bit." Then he pressed his right hand around my upper arm, leaving behind a tattoo of his imprint.

And seeing as Paula was pretending we weren't there and had her head in the refrigerator, I strode to the sink, squeezed the cool berries in my hand, felt the juice coat my fingers, and planted my hand on his upper arm.

"You own me now," he'd said, and he grabbed the bottom of my shirt, balled it up, and pulled me toward him. It was stained now, I was sure. I squirmed away from him, because his mother was *right there*, and also because he was ruining my shirt.

I turned my back to him and washed my hands in the sink. And then I felt him beside me, sharing the same water.

Then a boy in nothing but boxers barged into the room. "What the—"

Paula spun around, cutting his sentence in half. "Dylan, this is Brian's friend, Mallory."

"Yeah, I know who it is. I'm just wondering why my lab partner from chemistry is in my kitchen at nine in the morning." And there was another question lingering in the air as he cut his eyes from me to Brian.

Paula narrowed her eyes. "Your lab partner?"

I looked at the floor, not because of his mom's question, but because of Dylan's look. And because Dylan was in his boxers. With Brian standing right there. Like Brian might see something in the way Dylan was looking at us, or he might see something in the way that I was looking at Dylan. I leaned into Brian's side, hoping it hurt Dylan to see.

It did. I could tell. "Seriously?" Dylan said. And I was worried he wasn't going to stop there.

"Brian," Paula said, "a word, please?"

Brian laughed and ran a hand through his hair. "Don't worry, Mom. She's eighteen. Right, Mallory? Tell my mom so she'll get off my case." I liked Brian. I liked Brian in the way that girls like boys when they see them surfing. And the way girls like boys slinging their arms over them in front of their friends. And I liked the way he reminded me of Dylan, only he was Dylan times two. More outspoken, easier to read. And best of all, he didn't already have a girlfriend.

Maybe I'd come to like him more than that, but I didn't know him well enough yet. We'd never crossed paths when we were in the same school, and he'd been away at college this past year. He'd be going back there soon enough. I was still New Girl, and he was still a little intimidating, which was something I wasn't used to.

"Eighteen," I said, my breath coming too fast. "I'm just pretty bad at science."

Brian laughed at the lie and Dylan cringed, while Paula's eyes moved from me to Dylan to Brian to me again. Like she was assessing my age, holding my face next to each of her children for comparison. I knew she could tell. I should've been with Dylan.

"I didn't realize you guys knew each other," Brian said.

"Just a little," I answered, because after that first lie, the next came easy.

"Yeah," Dylan said, like he was trying to mock me, but it didn't come out right. I couldn't understand how Brian didn't notice. Probably because he didn't pay that much attention to his little brother. Or maybe I had just spent way too long paying way too much attention to Dylan, trying to pull meaning from every shift of his expression. I was still doing it right then, trying to decipher his words: was there an inflection where there shouldn't have been? Was he secretly directing his words at me? Was there meaning just below the casual phrase? I'd always thought there was. But maybe I'd been imagining it.

Brian planted a kiss on his mother's cheek and pulled me down the hall again. And when I said good-bye, her mouth was a tight line. Her eyes creased. Her shoulders tensed. It was like, even then, she knew I'd somehow ruin his life.

She was right.

I'd marked him with my handprint. And two weeks later, he was dead.

Now she had marked me.

The stain on our door was dry. I picked up a rag from the sink, doused it in vinegar, and started rubbing. That's how I got his handprint off my arm later that day. Brian kept his on. It took three days to fade.

"Stop," my mother said as I scrubbed the back door. "Stop. The fingerprints. You're ruining it."

Seemed to me like I was fixing it.

Semantics.

Dad helped me scrub, but the stain wouldn't budge. And the whole time, I felt this prickly feeling along my back, the kitchen charged with this energy, and it grew and grew until it felt like the entire room would burst from the tension.

I threw the rag on the floor and retreated to the living room. Dad said, "I'll take care of this," like it was up for discussion or something, and disappeared into the garage. He returned with a bucket of leftover white paint and applied a thick coat over the entire door before he left for work. I watched from the safety of the living room.

We had to leave the door open for the paint to dry, so Mom sat at the kitchen table, staring out the open door.

Mom used to fight to keep the doors open as soon as spring hit. "Let the outside in," she'd say.

Dad would position himself in the entranceway, like he was doing the door's job, and say, "The bugs, Lori."

She'd turn to me and mouth *the bugs*, and I'd smile. "They won't stay forever," she promised. But Dad hated bugs. Stomped them with his work shoes, using twenty-thousand times the necessary force. Or he'd chase them around with a flyswatter, stalking them from room to room.

But he always caved to her. We both did. Everyone did. I think maybe it was her smile. Or maybe the way she'd laugh at you, but also kind of with you. Or the way she'd just declare something and expect that that would be the end of it.

But now she was terrified of what might come through open doors. Or open windows. Even unlocked bedroom doors.

The new version of my mother had two gears. One where she sat still and stared off into the distance, like now, and another where she fluttered unpredictably around the house, never making eye contact. She fluttered when she woke—paused through the middle of the day—and fluttered again before bed. She darted from window to window, diagonally across the room and back again, with no real pattern. She revisited the same window two, three times. She flipped the locks, open, closed. She turned the deadbolts, unlocked, locked. She checked the upstairs windows.

And three nights ago, I waited in the hall outside my bedroom door. I waited for her to finish and retreat into her room. I held out my hand to steady her, to ground her again. To make her look at me. I touched her elbow and she flinched. I drew back my arm.

Then she locked eyes with me for a fraction of a second and said, "Good night, Mallory," backed into her bedroom, and shut the door.

And then she turned the lock.

That's when I learned that hate is a funny thing. It can manifest out of nothing in an instant. It can jump from there to here. Like how Dylan taught me in chemistry, electrons jumping from cloud to cloud, never passing through empty space. It doesn't take time to grow. It's just not there. And then it is. Effortless.

So I backed into my bedroom, bubbling with hate, and turned my own lock.

After the paint on the back door was dry and my mother shut and locked it, she settled into her lifeless state. She was perched on the edge of the white sofa, staring through a crack in the lace curtains. Every time a car drove by, she'd suck in a breath and stare out the window even harder. I tried to see what she saw, but everything was muted by the white curtains. Filtered somehow. A little more abstract, a little less real.

There's nothing ominous about white. White walls, white tiles, white furniture. It's clean, pure, innocent. Nothing hides in white. Except sometimes when the sun is directly overhead, nothing casts a shadow. And it's hard to tell where the wall ends and the floor begins. Like there's just this expanse stretching outward, curving back around. Like there's no depth perception. It feels like the opposite of claustrophobia.

"She'll stop when I leave," I said, standing behind her.

"I don't . . ." No smile. No laugh. No declaration. Just this uncertainty. Half a sentence. I hated her for it. And suddenly I couldn't stand the thought of seven hours in the car together. Of Mom staring out the window or maybe fidgeting with the lock, and Dad telling all these stories about his time at Monroe, hearing about so-and-so's son or daughter, or so-and-so's second cousin twice removed. Of saying these formal good-byes—all fake smiles and fake words and fake everything.

"I'm ready to go now." But the words came out quiet and unsure.

She shook her head. "We'll drive up together tomorrow."

"I've taken the train before, you know."

"Not that far. You'd have to switch lines in Boston and you'd be all alone . . ." Her voice trailed off at the word. I'd be *alone* for the entire school year.

"Your father's at work," she said.

I tried to think of how to appeal to her senses. "I'm scared," I said, which, as it turned out, was the most honest thing I'd said to my mother in weeks.

She stayed silent, doing the staring-off-into-space thing. Then she snapped to attention, nodded vigorously, and grabbed the keys off the holder next to the front door.

We left.

I didn't call Colleen. I didn't leave a note for my father.

I didn't lean my head out the door and scream, "I'm leaving!" at Brian's mom, wherever she was. I didn't tell anyone. I just grabbed my bags and walked out the front door into the stifling heat. One last glance toward the kitchen, to the white spot on the floor.

Good-bye.

At the train station, Mom handed me several twenties. Then she leaned across the center console, a halfhearted attempt at a halfhearted hug. "Be good, Mallory love," she whispered into my ear.

It was the type of thing she'd never said to me before. It was the type of thing she never felt the need to remind me of before.

I felt the hate again, flashing from nowhere. Light off. Light on.

And then I walked away from the car.

My hands shook as I handed the money to the cashier. I didn't know why. Colleen and I used to take this train into the city several times a year. And, really, I was glad to leave. Brian's mom was always waiting, two hundred yards away. And there was that *thing* in my house, waiting for me. Coming for me.

I should've felt relieved as I boarded the train. Free. I was free. I whispered it to myself, like this whole thing was my idea, and by the time I reached Boston, I almost believed it.

I transferred to a bus, dragging my luggage behind me. There were so many people, and nobody paused to give me a second look. Most people here never even gave me a first look. As I boarded the bus for the middle of nowhere, New Hampshire, I thought that maybe my parents were right. Maybe a fresh start was all I needed.

Maybe next time I went home the grout between the tiles would be dirty and I wouldn't see the outline of Brian's body. Maybe my parents wouldn't flinch when I reached for a steak knife. Maybe Colleen would be allowed to see me. Maybe Brian's mom would move away.

I was downright saturated with the hope of the Maybes when the bus screeched to a halt in the middle of the road a few hours later.

The doors opened and the light flickered on inside, making the dusk outside seem even darker. "Monroe," the driver announced, with his finger extended down a fork in the road. "This is as close as I get."

I walked down the steps, and he pulled my bags out from the storage area underneath. "Quarter mile down the road, honey."

The bus shifted into gear and rumbled away. I couldn't see anything past the curve in the road ahead of me.

Maybe.

An engine idled nearby, and though I couldn't see the car,

a horrible chill ran down my neck and across my shoulders. I was convinced it was pine green. I was convinced it was waiting for me.

I walked along the shoulder of the road, which wasn't really a shoulder at all, just the cracked, uneven edge where pavement ended and the woods began. I walked against traffic like I was taught, but it probably wouldn't make a difference. The road was too narrow and the curve too sudden for a car to maneuver around me in time. So I walked fast, listening for the sound of oncoming cars. But the only sound I heard was the idling engine. Waiting.

I reached the corner and rounded it quickly and the car took off, a blur of red taillights and nothing else. The only thing waiting for me was the gate ahead, the ivy creeping upward, gripping the iron bars.

The scarlet *M* looming over top, just for me.

CHAPTER 3

Dusk was darker in the woods than on the coast. Too many trees to see the horizon. Light filtered through at odd angles, stretching and distorting the shadows. There were two archways carved into the gate, which made the whole gate thing kind of pointless.

I walked through the one on the left, which was narrower than I'd thought, and I felt myself shrinking down as I passed through it. In front of me, the brick walkway diverged into three paths snaking through the trees and the buildings. I couldn't see where anything led, so I rested my luggage against the iron bars, took out my cell phone, and held it toward the sky.

"Come on, come on," I mumbled. I probably should've cleared this with Dad after all. I'd been so preoccupied with the getting away part that I hadn't thought about what to do when I actually arrived. I paced to the other end of the gate, walked back through it, around it, and finally stood on a stone bench. Still no signal.

The wind blew strongly and I nearly lost my footing on the edge of the bench. Leaves rustled and a flag whipped around on the top of the building to my right. And then a vision came waltzing down the middle path. Brown hair, bouncing. Hips swaying. My heart skipped a beat and I thought, *Colleen.*

But it wasn't Colleen. This girl had a splattering of freckles across her nose and overarched eyebrows, and when the shadows shifted and the light hit her hair, I could tell it was more red than brown. I hopped off the bench. And then another girl came skipping after her. Skinny and blond and all frail boned. Just a wisp of a person.

"It's a dead zone. Because of the mountains," said the girl with the curls. "That's what they tell us anyway. Seems awfully convenient." Then she extended a short, manicured finger in the direction of the bus stop. "About a mile that way I can get some signal. At the gas station."

The blond girl shuddered. "Not worth the risk. The locals are inbred." She opened her eyes wide and leaned forward, like a warning.

"They just don't have dental insurance," Curls said, waving her off.

I smiled at Curls, but neither smiled back. Blond Girl had a fine white scar running across her chin, and she raised her hand to touch it, like she knew I was looking.

"Well, anyway, I have a satellite phone," said Blond Girl. Curls blinked heavily and shifted her jaw back and forth.

"Early arrivals need to check in with Ms. Perkins. Housemaster." Curls pointed up to the top of the building with the whipping flag.

"On the roof?" I asked.

Curls cocked her head to the side and pulled her lips into a hideous grin. "Oh look, a funny one."

And then they left.

I dragged my luggage into the building on the right. A dorm, I guess. But for the money my parents were spending, I expected a little more. Automatic doors instead of the heavy wooden ones that creaked when they opened. Fancy artwork instead of wood-paneled walls. For Christ's sake, the lobby didn't even have a television. Just a handful of couches tossed haphazardly around the room. I wouldn't have been surprised to see a moose head mounted on the wall.

Through the window on a thick wooden door, I saw a hallway stretch down to my left, door after door after door. Like some asylum. There was a staircase at the back of the lounge, wall sconces illuminating the way up and down.

I left my bags and went up, my flip-flops slapping at the steps. The stairs ended at the third floor with a single door.

A woman not much older than me in sweats and a ponytail

answered when I knocked, looked me over, and pushed her glasses up onto her nose. "You must be Mallory," she said, with no inflection to her voice whatsoever. I must've look surprised that she knew who I was, because she said, "Your father spoke with the dean of students earlier today." Then she nodded and said, "Very well then," like she was playing some part and going back to her script. She pulled a blue stretchy bracelet with a key attached off the table along the entrance wall. "Room 102. Do you have a laptop?"

Was I supposed to have a laptop? "No."

"You'll get one tomorrow during orientation. And the cellular service is appalling. There's a pay phone in the hall and vending machines in the basement. The cafeteria doesn't open until tomorrow, I'm afraid."

I slipped the key bracelet onto my wrist.

"If you need anything, don't hesitate to ask." And yet, as she said it, she slowly closed the door in my face.

My steps echoed throughout the stairwell as I descended. Fresh start, like hell. Like this place could be anyone's fresh start. Full of snotty people and arrogant buildings and way too many trees. God, there were so many freaking trees.

I entered the barren lobby, void of all sound except the low hum of electricity buzzing from the lights, and I felt it.

It. Him. Here, hundreds of miles from home. Here, in this emptiness. It was here, like a suffocating fullness to the room, humming along with the electricity.

I didn't understand. There was no reason for his soul or presence or whatever to be here. He'd probably never set foot here in his life. This place meant nothing to him—to us.

And then I backed slowly into the stairwell again. Because I realized that whatever it was—a ghost, a soul, a ripple in the atmosphere—it wasn't tied to my kitchen. It was tied to me.

I took shallow breaths so nothing could really register in the pit of my gut. Colleen. I needed Colleen. I stumbled down the last flight of stairs, and I kept casting glances over my shoulder but there was nothing there. Except every time I turned back around, I felt something, or this *almost* something, pressed up against my back, mirroring my every movement as I scampered down the hall past the vending machines.

But every time I looked there was nothing, like it was in my blind spot. Just out of sight. But there.

I ran into the laundry room, where everything smelled like dryer sheets and felt like excess heat, and that muffled the feeling a little, though it was still there.

Everything was coin operated. I ran my bills through the coin machine until my bag was half full of quarters because I had no idea how much it cost to call New Jersey from the middle of nowhere, and the sound of the money sloshing around made me feel a little better, for no reason at all, really.

But not that much better because my hands were still shaking when I inserted half the contents of my purse into the pay phone upstairs. And that feeling was practically on top of me, like someone was pressed up against my back, eyes on the back of my head, arms at my sides, deciding what to do.

The phone rang three times and Colleen picked up, breathy and quiet. “Hello?” she said. And the feeling retreated for the moment.

“Colleen?”

“Oh my God, Mallory?”

“In the flesh. Well, not really.”

“What the crap? Caller ID said unknown caller, New Hampshire. You’re already there?”

“Yes. And I’m on a pay phone in my dorm. A pay phone!”

“They still make those?”

“Are you ungrounded?”

“No.” Her voice dropped lower. “The parental unit is in the shower. *Was* in the shower.”

“Colleen?” a voice in the background asked.

“Shit. Okay, give me the number. I’ll call it when I can.”

I found the numbers on top of the keypad. “603-555—”

“Colleen Elizabeth, hang up this instant.”

“One sec, Ma. Okay, 603-555 . . . ?”

“23—” And then I heard a dial tone. I listened to the tone for a minute, willing the numbers across the connection.

I went back to the lounge and grabbed my luggage. The feeling was gone. All that was left was me and my luggage and the faint hum of electricity. I pulled my bags down the hall to room 102—the corner room, next to a secondary staircase, narrow and dark. I let myself into my room and I swear I could smell concrete. Because that's all there was. White walls, two standard-issue twin beds with white linens that blended into the background. White on white, just like home. Minus the home part. There were desks in each corner, a light oak. But with the poor lighting, they almost looked the same color as the rest of the room.

I opened the closet door and found a low dresser shoved into the bottom. Brown and worn. Like the unseemly stuff was hidden from sight here.

I turned on the overhead light, but it was yellow and dim. So I flung open the shades, but the room faced the woods. And all that was out there now were dark shadows against a darker sky. So I propped the door to my room open with my bag and let the fluorescent light from the hall shine in. And even after I didn't need the light anymore, I kept the door open, waiting for Colleen to call back. It didn't matter that I couldn't get the number to her. She'd figure it out.

I knew she'd find me.

She could always find me.

She found me that night, when Brian died. When the cops couldn't find me, when my parents couldn't find me. After I'd run. After.

I heard her steps splashing toward me, over the sound of the rain falling into the ocean, where I sat in a few inches of dark water, seaweed, plastic bottles, and remnants of blood.

"Mallory," she called before she was really close enough to know it was me.

But of course it was me. The first time we hid here was in eighth grade, when Colleen's mom wouldn't let her date a boy in high school. We'd camped out under the boardwalk, which was not at all romantic but kind of foul, so we moved back home and Colleen learned to sneak out her bedroom window instead.

"Mallory." She crouched in front of me. "Oh God, Mallory, I'm sorry," she said, but I still wasn't looking at her.

I felt her arm reach under my knees and she grunted as she tried to lift me, but instead she sunk down, tangled up in me. She wrapped her arms around me and said, "You need to stand up." But the only thing I needed to do was sink farther into the wet sand under the murky water.

There was a shrill ringing down the hall. A second later, I heard it again. *Colleen.* I ran out of my room and down the hall and skidded to a stop at the pay phone. "Hello?"

"Mallory." Not Colleen. My father. I plopped in the plastic chair beside the phone.

"Yes."

"You shouldn't have left. How could you just leave like that?"

"Mom let me. She drove me to the train station."

"Your mother is in no position to be making those kinds of decisions." Whatever that was supposed to mean.

"Well," I said, "I'm here. And everything's fine."

Dad let his disappointment linger in the silence before he spoke. "I'm going to set up an 800 number for you to call home for free."

"Great," I said, extra emphasis on the *T*.

"And I'll set up an account there in case you need money."

"Perfect."

"And don't you ever do something like that again."

"Yes, sir." Then I hung up and felt the hate flashing again. Light off. Light on.

Now they could get on with their lives. Move on. Problem solved. I narrowed my eyes at the phone and watched my distorted reflection scowl back. Then I felt a presence behind me and my muscles tensed. I stayed perfectly still. A streak of blue passed behind my reflection. I jumped up, back to the phone, as the chair scraped against the floor with a high-pitched shriek.

There was a guy in the hall, blue shirt and khaki shorts, watching me.

I cleared my throat. "I'm done with the phone."

"I'm not waiting for the phone," he said. He was built tall and thick, with a cocky stance and a lazy grin.

"I thought nobody was here yet."

"I live here. I'm Jason. Mallory, right?"

I searched my memory for his face, for his name. But I couldn't remember seeing him at any of Dad's alumni events. I didn't remember any Jason. It'd been two years since I stopped going, though. He could've been anyone. "Sorry, I don't remember you."

I looked around the empty hallway, wondering if this Jason character was supposed to be wandering the girls' dorm at night. He saw my expression and his grin stretched wider. It was the type of smile on the type of face that said he usually got exactly what he wanted. And in that moment, it looked like what he wanted was me.

I tugged down the ends of my shorts, which were now decidedly too short.

He laughed. "No, I mean I know who you *are*." He stayed against the wall, but he smiled in a way that made him seem closer. "My dad is the dean of students."

Which was his way of telling me he knew everything. Everything.

All the air drained from the hallway, my fresh start rapidly disappearing.

I walked toward my room, and he backed down the hall

in front of me. "There's nothing to do around here tonight. We should hang out."

"Jason," I said as I strode by him into my room. He knew who I was. He knew everything about me. I gathered my voice and said, "You should know better."

He grinned again as I shut my door in his face. He tapped his fingers against it twice and said, "See ya, Mallory."

I turned the lock. Ridiculous, really. I wasn't naive enough to think a lock would prevent someone from getting in if he wanted to. But I ran across the room to the window and checked that lock too. The outside was blackness now. No moon. No lights. I couldn't even see the trees. Just darkness, stretching forever.

I pulled the off-white shade down to the sill, rummaged in the smaller suitcase for my vial of sleeping pills, and swallowed one dry. The lock kept Jason out. But not that other thing. I heard it coming as I lay on the starchy sheets.

Boom, boom, boom.

Inescapable. I felt it like a jolt of cold air as it seeped through the crack at the base of the window and spread out along the floor.

The room throbbed with the *boom, boom, boom* just like at home. Same as always. But this time my eyelids fluttered open and I saw it hovering in the corner, starting to take shape. Like a shadow in the darkness, darker than all the rest.

I squeezed my eyelids closed again and I thought, *Sorry, I'm sorry, I'm sorry, I'm sorry, I'm sorry* . . . because it was the only thing I could think.

But it didn't matter because I already knew those words meant nothing.

And as I drifted away, I felt the shadow coming closer . . . closer . . .

I woke to whispers in the hall. Fast-moving words, sharp laughter, an indecipherable string of syllables. Gossip. Girls moving in.

The clock told me what I already knew by the amount of noise in the hall—I'd missed breakfast. And I hadn't eaten dinner. My stomach clenched. I slipped my key bracelet onto my wrist and padded down the narrow set of stairs near my room. I got a bag of pretzels and a soda from the vending machine in the basement and tore into the bag as soon as I pulled it from the dispenser. Then I heard doors slamming around in the laundry room.

I walked over to the entranceway and saw Curls slamming the dryer shut, leaning into it with her hip.

Blond Girl was sitting on top of a washer across the room, filing her nails. They were both in pajamas still. Blond Girl spoke, still looking at her nails. "I don't know why you don't just do it at your uncle's place."

Curls put her hands on her hips and said, "I'm not lugging this across campus."

"Well then, at the very least you could send it out like I do."

Curls opened the door again and slammed it shut, and this time it latched. "There," she said. Then she turned to Blond Girl and said, "Stuff always goes missing when I do that." Then she motioned for Blond Girl to follow her. "Time to get ready," she said.

I backed away before they could notice me standing there.

Someone had slid a schedule for the day under my door, along with the Monroe Student Handbook. I spent the morning reading the handbook while everyone else moved in. Learning about the consequences as dictated by Monroe for various offenses. I wondered what would happen if I refused to wear those ridiculous red shirts, but I couldn't find the answer.

There were two long folding tables set up at the end of the path in front of a large academic building, and two identical girls stood behind them. As I got closer, I noticed the girls were not at all identical, despite the red shirts and khaki pants and hair pulled up into taut ponytails. And, in fact, I knew them. They were the girls from the laundry room, from last night. Except now they were all smiles and perkiness, and they greeted me like they'd never seen me before.

"Welcome to Monroe!" said the girl with the reddish curls.

She was looking at me, but I got the feeling she was looking right through me. It was unsettling. Her name tag said KRISTA. "Last name, please."

"Murphy," I said as she rifled through the stack of red folders. Her eyes briefly flitted up to mine. The blond girl, who had been smiling at someone in the distance, stopped smiling. Her hand froze midwave.

"Taryn," Krista said, looking directly at me. "I think you have this one."

Taryn cleared her throat and rifled through the folders. I walked to her side of the table, but she passed the folder to Krista instead. And then we all stood in this awkward triangle: me with my folder, Taryn looking purposefully away, Krista looking purposefully toward me.

And then a voice from somewhere behind the table said, "Computer room next."

Krista looked at a guy sprawled out under the nearest tree and said, "I was getting to it, Reid." Then she turned back to me and said, "Computer room. Laptops." Fake smile.

She gestured over her shoulder to the building behind her.

But I was looking at the boy under the tree. Reid. I knew him—I used to know him. I hadn't seen him since freshman year, when I was an awkward fourteen and he was a cute fifteen, as long as you didn't look too closely at his uncontrollable hair.

Reid wore sneakers and khaki shorts and that ridiculous

red polo, and I started to worry I wouldn't be able to tell anyone apart. When I passed close by him, he raised himself up on his elbows and smiled, and not only did he have that ridiculous shirt, he also now had this ridiculous brown hair that curled at the bottom. Not even close to the uncontrollable mess I remembered.

"You got taller," he said.

"You got all . . ." I waved my hands around my head. "Nice hair."

Reid laughed and stood up. "So you *do* remember me."

Hard to forget the guy whose father—who also happened to be Dad's oldest friend—died in a freak accident, or the funeral your parents dragged you across three states for, or the fact that you sat with him in his room while everyone else mourned for his father downstairs. Hard to forget the first guy who rejected you.

When my lack of speaking turned awkward, Reid shuffled his feet and asked, "Need help orientating?"

"No thanks," I said. I would've thought that after two years, I wouldn't feel the pit in my stomach when I looked at him. Wouldn't feel the urge to spin on my heel and self-righteously walk away. And definitely wouldn't feel the urge to close the space between us.

Walk away, Mallory.

I spent the rest of the morning orienting myself at the computer lab and the student banking center and the registrar's office. Then I spent the afternoon orienting myself at the cafeteria and the bookstore. The new kids stood out—we hadn't assimilated yet. Hadn't learned how to wear our hair or carry our books. Hadn't put on the red shirt and adopted the sameness yet. So when they smiled at me, I smiled back, like we were in this together.

I had my laptop bag swung over my shoulder and a stack of books propped between my arms and my chin as I moved slowly back toward my dorm, rocks getting stuck in my flip-flops every few steps. Reid was still under that same oak tree, like there was nothing worth moving for, but now he was eating a giant sandwich.

He was watching me, but I didn't know whether he was staring because he'd heard about what I'd done or whether he was remembering me, reconciling the Mallory in his head with the Mallory in front of him. Whether he was remembering the same moment I was: his hand in my hair and his face an inch from mine the moment before he walked away.

Or maybe he was staring because I had to stop every few steps and shake my feet while simultaneously balancing a stack of textbooks. He put down the food as I passed by again. "Hey," he said.

I kicked off my shoes and started walking faster.

There was a girl in my room. Actually, she was only half in my room. The upper half of her body was leaning out the window, blowing smoke toward the trees.

She turned around when the door slammed shut behind me but held her cigarette out the window. She had blond hair cut blunt at her shoulders, a heart-shaped face and jeans that fit her perfectly, and a T-shirt that fit too tight, but guys probably wouldn't agree.

She watched me, expressionless, until I dumped my gear on the bed and said, "Hey."

She smiled, which I guess meant I had passed some test. She held up a neon-pink lighter from her other hand and said, "You want?"

"I'm good," I said, and she ground the cigarette onto the bricks outside the window and flicked it somewhere toward the forest. Apparently not worried about being caught. Or starting forest fires.

"So," she said, quirking her mouth to the side and leaning her back against the wall. "Like what I've done with the place?" She had hung band posters over the other standard-issue bed, and there were stand-up lights in the corners of our room now. She walked over to me and stuck her hand out all formal like. "Brianne Dalton. Bree."

I shook her hand and said, "Mallory Murphy. No nickname."

She stepped back and looked me over, scanning me slowly

from my bare feet to my bare shoulders and raised an eyebrow at me. "Hmm. Well, you don't need one. You new here?"

I nodded, searching through my suitcase for another pair of flip-flops, feeling her eyes on me.

"Me too. Transferred from Chelsey. You know it? No? All-girls school. Can you picture me at an all-girls school?"

Actually, I could. Probably how she learned to make other girls uncomfortable just by looking at them. She reminded me of Colleen, even though they looked nothing alike. Colleen was the one who taught me how to walk when you know someone is watching, and how to walk to make someone watch. She oozed attraction just by being in a room. Same as this girl.

Bree looped an arm through mine and led me back into the hall. "Come on, orientation tours are about to start. And trust me, you are in for a treat."

I looked down at the registration paper. Bree's idea of a treat was my idea of perpetual humiliation.

"I see you made it unscathed," Reid called to me as we approached the grass. *Unscathed.* Who says unscathed? Prep school boys, apparently. With perfect hair. Who reject you.

Bree leaned closer into my side. "You know Reid?"

"Not exactly," I said, because it was true. I knew him two years ago, when his hair stuck out in every different direction. I knew him before his father was taken from him, before all of this. I didn't know him anymore.

"Whatever," she said. She kept her arm looped through mine, but I felt her pull away.

The whole quad area between the dorms and the school buildings took up the space of two soccer fields. Students were scattered in circular groups, like they were singing "Kumbaya" or something. Reid was already surrounded by two guys and one other girl. He must've been the leader since he was the only one in uniform.

Reid held my flip-flops out in an extended hand. "Hey, Cinderella, you lost your shoes." He smiled and showed his dimple, which I'd forgotten about until right that moment, and suddenly I was back, three years earlier, a year before Reid's dad died, walking into Dad's twenty-fifth reunion and pushing through the crowd until I'd found Reid, and he was saying, "Miss me?" with that same dimple, and I was saying, "Hardly," and trying not to smile.

Now he was holding my shoes and smiling, like this whole thing wasn't horrifically awkward. "I didn't lose them. I left them right there."

"Well then, you're welcome for keeping them safe. There's a big demand around here for worn-out flip-flops."

Or maybe this wasn't awkward for him. Maybe two years was long enough to forget. Maybe he started the process of forgetting as soon as he walked out of his room. Not that I blamed him. He'd had enough going on that day, and in the days that followed. And if I could've made myself forget that, I would have.

I took them from his outstretched arm. "They're not worn out," I said, careful not to touch his fingers. But I threw them back onto the ground because I was pretty sure they actually were. I'm also pretty sure I was grinning.

Bree caught sight of someone over my shoulder and smiled a "hello, I'm cute and somewhat mysterious" smile that, as it turns out, was not at all mysterious. Must've been a boy. A cute one.

"When's the tour start?" My shoulders tensed because I recognized that voice. I turned around just in time to see Jason, nighttime dorm lurker, skillfully pull out yet another obnoxious grin.

Reid narrowed his eyes and looked around the group gathered in front of him. "What do you want, Jason?" he asked. For the moment, I trusted Reid's untrusting expression.

"Hanging with my new friend, Mallory." He rested a hand on my shoulder.

I slunk down and stepped away. "New friend, huh?" Reid asked. But before I had a chance to throw an "I'd rather have my teeth pulled" expression his way, Reid shrugged, and it didn't seem like the shrug was directed at me.

"This is the quad, obviously," Reid said as he started walking backward, like he owned this place.

Jason leaned in close as we followed Reid. "I get the feeling you don't like me."

I didn't answer.

"Didn't mean to scare you last night. I wanted you to feel welcome."

I grabbed Bree's arm and said, "This is Bree. She's new. Welcome her."

Bree dislodged her arm and rolled her eyes. She was nobody's second choice. And she sure as hell didn't want my leftovers.

We walked out the gate with the *M* over the top and started walking around the perimeter. Reid said, "This is the West Gate—what the town considers our main entrance, but our main entrance is actually farther down this road." He pointed behind him as he walked backward, and we all strained to see. Apparently there was a gate in our immediate future, but the only thing I could see was the car pulled off the side of the road, engine off. Same color as the surrounding weeds.

Jason was trying to say something again, but I had stopped moving. "Mallory?" Reid asked, shooting a glance from me to Jason.

They were all still moving toward the car. I turned around, picked a spot in the distance, woods on woods on woods.

And, like always, I ran.

CHAPTER 4

I ran past the scarlet *M* again, past the corner of campus, and then I kept running as the sidewalk turned into packed dirt, roots, and stone mangling the ground. And again my flip-flops held me back, so I kicked them off and ran some more. The path narrowed, twigs and briars reaching toward me, and then suddenly opened again to a large clearing.

I bent over at the entrance, still sheltered by the trees, and sucked in some air. Then I held my breath so I could hear the noises around me—wind filtering through the trunks, leaves rustling up high, faint scurrying below. But nothing human. So I rested on the side of a fallen tree and took in the unnatural scene in front of me: a dilapidated brick building, half-walls standing, piles of bricks scattered around the floor of the clearing.

Those half-walls were the perfect place to hide, so I balanced myself on the piles of bricks and carefully stepped my way to the building, watching for nails or sharp rocks as the bricks dislodged and scattered below each step. Then I crouched at the spot where two of the partially standing walls still stood and leaned back into the corner.

I closed my eyes, but in my mind I could still see through the back window of the car, and I pictured her hair poofing over the top of the seat. I imagined her turning and watching me with those eyes, red and dry. I could see her rise higher still, pulling herself over the seat, and I could see her clenched jaw and the vein fighting to escape her neck, pulsating and pulsating.

Like I saw at Brian's funeral.

Brian's mom didn't see me then. Nobody saw me. Not even Colleen, who didn't tell me she was going. But there she was, squeezed between Cody and either Joe or Sammy—I couldn't tell from the distance. I didn't know whether Colleen was there for Cody or as some sort of atonement for herself. Or if maybe she was there for me. Colleen had her hand cupped over her mouth, and I could tell, even from between the pickets of the fence across the street, that she was doing that thing where she wasn't really crying, but her body was still shaking like she was.

Brian's mom wasn't paying attention. She looked like she was, but if you were staring, like I was, you'd see she had her head tilted to the side like she was listening to something. Listening for *something. Dylan stood next to her, his fists balled up. Staring at the ground like he was furious with it. Like it had taken something from him. Which, I guess, it had.*

Then they all walked up to the hole in the ground. His mother dropped a handful of dirt into it, and someone, I'm not sure who, but someone released this noise. *This horrible, unnatural sound—a* wail. *It traveled across the field and through the pickets of the fence. And it buried itself deep within my stomach, like grief was a concrete thing. It settled inside me, and there wasn't room for anything else, not even air. I was suffocating. I turned around with my back pressed up hard against the fence, and I felt hot and cold all at once, but then only hot. And I vomited into the bushes behind me.*

Then they were coming. They all crossed back over the street, finding their way to their cars parked along the curb. I held my breath between the fence posts. Brian's mom was right there. I could reach out and touch her between the slats. I couldn't see her face, but she paused right in front of me and tilted her head to the side. Like maybe that whole time she had been listening for me. Then Dylan was beside her, pulling her along. I saw her jaw tense, and that vein, seething.

Later that night, when Colleen snuck over to see me, I said, "The funeral was today," because I wanted her to tell me why she went.

And she said, "Really? I thought it was next week." I still didn't know why she went, but at least I knew why she wouldn't admit to it then: there was nothing quite like watching Brian's body being lowered into the ground to fully understand the horror of what I had done.

Someone was running up the path. Heavy steps, stomping the dirt. I crouched lower. And then a muffled voice said, "Shit." A decidedly male voice. I scrambled to my knees and peeked over the top, breathing in the dust from the bricks under my nose. Reid was scanning the woods beyond, my second pair of flip-flops in his hands.

I stood up, brushing the dust and debris from my shorts.

"God, are you trying to kill me?" He stepped over the piles of bricks, but froze a few feet away. He shook his head to himself and stared at the bricks. "I mean, you could've gotten me in a lot of trouble." He held my shoes toward me again, like a peace offering.

I took the shoes and slid them onto my feet. "I guess it's no secret, huh?" At least I knew why he'd been staring at me when I crossed center campus.

He had the decency not to act like he didn't know what I was talking about. "It is and it isn't," he finally said. "Jason's dad is Dean Dorchester, so no luck there. And Krista's part of the family, though she was away for the summer, so I don't know if she knows yet." She did. She definitely did.

"Siblings?" Made perfect sense to me. They had the same hair color and, from what I could tell, the same cold attitude.

Reid shook his head. "Cousins."

"What about you, Reid?" It's not like our dads could confide in each other anymore.

He looked away. "I heard from Jason."

"You're friends?" I didn't know why I assumed they wouldn't be—it's not like I knew him all that well. And even when I did, I never saw him with his school friends. He could've been an entirely different person with them. Like how being with Colleen made me bolder, more sure of myself, more confident.

Reid paused, like he was thinking really hard about the question. "We're teammates. And secrets are like currency here. You tell one, you're owed one. There's a hierarchy to it."

"You're high up?"

He shrugged. "I'm high up."

Reid's eyes skimmed the trees as they rustled, like the wind was a thing and he could trace its path. "You shouldn't be here. It's not safe."

I looked around. The remaining walls were kind of unsteady, but nothing seemed dangerous about it. Reid continued, "This is the old student center. You know what's past here?"

"No," I said.

"Nothing. Well, not nothing, just nothing you'll ever find your way out of again."

"It's just trees."

"No, not trees, a forest."

Now that was something I could understand. The way a bunch of little things can become something bigger—something more than the sum of its parts. I stared off into the distance, no longer seeing the trees stacked up behind one another, but seeing this big *thing*—a forest, a living, breathing single entity.

"Once you get going," Reid said, also staring off into the distance, "it's hard to find your way back out again. There's this story about this kid, Jack Danvers, who got lost during initi— Anyway, he wandered off one night and didn't come back."

A chill ran down my spine. "What happened?"

"Don't know. They never found a body. I tried to look it up but couldn't find anything. Didn't you notice that form you had to sign about not going into the woods? It basically excuses the school from liability. And a few years ago, the school finally raised enough money to build a new student center so we could stay more centralized."

I stared off into the trees, thinking about that kid who disappeared. I wondered what the end was like for him—was it fast? Slow? Was he scared? Resigned? Was it violent? Gradual? But then I realized it didn't matter. Dead is dead is dead.

The wind blew and Reid narrowed his eyes at the woods. "Sometimes I think I can feel . . ."

I shivered and cleared my throat. I didn't want to talk about ghosts. "Anything else I should know?"

"Jason's an ass. Don't let him get to you."

I shook my head, about to explain that it wasn't Jason I was running from, but I wasn't about to offer up yet another secret for distribution. If secrets were currency, I was holding onto the ones I had left. "Noted," I said.

"So come on," he said, holding his hand out for me. I stared at his open palm, at the lifeline running down it.

Colleen traced mine once, back in middle school. She ran the dark nail of her pointer finger along the crease toward my wrist and said, "Better live while you can." I had laughed uncomfortably, and Colleen had smiled, even though she'd been trying to keep a straight face. "Just kidding," she'd said. "We're going to live forever." Because that's exactly the type of thing you think when you're twelve.

Reid's arm eventually dropped to his side. "Come on," he said again, but this time without the open palm.

I pictured us walking back together, side by side on the narrow trail. Either in awkward silence, where I'd be thinking about how he used to be, or with him telling me stories about Monroe, like almost kissing me wasn't something worth remembering.

"I like it here," I said. "Quiet."

He dug at the dirt with the toe of his shoe, but didn't make any move to leave.

"I won't get lost. Promise."

"Okay," he said, making his way through the rubble again. "So I'll see you later?"

"Later," I said.

After he'd left, after I couldn't hear his footsteps, even in the distance, and after I couldn't really even hear the scurrying of animals anymore, I maneuvered my way back over the piles of bricks and shuffled down the dirt path, back toward Monroe. I stood in front of the apparently not-main gate watching the students weave around in pairs and clusters. But before I went back through the gate, I had to know. I had to get close enough to check the license plate—check to make sure it was her. Before I called Dad. I skirted the edge of campus, easing my way slowly down the street, watching for the car.

I kept moving until I could see the main gate that Reid had been pointing out. Smaller and single arched, but smack dead in the middle of the school. From here to the gate, no car. And beyond, as far as I could see, no car. I squinted, straining to differentiate the shades of green on the shoulder of the road. The sun had sunk below the tree line, and the shadows loomed again. I tiptoed down the road, the noises from campus getting farther away, and eventually darted to the other side of the street, where I was sure I'd seen the car.

Weeds tickled my calves and the backs of my knees as I made my way through the underbrush. Nothing. I turned around to go back, wondering if I had imagined it all, if my brain put it in my head—like how I'd see Brian's shadow against my furniture in the dark. And then I stepped into a hole. A flattening of weeds. And beside it, another. And ahead, two more. The indentations from the tires of a car.

I whipped my head over my shoulder and stared into the trees—no, into the forest. I closed my eyes and listened for sounds from a car. The shadows stretched farther, crisscrossing the street, making the gate to Monroe contort backward, concave, like a spoon. I swatted at a mosquito on the back of my arm. And then the first firefly of the evening flashed in front of me. Light on. Light off. Here and not here. Like a signal to the rest, they lit up the roadside.

One flittered in front of my face, black as night. Light off, it flew.

The night Brian died, Colleen was catching fireflies on my back patio when I stepped outside. She had one cupped in her hand, and when I walked down the steps, she released it into my face, laughing as I swatted it away. "I think that's bad luck," she said. "Like breaking a mirror or walking under a ladder or something."

"I thought you were grounded," I said, looking over her outfit: black miniskirt, tight blue top.

"I was. Until Martha next door got in a fight with her husband and my mom went over, and my bedroom window just happened to slide open a little, and I just happened to fall out of it. And then I just so happened to remember that Brian is having a party this very instant."

"There's late, there's fashionably late, then there's God-where-were-you-you-missed-everything *late. Guess which one we are."*

"He's your boyfriend. Or something." She smirked.

I grinned. "My parents will be home in two hours. What's the point?"

"What's the point? What's the point*?" She gripped me by the shoulders and shook. "Cody fucking Parker, that's the point!"*

"He called?"

"No, he texted." She fumbled around in her bag and pressed a few buttons on her phone and held it in front of my face, the screen illuminated like the firefly.

where U at

Classy.

"I'm not ready," I said.

"So get ready."

I smiled. Colleen smiled back, big and toothy. "Two minutes, Mallory."

I took three. Exchanged my boxers for a jean skirt and threw on a black tank top. Since we were God-where-were-you-you-missed-everything *late, we didn't walk up to the beach, down the boardwalk, and cut back in, even though it was safer according to my parents, who didn't like me walking in the alleys after dark. Especially since people came and went so quickly in the summer, renting homes for a month, or a week. Then they'd be gone and replaced with more people we'd never get a chance to know.*

So as we walked, Colleen took out her black mini canister of pepper spray with the key ring on the end and swung it around on her pointer finger.

"It's probably not effective if they know you have it."

"This is preemptive," she explained. "They see I have it and that I'm not afraid to use it. You should get one."

"That's why I have you," I said. Also, I never carried a purse if I could help it, just stuffed my back pocket with a few dollars and hid my house key at the base of the gutter beside the front porch.

Colleen skipped ahead, spun around, and struck some made-up martial arts pose. "You wanna mess with this? Do ya?" Then she tilted her head back and opened her mouth, and her laughter echoed down the alley, across the ocean, and back again.

I crossed the street and entered campus through the main gate. As I walked back toward my dorm, I noticed a few people looking at me. I finally understood Colleen's feeling of power as she walked to the party that night. I could walk across campus and people would know. They'd know what I was capable of.

And I didn't even need the pepper spray.

A girl with long black hair, short black bangs, and thick black eyeliner put her hand on my arm as I walked through the lounge. "Do you remember me?" she asked. She moved a piece of gum from one side of her mouth to the other. "Chloe. Remember? You came to my mom's wedding. I was a bridesmaid. Orange dress. Big bow. You can't forget something like that."

Her hair had been lighter and shorter, and that had been before her discovery of eyeliner, but she was right: hard to forget an orange dress with a giant bow.

"The chocolate fountain," I said, because that wasn't something you could forget, either. Especially since I got it all over my dress. Actually, *Reid* had gotten it all over my dress. Chocolate-covered-strawberry handoff gone wrong.

Chloe smiled. "Exactly. My mom told me you were enrolled this year." I wondered what, exactly, her mother had told her, but I could tell from the way she didn't ask that she already knew. "Come sit with us at Preview?"

"Preview?"

"Yeah. Fall Preview. It's like a dinner-dance thing in the dining hall the day before classes start every year. Kinda lame, but, you know, tradition."

"Oh, I can't go," I said, because I was fairly certain I'd never go to another party again.

She scrunched up her mouth. "All right. Well, I'm in 233." She pointed straight up. "Come visit sometime."

"Okay," I said, and Chloe left through the front door. I walked down the hall toward my room. I wished it was that easy. Walk up the stairs to room 233 and talk about her hideous bridesmaid dress. Be friends in that easy, simple way. Talk about easy, simple things.

Think about easy, simple things.

My dorm room was empty—*emptied*. I guess this was just another part of consequence, like my grandma had warned me. Everything we do has consequence. This was just another.

My bed was piled high with my stuff, but the other side of the room, where Bree had been, was now consumed with an emptiness. Her bed was stripped. Her desktop was bare. The lights were gone. The posters were down. The only thing remaining was the sticky tack where the posters used to hang.

I unpacked and set up my room, trying to spread everything out so the emptiness wasn't so overwhelming. It wasn't a big room, and it hadn't felt empty when I'd first arrived. Only after Bree came. And left. People are funny like that.

I booted up the laptop and followed the instructions to set up the Internet connection and a school e-mail account. Then I composed a message to Colleen:

1 ex-roommate.

1 creep.

2 bitchtastic girls.

79 days till Thanksgiving break.

I hit send, pressed my thumbs into my temples, and felt this chill along the base of my neck. I squeezed my eyes shut and thought *No*, but that doesn't do anything either. My laptop made a tiny ping—a message from Colleen:

Miss you too. Will come as soon as detainment is over.

And that was just like Colleen. She didn't send cryptic messages, saying anything but what she meant. If she loved you she said I love you. If she hated you she said I hate you. She said what she meant.

And she did what she wanted.

We were a block away from the party that night when she stopped walking. She'd put her hand on my arm while I was re-tying a ponytail that I'd just undone. "You're nervous," she said.

"My hair won't cooperate."

She reached up behind me, pulled out the elastic, and threw it to the ground. "It's perfect." Then she put her hands on her hips and lowered her voice. "Mallory, it's no big thing. You do what you want to do and you don't do what you don't want to do. No biggie." Then she shrugged her shoulders and fluffed my hair with both hands.

Easy for her to say. Turns out Colleen mostly wanted to do everything anyway.

"Hey," she said, her hand on my elbow. "We don't have to go."

"But Cody Parker." I grinned.

"I like you better," she said.

Then I was laughing and not as nervous anymore, which I guess was her point, and we continued walking down the alley.

She hung an arm over my shoulders and pulled me in close for a few steps. I could hear the smile in her voice. "Dylan's gonna freak," she said. "You know he dumped Danielle last week."

No, I hadn't known.

People in the dorm were getting ready for Fall Preview. Whatever that meant. Were they previewing the new kids, like some meat factory? Did they bring a pen and take notes for later? All I knew was the bathrooms were overrun with girls spending hours trying to look like they hadn't spent any time getting ready.

I saw Bree skip across the hall, following Taryn into her room at the other end, near the lounge. I guess they were roommates now. If she noticed me, she didn't let on. I went back to my room and made a list of things I'd have to buy at the campus store tomorrow. First on the list: lights.

I thought about sending Colleen another e-mail about this ridiculously pretentious school that calls their lame-ass dance a Fall Preview, but I couldn't concentrate enough to compose a coherent sentence. Something was scraping my outside window. A tree branch, probably. And there were footsteps. Quiet, shuffling back and forth. Some guy waiting outside his girlfriend's window, probably.

Probably.

But in the back of my mind—no, in the front of my mind—I kept picturing that car. It was somewhere nearby. And if the car was nearby, so was Brian's mom.

My room was nestled into the corner—far enough so the noise from the hall didn't really bother me. Also far enough so nobody in the hall would hear me either. So I left the room, locked the door behind me, and walked through the cluster of girls streaming back and forth down the hall. I pushed through the door leading to the lounge and found a couch tucked away in the back corner. I watched the people waiting for their friends to show up, or waiting for their friends to come out of their rooms. So they could walk over together, I assumed. Like Colleen and I would've done.

Krista and Bree came through the hall door, side by side. And Taryn came tagging along right behind them. Jason barreled through the front door, pushing the wooden doors so hard they ricocheted off the wall and bounced back toward him. He stopped them with his open palms held out at his sides.

He stood in the entrance, scanning the room, scanning right over me, until his eyes landed on Krista. "Lovely, as always."

Krista curtsied and Bree smiled her nonmysterious smile.

"Who's this?" Jason asked, scanning Bree from head to toe.

"Bree," said Bree, even though I'd already introduced her as Bree not half a day earlier.

He looked between Krista and Bree and rocked back on his heels. "So are we going or what?"

"We're going," said Krista, with Bree on her arm and Taryn trailing behind.

But as they crossed the threshold, I saw Krista reach behind her and take Taryn's hand, pulling her along.

And for a second I thought that Krista was all right. It's the kind of thing Colleen would do for me. Making sure I was included. Making sure I was with her. Making sure I knew she was thinking of me.

She'd done it that night. When we left the alley and stood on the corner of Brian's street, she took my hand and pulled me toward the front steps.

CHAPTER 5

I didn't know Brian at first. First, there was Dylan. My lab partner in chemistry, and something else, something lingering under the surface, waiting to bubble over.

Which it eventually did.

Dylan liked me. I liked him. He knew it. I knew it. But there was the small issue of his girlfriend. Even she knew it, which is why she scowled at me whenever she passed me in the hall. Colleen told me to be bold. But I thought I already was.

I spent the semester giggling at his jokes, purposely bumping into him, and leaning too close while he used the dropper to fill a test tube—like it was the most fascinating thing I'd ever seen.

And he spent the semester looking me over. And over. And over.

Sometimes he'd text me in between classes, from down the hall, where I could see him standing with his group of friends. He'd look up and smile at me, and then I'd feel my phone vibrate. I didn't even have to check—it would say: I didn't do my homework. *I'd write back:* me neither. *He'd write:* library? *And we'd meet there for study hall. I was pretty sure we were both purposely not doing our chemistry homework just to have an excuse to hang out during study hall.*

But nothing ever happened. He kept his girlfriend, and our homework always sucked. And then we were failing. And that's when I got bold. Because everything suddenly felt so frantic, so urgent. We couldn't get our year-end project to work. The test tubes kept fizzling out and dying. So we stayed after school, and Dylan scribbled in his notebook and squinted at a calculator. Finally he said, "You don't want to know how many decimal places we were off by."

Then Dylan measured things out, and I leaned too close to the dropper, like I expected to remember any of this after the final exam, and finally our solution bubbled over, spilling out the top.

I leaped off my stool, spun around, and high-fived him.

Then I started laughing and said, "Oh my God, did we just high-five? Over a chemistry experiment?"

And he'd said, "No way, you misinterpreted my raised hand. I was waving at someone in the hall. And then you slapped it. Very uncool, Mallory. Your social status is plummeting as we speak."

I perched on the stool beside him. "Am I ruined?"

He smirked. "I could be convinced not to tell."

I didn't wait for him to elaborate. I leaned in and kissed him.

He didn't kiss me back. I mean, he didn't push me away or anything, but he didn't really put forth the effort. It was like he was undecided about the whole thing. And then there were footsteps in the hall. He'd glanced toward the door and said, "I'm supposed to meet Danielle." Right.

I thought maybe they'd break up, once he had time to think about it, but the next day they were walking down the hall together. The day after that too. Weeks of them walking down the hall together and kissing by her locker. Until school let out for the summer. And one day, I saw this guy on the boardwalk. I could've sworn it was Dylan. But it wasn't. This was an older version with a broader smile, and something else in his eyes. He saw me staring. And the first time he looked at me, I knew. He'd kiss me back.

He was a way to forget.

Forgetting wasn't really an option anymore.

Everyone had already left for Preview at least an hour earlier—even the stragglers were gone. My eyes were closed, not that I was sleeping. Not that I could ever sleep on my own anymore. But I could feel that *thing* coming. The way the room suddenly felt alive and charged. So I kept my eyes closed. Something grazed my arm. I opened my eyes and jumped up.

"Sorry." Reid was standing back, his hands held out innocently. "Didn't know if you were awake."

"I'm awake," I said, waiting until I couldn't hear my heartbeat pounding in my head anymore. I pushed the hair out of my face and scanned the empty room. Just me and Reid. I stared at my arm, where he had touched me, and wondered how long he'd been standing there. Wondered why, if he wanted to see if I was awake, he didn't just say my name.

"You're waiting for someone?"

"No," I said, checking out the room again. Then I looked at Reid again and said, "No, no one."

"Oh, I just figured since you were sitting out here, and, you know, you weren't *there* . . ." Reid was still standing on the other end of the couch. He was dressed up, I assumed. Hard to tell at a prep school.

"I wasn't where?"

"Fall Preview."

I sat back down and pulled my legs underneath me. "Wasn't really in the mood to preview. Or to be previewed. What, did you think I got lost in the woods or something?"

"What? No . . ." Reid's eyes jumped from bare wall to bare wall. "I said I'd see you later. You said 'later.' But you weren't there."

I started to smile. I couldn't help myself. I stood up and pointed my finger at his chest. "You did. When I wasn't there, you thought I got lost."

"I did not—"

I tilted my head back and laughed. "You thought you were gonna get in trouble."

Reid threw his hands up. "Okay, fine. *Fine.* I wanted to make sure you got back okay. Happy?" But he was laughing too.

I cleared my throat. "Well, look," I said. "I'm here and I'm alive. Your reputation as a responsible tour guide remains intact."

I walked past Reid, pushed open the hall door, and heard the buzzing of the fluorescent lights in the ceiling. And I paused because it reminded me of that feeling that was following me, waiting for me. Reid took a quick look toward the stairs on the other side of the lounge and then scanned the empty room. "Can I come in?"

"Does that line usually work for you?" I asked over my shoulder.

"That's not what I . . ." I couldn't see his face, but I imagined it turning red during the pause that followed. "Do you remember my dad's funeral?" he asked a moment later.

I kept myself turned away from him because I did remember. I remembered everything about it. It was the first funeral I'd ever been to, and I'd felt oddly detached from reality. Like time was moving slower, or faster—like what happened there didn't have any effect on the outside world. I had the feeling that if I'd wanted to run, I wouldn't have been able to. Like a dream where your legs never really touch the ground.

"Do you remember?" Reid asked. "You knocked on my door and said, 'Can I come in?' I said no. But you came in anyway."

And now I was too embarrassed by the whole thing to look him in the eye. "So you're going to come in even if I say no?"

"No," he said. "That would be creepy."

I felt him coming closer, in the way the air got thicker, warmer. "You know, you were the only one who came in my room that day." It felt like we were back there, two years earlier, exactly where we'd left off.

I turned around. He was coming closer. Like the moment was unfinished, and he needed to finish it. "Because your uncle told everyone you wanted to be left alone." I put my hands up, and he stopped walking. The whole thing was *mortifying*.

"And you're the only one who didn't listen. God, you were so bold . . ." Reid stared past me, down the hall, like he was remembering this other version of me and not the me who was standing in front of him.

I stepped into the hall, the door balancing against my hip. "Is that a yes?" he asked.

I thought about my room, and the emptiness, and the *thing*, and Brian's mom somewhere nearby. I thought about all the reasons I should say no, but all the reasons I wanted to say yes outweighed them. I turned back for a moment, and caught him looking at me like he did that day in his room. My stomach flipped, same as it did that day. "No," I said, as the door slammed shut behind me.

Because I remembered the next part too.

After he told me not to come in, and after I went in anyway, I sat beside him on the floor, our backs resting against the side of his bed. He threw a rubber ball against his wall and caught the rebound. I reached my hand across and intercepted the next bounce. Then I threw it against his wall, back to him. We did that for minutes, or hours, with nothing but the rhythm of the ball hitting the wall, then the floor, then our palms, filling the room.

Until Reid pulled his feet closer and flung the ball against the wall. He meant it to go nowhere. Anywhere. Straight through the wall, maybe. But it bounced back and smacked me in my upper cheek.

"Oh, shit," Reid said. He was on his knees in front of me, pulling my hand away from my face. It hurt, but the tears were from the surprise, and I swiped at them with the back of my other hand. "I didn't mean—"

I started to laugh, or I pretended to laugh, so he wouldn't think I was crying. "Girl, fourteen," I said in an official voice, "injured by rubber ball at funeral."

The side of Reid's mouth quirked up, just a bit. "The accused asserts that the victim had slow reflexes. He said he'd never seen such pathetic reflexes in his life." And then I laughed for real.

"On the contrary, the victim had amazing reflexes. In fact, she dove in front of the accused to protect him. That's how fast she is."

Reid was smiling. Smiling and laughing. "The accused would like to point out, for the record, that he told her not to come into his room in the first place."

Reid's hand was still on mine, from when he had pulled my arm away from my face. We seemed to notice it at the same time, because he looked at his hand. But he didn't move it away.

"Don't blame her. The victim only wanted to make him smile."

And then he stopped smiling. And he took his other hand and brushed the hair away from my cheek. Ran his thumb across the spot where I'd been hit. Then moved his hand back to my hair, moved his face closer to mine, and I held my breath, thinking, He's going to kiss me. *I remembered Colleen telling me to close my eyes, so I did.*

"What the hell am I doing?" he said, and the air around me felt empty. I opened my eyes and Reid was backing away from me. "I'm sorry," he said.

He walked out of his room. I stayed there until my heart rate returned to normal, until my face wasn't red from embarrassment. Then I walked down the stairs and waved to my parents.

We left a half hour later, and that was the last I'd seen of Reid. Dad stopped going to events after that—like the absence of his closest childhood friend, his high school roommate, was too much to endure.

Funny how two years can feel like nothing. How one moment can feel like eternity.

Two years, like they never even existed.

One moment, like there had never been anything else, would never be anything more.

Boom, boom, boom.

Someone was knocking. A dull thud, like someone was using the side of a closed fist instead of knuckles. I pictured Reid on the other side. Being bold, like I had been. "I told you no," I said, but this stupid grin was spreading across my face.

I opened the door to nothing. No, not nothing, *no one.* Because there was definitely something. Red and globbed and smeared across my door. Drops sliding downward, like tears. A small puddle on the linoleum floor, spreading like blood.

Everything inside of me froze, until I felt the hallway fill up—felt it practically vibrate with his presence. My eyes darted around the empty hallway until it seemed to constrict. And the entire feeling contracted into the space behind me. A wave of chills started at my scalp and slid down my arms, my spine, my legs.

My senses went on high alert—like I could see more clearly and hear more sharply—and I smelled something off, not quite right. Something chemical. I stepped closer to the door, bent down, and dipped my fingers in the puddle on the floor. Cold. Nothing like blood. I brought my red fingers to my face and breathed in through my nose. Paint. This was paint.

There were voices in the distance—girls laughing and a guy talking too loud—probably on their way back. I ran to the bathroom, and as I pushed the door open, I got this flash in my mind. Red handprints. Everywhere.

But I squeezed my eyes shut and thought *No*.

I brought wet paper towels back to my room and saturated my door. I squeezed and squeezed until the puddle at my feet was thin and the paint streaked unevenly through the water. Then I wiped it all up and buried the evidence in the bottom of the trash in the restroom. I couldn't see the red anymore, but there was still this dark spot. A water mark. A reminder. So I got more paper towels and started scrubbing harder.

And the whole time, I felt that presence pressed up against my back, and I could imagine his mouth, breathing against my neck through his teeth.

Like I could feel him smiling.

I didn't meet Brian that day on the boardwalk. We'd almost met. He smiled and stepped toward me, and I was wondering what to say. Sorry I was staring, I thought you were someone else? Sorry I'm still staring? I'm not sorry I'm staring because I still can't look away?

I tried to pull myself together because he was heading straight for me. Then this guy on a skateboard crashed into him. Came out of nowhere, music so loud I could hear it from his earbuds through the crowd. Brian stumbled backward and the skateboard slid out from under the other guy.

And then Brian yanked the earbuds out of the guy's ears and punched him in the face.

Just like that.

And, just like that, a circle formed around them as the skateboard guy, twice Brian's width, took a swing back at him. Brian ducked, smiled, and attacked. And then there were fists flying and blood spurting and people yelling, and I still couldn't look away.

Until two cops came and pulled them apart and started leading them down the boardwalk. But Brian turned and scanned the crowd for me and he smiled. After all that, he was still looking for me. He yelled out, "Meet me here tomorrow," like he was so sure this whole cop thing was no big deal. Like it happened all the time.

And like I should know what time he meant.

So that next day, even though I told myself I wasn't looking for him, I showed up early, before lunch. Just in case. And that's when I fell for him. Because he was already there too. He had a cut over his right eye, and there was a dark bruise underneath it, but he was there. Waiting for me.

Like he was still here now. Waiting. And smiling.

I heard voices in the lobby. The slow, monotone authority of Krista's voice. And the rise and fall of Bree's words coming straight from her brain out her mouth. I slipped into my room and shut the door behind me.

"Is it weird, though? Since he's your cousin?"

A pause. "Not at all," she said. The words were clipped, pronounced perfectly. Almost rehearsed.

"Because you could tell me, you know. If it gets weird, I mean. Or if it's weird for me to talk about him."

"Jesus," she said. "He asked you to hang out after class, not have his babies."

"Ha," Bree said. "It does bother you."

"Bree," Krista said, in this way that suddenly made me understand what it meant to speak carefully. "I doubt anything you do will bother me."

Bree laughed and started talking faster, like she was excited, but the way Krista said it didn't make it sound like a good thing. It sounded like Bree was inconsequential. Like she didn't matter enough to her at all.

And then a third voice, quieter, said, "He doesn't have the best reputation." Taryn, I guessed.

There was this beat of silence before I heard Bree laugh again. "Yeah, well, neither do I."

The door shut behind them and I was left with the silence again. With nothing but Bree's words lingering in my head.

Because Bree didn't have a reputation yet. So I guess what she was really saying was *neither will I.* Like that was the whole purpose.

Which was the type of thing someone said who had never truly had a bad reputation before.

This is what the people with the bad reputation do: they take a sleeping pill and hope that their ghosts won't come for them each night.

But all the hoping in the world doesn't change what happens.

The ghosts always come.

It starts in the distance.

Boom, boom, boom.

CHAPTER 6

Something wasn't right. I could sense that even though I was nearly asleep. I shouldn't have taken the sleeping pill. Someone was out there. Someone had thrown red paint on my door, playing a joke on me. Or maybe it wasn't a joke. Maybe it was Brian's mom. And here I was, sleeping. Almost sleeping.

The heartbeat filling the room paused, the room still buzzing with energy, and then there was a harsh whisper. "Mallory," it said, sounding far, far away.

Something grazed my shoulder. Just barely. Like I might've imagined it. And then fingers tightened around my shoulder and I felt warm breath on my ear. A whisper. *Wait.*

My eyes shot open.

Morning. The alarm was blaring beside me. I fumbled until I found the snooze button, then rubbed at my left ear, where I still felt the warmth. I jolted upright and moved my arm in a giant circle, stretching my shoulder. But when I stood up, I could still feel it. The spot where four fingers had pressed down on the front of my shoulder. The feel of a thumb on my back.

Something lingered in my room. Like the dust hovering in the slant of light beside my bed. Like the air before a thunderstorm. The threat of something coming.

I ran to the bathroom and stood in front of the mirror, the neck of my shirt jerked down past my shoulder. I stretched the skin and squinted at the mirror. I thought I could just barely make out four pink marks.

Taryn barreled through the bathroom door, half awake. She glanced at me, quickly looked away, and went to a shower stall on autopilot.

The mirror fogged up as I bent close to the sink, straining to see. I pulled at the skin of my shoulder repeatedly and wiped at the condensation on the mirror, but everything was muted. Filtered. Like viewing the world through white curtains.

Another girl came into the bathroom, pointed to the other shower stall, and said, "Are you using that?"

I took a step away from the mirror. And then another.

"Hey, I asked if you were using that shower."

"Huh? Yeah. Um, I need to get my stuff," I said, stumbling by her.

"Somebody needs some coffee," she mumbled as I passed.

Shower. Khaki pants. Brown shoes, not broken in yet. Scarlet shirt. I grabbed breakfast in the cafeteria on the way to first period and saw Reid in the student center with a group of guys, including Jason.

Reid patted someone on the shoulder and excused himself, and I walked a little faster. I felt Jason's eyes following me.

"Mallory," Reid called. "Wait."

The hairs on the back of my neck stood on end, and I backed into an alcove behind a column. The whole hallway seemed to throb like my room at night, when I wasn't fully awake.

Reid jogged over to me. "Hey," he said.

But before he had a chance to say anything else, I said, "Did you see anyone last night?"

"Huh?"

"In the dorm. Around the dorm. Last night." Because there was red paint on my door. Because something grabbed onto my shoulder.

"Not that I noticed. What happened? You don't look so good."

What happened? I wasn't sure. I wasn't even sure if I was seeing clearly. I yanked at the collar of my shirt, pulling it down over my shoulder. "Do you see something?" I asked.

Reid smiled, then tried not to smile, then smiled again. "Um." I followed his gaze to the black-and-silver bra strap.

Damn Colleen and her proclamation that the only thing more boring than a white bra was a sports bra. I released the neck of the shirt and shrugged it back up over my shoulder.

"I meant like marks or something. On my shoulder," I said, looking at the people rushing past, but not really focusing on them.

His forehead creased and he leaned closer. "Did someone hurt you?"

I shook my head. *Maybe. No. I don't know.* "Never mind." I looked at his hands, which were kind of hovering between us, like they were undecided.

There was a chime from the speakers. "Warning bell." Reid started backing away in the opposite direction. "I have soccer later," he said, like I had wondered. "But I'll see you." Like I had asked. Then he turned and fell into stride with a sea of red shirts and khaki pants.

He disappeared.

Colleen said I disappeared when I was with Brian. Which at first I didn't get—because I was louder and more sarcastic and I laughed more whenever I was near him.

I was always on my toes, deflecting his friends' half flirts, half jabs. Reminding Joe that Sammy was the hot twin, without the busted nose. Making sure Brian saw me doing cartwheels at the waterline. I was me, and then some. I was me times ten. So I rolled my eyes the first time she said it. But then I realized she meant that, even then, I still paled in comparison to Brian's forceful personality. The way he demanded attention, demanded respect, demanded me.

"Mallory, come on," he'd said, while we sat with Colleen, Cody, and Sammy on the beach. "Show me your place."

I waited for Colleen to come up with an excuse for me, like she always did, because she could usually sense, without asking, that I wanted one. But she stayed silent, staring off at the horizon.

"Colleen," I'd said. "Don't we have plans this afternoon?"

"Yeah," she said, keeping her eyes on the distance. "We do." Then she turned to me and kept her face hard. "Sorry, I didn't notice you were here."

Bree was hard not to notice in English class. She was demanding attention too, laughing a little too loudly. Making sure everyone overheard her telling some story to Krista about some guy over the summer. I rolled my eyes, but I kind of understood why she was doing it. Krista sat directly across the room from me, on the other side of the *U* of tables, wedged between Bree, who wouldn't shut up, and Taryn, who was drawing in her notebook. There was this berth around them, almost like they were exclusive, except I got the feeling that nobody else wanted to touch them.

Chloe sat beside me. “Word to the wise,” she whispered. “Mr. Durham can make your life easy, or he can make your life hell. Choose wisely.”

“Thanks.”

“Also, we’re about to have a pop quiz on the summer reading. Happens every year.”

“I didn’t get the summer reading list.”

“Not good.” Chloe tore a paper from her notebook and started scribbling titles and names and half sentences. Quick plot summaries. Then Mr. Durham walked in the room and she quickly balled up the paper and stuffed it in her bag.

I was definitely going to fail.

I only saw Reid once during classes, and he didn’t see me. He walked into a science classroom down the hall from mine, laughing at something the girl next to him was saying, raising his hand in greeting as he passed his teacher. And that was all I saw of him. He was a senior, with senior classes and senior friends, and presumably a better lunch slot than me. Seriously. Who eats lunch at eleven in the morning?

And after school, with nothing better to do, I worked. Well, first I changed. Then I worked. I made a serious dent in the summer reading list even before study hall began. After Ms. Perkins made the rounds and checked that we were all in our rooms for the mandatory two-hour study-hall block, I sent a quick message off to Colleen: Day 1: success. And by "success" I mean "survived." 78 days left. I ran through make-believe responses in my head: telling me how much her day sucked maybe, or sharing some piece of mindless gossip—real or imagined—about someone we both knew.

I picked up *Lord of the Flies*, waiting to hear a chime from my computer, but nothing came. So about halfway through study hall, I started writing another email, this time about Reid. Except I realized I'd never once mentioned him to her. And I wasn't sure why.

There was a knock at my door, and I froze. Could the faculty sense when we weren't studying during study hall? Someone jiggled the door handle, and I slammed my laptop shut. "Hey, it's me," a voice called. Like I should just know who it was. Which, okay, I did.

I opened the door and Reid wedged a triangle block underneath it, propping it open. Part (b) of visitation rules as stated in the Monroe Student Handbook.

"You carry those around?"

"Ms. Perkins hands them out at check-in," Reid said. Right. Part (a).

"Oh." Then I stood in the doorway, wondering what I was supposed to do. Reid brushed by me and sprawled out on this particularly unattractive orange shag carpet I'd found that afternoon in the closet of spare furniture beside the laundry room.

"God, this is hideous," he said. He flipped a textbook open, stuck a pen behind his ear, and said, "By the way, I'm helping you with math."

"I don't need help with—"

And then Ms. Perkins was standing in the entrance to my room. "I wasn't aware you were taking senior courses, Mallory."

"Oh, I'm not." Reid was giving me a Look. I opened the top drawer to my desk and pulled out my calculator. "Reid's helping me with math."

He smiled at Ms. Perkins, dimple and all. "That's very generous of you, Reid."

He shrugged, like it was no big deal. "Yeah, well, we used to be friends."

Ms. Perkins left and I stared at the blank screen of my calculator. *Used to be friends.* Is that what we were? Were we ever anything, really? "Mallory, I didn't mean—"

"Why are you here, exactly?"

He glanced toward the hall again, where Ms. Perkins was making the rounds from room to room, and scribbled absently in his notebook. Or maybe all those letters and numbers meant something to him.

"How was your first day?" he asked, without looking up.

"I already failed my first quiz."

Reid smiled and put his pencil down. "Durham, right?"

I nodded. "And I eat lunch at eleven."

"The horror." He looked down the hall again. Empty. "So, here's the thing." Reid lowered his voice so I had to lean forward off my chair, and I still could barely hear him. "Tomorrow night—"

"Knock, knock." Chloe stood in my doorway, something clutched to her chest. Her eyes moved from me to Reid to me again, and she grinned. "Am I interrupting something?"

"No," Reid said, before I could even open my mouth. He went back to scribbling intensely in his notebook.

"Oh good," Chloe said. She stepped inside the room and pressed her back against the wall, out of view of the hallway. "I come bearing gifts." Apparently whatever she was clutching to her chest were the gifts. Looked like a stack of yellow books. Then she turned them around so they were facing out. CliffsNotes for all the summer reading.

"Oh my God," I said.

Reid glanced up. "Prep-school porn." He laughed to himself and started packing up his stuff. "I can't indulge this behavior. It's appalling. What would your parents think?"

Chloe was shaking with laughter. "Leave already so we can close the door."

"I'd rather be caught with a girl in my room than that," he said, hands held up.

"You mean Mallory?"

I looked at the floor, so unlike the version of me he remembered. As far as I could tell, Reid ignored the question. "Hey, I need to talk to you tomorrow."

"I have e-mail, you know."

"Oh no," Chloe said, "that doesn't really belong to you. Don't send anything you don't want *them* knowing." She pointed to the ceiling, like they were all-powerful, all-seeing.

"Will you be here tomorrow? Same time?" Reid asked.

"Not like I can be anywhere else." I pointed to the Monroe handbook on my desk. "I think every hour is regimented."

Reid smiled as he backed out the door. "Nah, Mallory. Those are only suggestions." It sounded exactly like something Colleen would say. And before I could stop myself, I was grinning ear to ear.

Chloe closed the door behind him and threw the books on my desk. "I *suggest* we get to work." She pointed to the Cliffs-Notes for *The Grapes of Wrath*. "This. This is a particular brand of torture I can't let anyone endure. Start here." I searched for a pen. "And Mallory? Write fast."

When Chloe left with her books at the end of study hall, the emptiness of the room was overwhelming. I started to see things, like I used to at home. Brian's shadow on the dark window. A handprint on the wall.

Ms. Perkins came around to give the lights-out notice, and I held the vial of sleeping pills in my hand, thinking about the hand on my shoulder when I was half conscious. I started to worry that maybe someone *had* been in my room—someone real. I tilted the vial back and forth, listening to the pills fall against one another. Then I threw them in the bottom drawer of my desk and slammed it shut.

My mind raced with possibility. That green car. The red door. The restraining order. Was it only good in New Jersey?

The alarms on the outside doors were armed at night, at least.

But the window. Crap, the window. I checked it and double-checked it, like Mom would do at home.

I sat on my bed and stared at the door, the window, the door again. The dorm settled into silence.

And then it started, in the distance. Even though I wasn't sleeping. Even though I wasn't in the in-between. I was wide awake. Sitting upright. Staring at the door. And it started.

Boom, boom, boom.

I stared at the light framing the door, which seemed to pulsate brighter with each beat of his heart, coming closer.

I used to have nightmares when I was a kid. The kind where you wake up, but you still see the dream. Back then, I used to close my eyes from it. Remembering what Mom always told me—it's only real if you let it be. So I'd close my eyes until it passed.

The air changed in my dorm room. It started throbbing

with the slow and steady beat. And because I was a coward, I ran for the desk. I threw open the bottom drawer, snatched the vial of sleeping pills, and took one.

I buried myself face down on my bed and covered my head with my pillow, but sleep didn't come quickly enough. I felt something taking shape behind me. And this time, I swear I could hear it laughing.

I felt the hand on my shoulder, fingers digging in, as it held me down.

There were marks the next morning. I saw them in the shower. Red and thin, like fingers. I thought of Mom sitting by my bed, stroking the hair away from my sweat-drenched forehead, saying, *It's only real if you let it be.* I looked away from my shoulder. If I didn't see it, it wasn't real.

Mr. Durham perched on the edge of his desk and took out his tattered copy of *Lord of the Flies.* I'd read most of that one on my own yesterday. And not the CliffsNotes version. Everyone took out their crisp copies and placed them on the tables in front of them.

"So," he began, licking his finger and thumbing through the pages, "I think we've already established that Golding was saying, underneath it all, that without civilization, we are essentially savages."

I opened my notebook and wrote, *We are savages.*

Mr. Durham stopped flipping pages and smoothed down a corner. "They stop thinking for themselves. When they kill Piggy, do they know it's Piggy? Do any of them know?"

Krista spoke. "They had to know. How could they not? It's pretty unrealistic."

"Is it?" Mr. Durham asked. "You've all witnessed herd behavior."

I wrote, *herd behavior.* Yes, I had witnessed it. At the ice cream shop.

Everyone leaned forward a little over the tables. Everyone but me. This wasn't news to me.

"It can be as benign as shopping on Black Friday—haven't you heard of people stampeding to get the cheap televisions? Trampling others? And when you cheer at a sporting event, would you get up to shout or cheer or boo on your own? Or do you only do it because everyone else is doing it? Because you are part of something greater?"

Silence in the classroom.

"And trends," he continued. "I mean, really, who thought mullets were a good idea?"

A few of the guys laughed.

"Or blue eyeshadow," Chloe said.

"Or bell-bottoms," another kid said.

"Exactly," Mr. Durham said, nodding his head and smiling.

"But it starts somewhere," Bree said. "Right? I mean, blue eye shadow didn't just appear from nowhere. Someone had to start it."

"Yes, the idea comes from somewhere," Mr. Durham answered. "Is that person more culpable than the followers? Less? If one person says, 'Pull that person from the car and beat him to death,' and twenty people oblige, who's at fault?"

We stayed silent.

"And that, my friends, is why it's nearly impossible to convict a mob." He cut his eyes to me for a fraction of a second. I didn't know why he was thinking of me. I hadn't been part of a mob or influenced by group thought. No, it was just me. My decision. I chose death.

"So," Krista said, speaking carefully again, "*Lord of the Flies* is really just a metaphor for bad fashion decisions?" A few giggles escaped around the room.

Mr. Durham grinned. "Or maybe it's just one big allegory for high school."

Reid showed up for study hall again, as promised. He spread out his work across my floor, and then he put a finger to his lips and motioned for me to come toward him.

I crouched beside him and said, "What?"

"Tonight," he said in a voice that was so low I had to lean even closer. "New students get initiated."

"Initiated?"

Apparently I spoke too loudly because he glanced toward my open door. "Tradition. They're going to take you after lights out."

"And do what with me?"

"I'm not telling." He was fighting a smile.

"What the hell, Reid?" I sat cross-legged across from him, his notebook between us.

"Mallory, it's fun. I'm only giving you the heads up because . . . Because. We all did it. It's tradition."

"Tradition. You sound like my dad—at Monroe, it's tradition that blah, blah, blah."

"It's really not so bad here. And personally, I'd give just about anything to learn more about my dad."

Crap. There were words I was supposed to say now. But they seemed so worthless, so I pressed my lips together instead.

"Sorry," he said, like someone had to say it. "I'm just saying. This is practically my home. I like the traditions. You will too. I'm just giving you the heads-up. I feel like I owe you one."

Because we used to be friends. Right.

"Nobody's *taking* me," I said.

He started to speak, then stopped. Then grinned. "Are you fast?"

"Yes."

CHAPTER 7

Reid was right. I didn't need him to tell me when it would start. I heard the doors latching softly first, then the light padding of footsteps. Someone tested the handle, gently, but I had locked it. Then someone started knocking. Softly, but frantically. "Help," they whispered. "Mallory, help!"

I imagined them waiting on the other side of the door, waiting for me. Smiling at each other. Waiting to grab me. Instead I slipped on my sneakers, opened the window, and hopped out. It wasn't a far drop, but it was hard to judge in the dark, and my ankle rolled. I stretched it out, took a few shaky steps, and started to run.

Dark shapes came into focus against the brick of the building across the quad—Reid's dorm. Three people, dressed in black, hoods pulled up over their heads. They spread out in front of me, closing in from different angles. I couldn't tell them apart until Reid let his hood fall back, just a little off his face. I cut to the right, toward him, because I didn't know what else to do. He caught me around the waist, and we stood that way, both breathing heavy. This was the closest we had been since that day in his room. Closer, actually. But things were simpler in the dark. I couldn't see his expression and he couldn't see mine.

Then he said, "Someone tell the girls we have Mallory."

Reid's arm was still around my waist until I shook him off. Then he put his hand at the base of my neck. "Okay?" he asked. I didn't answer, but I didn't shake him off. "You're right," he whispered in my ear, "you're fast."

Behind the building, freshmen and the new transfer students were crouched along the base of the wall as Jason paced in front of them. They were wearing pajamas, huddled in dark blankets. Krista and Taryn, also dressed in black, turned the corner with Bree between the two of them. "We do it because we love you," said Krista. She laughed and deposited Bree with the rest of the new kids. Jason tossed Bree a blanket.

Jason got up in my face and said, "Looks like you skipped the getting-taken part." He looked at my sneakers, at my sweatshirt over top of my pajamas.

"She ran," Reid said.

Jason narrowed his eyes at Reid. "Yes, I can see that.

Doesn't seem fair, really." Jason pointed to everyone else against the wall: barefoot and underdressed for the cold night. He looked at Krista and held his hand out to his side. They shared the same knowing smile before she jogged around the side of the building. She returned with a hose.

"Jason . . . ," Reid began, before Jason raised his eyebrows at him.

Somebody else mumbled, "Dude, it's cold."

"So cold she sleeps in sneakers?" Then he grinned at me. "I *am* sorry to do this to you." Then he looked me up and down one last time. "Actually, I'm not."

I turned my back to him as a cold blast of water hit me between the shoulder blades.

Someone tossed me the same dark blanket—something cheap and feltlike—that everyone else was wrapped in. I wanted to let it fall to the ground, to pretend I wasn't cold, but I'm pretty sure the shivering gave me away. I wrapped it around my shoulders as they lined us up and marched us silently around the far edge of campus back toward Barringer Hall.

Something was behind me, right at my back, even though I thought I was the last in line. I thought about running. Just . . . running. Off into the woods somewhere. Anywhere but here. I tensed when I felt hands in my hair, twisting the ends around, until I realized it was Reid—that he was wringing out the water.

"I think I made it worse," he whispered over my shoulder.

I pulled the blanket tighter around my shoulders as we walked.

"You think?"

He put his hand on my side. "Just a sec," he said, as the rest of the line stumbled forward.

He took his sweatshirt off in one swift motion and said, "Here. Switch." He had a black T-shirt on underneath. I was trying to remember what I had on under mine.

"Mine won't fit you."

"Mallory, take the freaking sweatshirt." He glanced toward the line, moving farther away, and added, "Hurry."

I dropped my blanket, stripped off my top shirt, and threw on his sweatshirt before either of us had a chance to notice whether the shirt underneath was soaked through. His shirt was twice as long as mine and warm on the inside, and I pulled the sleeves down over my hands. "Think they'll notice if I skip it?"

He grinned. "They'll notice. Come on. Don't worry, it'll be fun." We jogged to catch up with the group.

One of the side doors of Barringer Hall was propped open with a brick. We entered and climbed the stairs in silence—but we didn't stop on the top floor. Jason pushed through the door to the roof and held it open as we all marched silently past him. The others, the initiators, I guess, stood in the doorway. Reid pushed my blanket back into my hands. "Take it," he said. "Trust me, it gets colder." He smiled at me.

I didn't smile back. But I took the blanket.

The roof was framed with a brick wall, about waist level. "Every one of us here has spent the night on the roof of Barringer Hall. Some, more than once." Jason smiled wide, and a few people snickered. "But it wasn't always this way. Initiations used to be held in the woods, until poor Jack Danvers wandered off and never returned. Which brings us to the rules. There's only one, really. Stay with the group. Unless you want a dorm named after you." Obnoxious grin.

The initiators started filing out the door, back down the steps. "Enjoy the sunrise, kids. Oh, and don't jump." Jason closed the door behind him, and everyone stood in silence, staring at it.

A freshman guy immediately started pulling on the handle, but the door wouldn't budge. A girl joined him and ran her fingers along the seams. "No hinges, either," she said.

"Son of a . . ."

A girl who looked way too young to be on a roof in the middle of the night said, "We could scream."

The freshman guy who'd been pulling on the door said, "Don't be stupid. If we get caught, they get in trouble, and then what? We're stuck with them for the rest of the school year. You want to be on their bad side? 'Cause I don't."

And with that sentiment, everyone settled into complacency. Some curled up around the edges under the bricks.

Bree folded her hands behind her head and closed her eyes. Like it was no big deal she was stuck on a roof for the foreseeable future. And some people took the opportunity to gossip, like it was some planned slumber party or something. Not like we were herded like animals, marched up here, and locked on the roof against our will.

I was surrounded by people who never worried, it seemed. Who never checked to see where the closest exits were or what they could use for a weapon if they had to. People who didn't worry about killing or being killed.

I walked the perimeter of the roof, stepping over a few freshman along the way. I peered over the edge every few steps. "Hey," I said. "There's a ladder." A few people rose to look over the edge with me. They leaned forward, ever so slightly, and peered down the three stories below.

"It stops, see?" one guy said. He was right. It stopped right at the next floor, like there used to be some sort of fire escape, but it had since been torn down. They all went back to doing nothing, but I kept walking and peering over the edge. On the opposite side of the roof, behind some chimney-looking thing, there was another ladder. This one stopped as well, but it ended right beside a classroom window. We were three floors up—not twelve or anything—so I carefully eased myself over the edge to investigate.

When I reached the bottom rung, I pushed on the window

with my foot, and it creaked open. No need for locks when the windows were so high. I pushed it farther, so it sat at a ninety-degree angle, and then I swung one leg into the building, eased myself from the bottom rung until I was safely straddling the sill, and then tilted my weight so I fell inward.

I was in a math classroom. Inside. On the floor. And I couldn't stop laughing. It sounded hollow and unfamiliar in the empty room. I stood up, brushed my pants off, and let out one last laugh. Then I listened to the silence buzzing in my ears.

The chairs, wedged up against each desk. Half a math problem on the white board. Unfinished.

Boom, boom, boom. In the distance, coming closer. I should've stayed up on the roof with everyone else.

Mallory. I should've stayed up there, with the things that were real.

Wait, it whispered, sounding way too close. I felt something, just out of sight, hovering behind me, and I didn't wait. I ran out of the room, down the hall, down the staircase to the lower level, where the door had been left ajar. I ran across the quad as fast as I possibly could. Faster even than I thought I could. I didn't stop.

I had been too pumped up to sleep by the time I crawled my way back through my dorm-room window, and it had been too close to morning to take a sleeping pill. But now, three minutes before English class was about to start, I couldn't keep my head off the desk.

Just as I was starting to doze, Chloe dropped her notebook next to my head. "How did you do it?" she said, leaning closer.

I sat up and rubbed at my face. "What?"

"You weren't on the roof when they went back. Everyone was freaking out. I heard they even checked the bushes."

"They thought I fell?"

"Or . . . Well, let's just say you gave everyone a freaking heart attack until Taryn saw you getting ready this morning. So how did you—"

"Ms. Murphy." Mr. Durham was standing over us. He placed my quiz, F, as expected, face up on the table. "Less talking, more reading."

Everyone stared at me for the rest of class. But this wasn't the type of stare I'd grown used to over the past two months. This was something else entirely.

Reid was waiting in the hall after class, and he looked angry. He gripped me by the elbow, so unlike last night. I ripped my arm away from him. "You scared the *shit* out of me," he said.

"You locked me on the goddamn *roof*." We weren't whispering. Actually, we were making a scene.

"We locked *everyone* on the goddamn roof," he said, remembering to lower his voice. "And we came *back* for them a few hours before class. You weren't there!"

To everyone else, it might not have been a big deal. But he didn't get how much I feared the very idea of being trapped. "Yeah, well, excuse me for not wanting to spend the night freezing my ass off with a bunch of people I don't know."

"That's the point of it, Mallory. To get to know everyone. It's like a bonding thing. It's supposed to be *fun*. Or, at least, it was for us."

"Who should I be bonding with? Let's see, there's the girl who moved out of our room the first day I was here, a bunch of scared little freshmen, people who talk about me behind my—"

Jason was suddenly between us. "Impressive, Mallory." Then he turned to Reid. "See? Told you she was fine." He turned back toward me again. "He was convinced you fell or something. So tell us. How'd you do it?"

But I was looking past him, at Reid, at his expression. Because I suddenly remembered how his father had died. A freak accident—he was chipping the ice off the roof because there'd been a leak underneath, and he slipped. Broke his neck. Not a fall that should kill you, but it did.

Of course he'd be thinking of that when I went missing. I guess he saw the realization on my face, because he turned around and left.

"I clicked my heels together three times," I told Jason, "and said, 'There's no place like home.' "

Home. I should've stayed home.

I shouldn't have gone to Brian's party. Shouldn't have left my house. As soon as I walked in, I felt the urge to leave. To click my heels together three times and magically transport myself home. We'd been late—so late—and things had already slid past the point of controlled or predictable.

Brian's house didn't look white or open or airy at night, filled with people and music and sweat. Colleen stood in the foyer and scanned the room. Cody was standing in the hallway, very tall and very dark and very worth sneaking out of the house for. His head was back against the wall, and Colleen walked straight for him.

She tossed a look over her shoulder, her eyebrows raised at me, before she reached him. I nodded. I didn't need a babysitter.

Brian's voice echoed down the hallway, like the blender that day with his mom, churning away above all the rest of the sound. I looked down the hall toward the kitchen and saw him pass across the doorway a few times. He was doing some routine, some reenactment, and everyone was laughing at him.

"Don't."

I spun around to find Dylan sprawled on the couch in the room beside the foyer. He had a red plastic cup in his hands and his feet were propped on the table, littered with discarded cups. Someone was unconscious on the couch across from him. And Dylan was looking at me with these alcohol-dazed eyes.

"I broke up with Danielle," he said.

"I know." I looked back down the hall and bit my lower lip.

"Please don't go down there."

I wanted him to understand. Because I understood. "You didn't dump her for me."

"I did."

"No," I said, more sure of myself. "No. You would've done it before. A long time before I was . . . with Brian."

Dylan chugged whatever was left in his cup and tossed it onto the coffee table. "Come on, Mallory. Brian isn't with *people. He's not* with *you. You're just* today*. Maybe tomorrow. Maybe not."*

If he was trying to hurt me, to hurt me like I had hurt him, he was doing a damn good job of it. Because inside, I had this inkling, this tiny feeling that he was right. That that's what had been holding me back, keeping me at a distance.

I looked at Dylan on the couch. He liked me and I liked him and, God, if he would just say the right thing, I'd change my mind right then. But he was making it so hard. He was being such an ass. And he wasn't saying the right thing. Probably because he didn't mean the right thing. And Brian was in the kitchen, larger than life—like Colleen—pulling me along in orbit. I could just let go, and I'd be swept along.

Neither was the right reason. "I kissed you," I said.

"I know. It's just that . . . we were together a long time. I was confused, you know?"

"It's not that complicated," I said. I held my breath and thought, Tell me you like me, tell me you liked me, tell me it was a mistake, that you should've picked me, that you want to take it all back.

"Today's my birthday," Dylan said. What did that *mean? Like I owed him something? Like I shouldn't be with his brother because it was his birthday? Definitely not the right thing to say. I felt pathetic, sick, and I realized there was a third option.*

I backed down the hall, let myself out the front door, maneuvered around the partially conscious bodies on the front steps, and left.

I folded my arms across my chest and kept my head down as I walked back toward the dark alley. The air was thick with the possibility of a storm. The night, about to break open.

Colleen picked up half a ring before the answering machine would have. I'd cashed in all my singles to get change for the hall pay phone and called during the hour between Colleen getting home from school and her mom getting back from work. She didn't sound out of breath, though. Not like she'd been racing to the phone. More like she'd been sitting there next to it the entire time. Debating.

"What's up?"

I imagined her staring at her nails. Resting the phone against her shoulder. Slouching into the corner of her couch. "General boredom. What's up with you, New Hampshire?"

"You didn't write back."

There was a pause, and I imagined her moving the phone from one shoulder to the other. "Is that the only reason you called? Geez, I only just got it. What, you think I sit around all day staring at the computer just in case you happen to send an e-mail?"

"No, I don't think—"

"And besides, it didn't even *say* anything. It said you were done with the day. That's it. Wow. Excuse me for not being inspired to respond."

"You're mad at me."

Silence. And then, "No, you asshole. I'm not mad at you." She sighed into the phone, and I felt it, I swear. And I wanted to reach through the phone. Sit cross-legged on the couch beside her while she painted my nails dark gray or hot pink or midnight blue. I ran my fingers against the silver cord of the phone, searching for words.

"To continue this call . . ." An automated voice broke the silence, jarring me back to here.

"I'm out of money . . ."

"I've got an end date: two weeks. Can't have your number showing up on the phone bill. Sorry."

"Colleen?" I thought of words, but they weren't the right ones. "I hate it here."

"I—" And then there was a dial tone. *What?* I thought. *I*

what? *I miss you* or *I'm hungry* or *I want to drop a penny from the top of the Eiffel Tower? What?*

Reid didn't show up during study hall. And really, why would he? He'd already told me what he had to say, and I thanked him by simultaneously scaring the shit out of him and insulting him. I wanted to send him an e-mail, tell him how I got off the roof. That it was safe, that I would've told him, if he asked. But he didn't ask. I also remembered that email wasn't necessarily private here.

Ugh. I shoved my work—and his sweatshirt—into a backpack and walked down the hall.

"Where to, Ms. Murphy?" Ms. Perkins tore a slip of paper off her permission pad.

Krista stood behind me, tapping her foot. "Danvers West," I said. And suddenly Jason's words from the night before made sense. *Danvers*. You disappear, you get a dorm named after you.

Ms. Perkins was still waiting. I cleared my throat. "Reid Carlson."

She tore the paper off the pad, but before handing it to me, she said, "Krista? Same?"

"Yep. Danvers West. Jason Dorchester."

Ms. Perkins handed us our slips of paper together, and I didn't really have any choice but to walk beside Krista.

Once we were outside, she spoke. "You shouldn't have left, you know. It's initiation. And you haven't been properly initiated yet."

"What, hosing me down with water doesn't count?"

"Oh, not hardly," she said. We walked across the rest of the quad in silence, and she entered the dorm in front of me.

Mr. Durham took our permission slips in the lounge. The dorm was the mirror image of mine, but the furniture was more worn, and the whole place smelled a little more like musk and sweat, like boys. Krista took off down the hall, but I stayed at Mr. Durham's makeshift desk.

"What is it?"

"I don't know the room number."

He grinned at me. "You're showing up uninvited?"

"No," I said. "He's expecting me." At least I hoped he was. "I just forgot to write it down."

"Right. Room 203."

The door to his room was open, and there were other voices coming from inside. By the time I realized that, though, he had already seen me and it was too late to turn around. Reid cocked his head to the side as I stepped into his room.

He was sitting on the black rug on his floor, surrounded by three other students from his grade. "This is Amy," he said, pointing to the redhead with freckles next to him. "Nick"—he pointed to the boy closest to me—"and Landon."

"And this must be Mallory," Landon said, standing. "Tell us how you did it."

I locked eyes with Reid, who was still on the floor, not smiling, and he raised his eyebrows. I pulled his sweatshirt out of my bag and tossed it to him.

"Thanks," he said.

I looked at the floor. "You too."

Nick cleared his throat and stood up. "Ohhh-kay." He motioned for Amy to follow him. "Relocating to my room when you're ready, Reid."

"Aw, man," Landon said. "But it's getting exciting."

He left anyway, waving at me as he passed.

"I actually need to do that work," Reid said.

I dropped my bag at the foot of his desk and sat in the chair beside it. I looked at his walls, with posters of bands I didn't know. And at his black-and-gray-striped comforter, thrown haphazardly over his bed. With everyone gone, I noticed there was music playing softly as well.

"There's a ladder," I said. "On the roof."

"No there isn't."

"Yes. There is. From when there were fire escapes, I guess. Really obvious, if you're looking for it. I mean, if you want to leave, you can."

"I've never seen a ladder."

"Well, it doesn't go all the way down. It's just half a ladder. A third of a ladder."

"A third of a ladder? And what about the missing two-thirds?"

"It ended right next to a window. A math room. And you know how those windows tilt to open? I tilted it. And that's that." Which sounded much more dangerous than it actually was.

He narrowed his eyes and spoke slowly. "You took a ladder and climbed through a window on the third floor? Of course you did. I can't decide whether you're brave or reckless."

I wasn't either of those things. I was anxious and unsettled and I wanted the hell off the roof. That's all. "No, I'm not—"

"Yeah, you are. You always were."

"Always? Reid, we saw each other three times a year, tops. You barely knew me."

"Right." He looked like he was trying not to smile. I was trying not to smile too.

"Hey, so, I'm gonna go back. I just wanted you to know . . . I mean, not like you asked or anything, but . . ."

Reid kept waiting, like he thought I was going to spell it all out for him. And when he finally realized I was done, he said, "Is that your apology?"

"Is this *yours*?" I asked, and this time I couldn't really stop the smile.

He stood up so he was taller than me, and I rolled his chair back a little farther, until it was pressed up against his desk. He stuck his hand out. "Friends?"

He didn't lower his hand just because I kept staring at it. Not like when he found me at the old student center. He held out his hand like we had no history. Like we were starting over. Which was really the entire point of my coming here after all.

I stood up and put my hand in his. I expected us to shake, but neither of us did. We just held on for a few seconds until I pulled my hand back.

I slung my bag over my shoulder.

"Are you coming to our game Saturday?"

"Um, not really my thing," I said, moving toward the door.

"What's not your thing? Soccer? Or me?"

I paused because there was really no right answer to that question. "Sitting on the bleachers."

He smiled. "Fair enough." I walked out the doorway, and when I was in the hall, he said, "So what is your thing?"

I thought of Colleen and the boardwalk, the beach and the sun, none of which were here, and I kept moving, because the truth was, without her, I had no idea.

After study hall I took a sleeping pill and raced the feeling to sleep. I wasn't fast enough. Like running away last night had flipped some switch. Almost as soon as I swallowed, I heard the noise. The *boom, boom, boom* coming closer. I closed my eyes, but I heard the voice. *Mallory*, it whispered. *Wait.*

And that's when the hand reached out and grabbed me.

Then came the dream, same as every night. I saw the choice, like the very first time: the knife, the door. Life, death. *Choose. Choose different.* But I didn't. I made the same choice every time. Even in my dream.

Reid fell into stride with me on the way to science class. "Hey."

"Hey," I said. "Were you waiting for me?" Bold.

"Just heading in the same direction." Half-truth.

"I didn't know you had science this period." Lie.

Silence as we weaved through the crowded hall.

"Word on the street is that you slid down the downspout."

"No!"

"There's a smaller faction who say you crawled through the ventilation shaft, but my class knows that's not possible."

"How do they know?"

"We tried that my year."

I stopped walking. "Hey, I thought you said being locked on the roof was *fun*?"

"It was fun trying to escape together." He smiled and shook his head to himself, then put a hand on my back for half a second as he started walking again. "Turns out ventilation shafts aren't big like they seem in movies. Or sturdy. At all. Jason got both his legs stuck. The orientation group had to get oil to get him unstuck. Almost got caught because of it . . ."

I stopped just inside the Science Center, leaning toward him to hear more. The warning bell chimed. "I have to go," I said.

He stepped closer, and people brushed past us, rushing to beat the bell. "So do I," he said. Then he raised his hand almost to my face, then dropped it to my shoulder instead, like he had patted his friend on the shoulder as they parted a few mornings ago. I winced.

He pulled back his hand and stared at it, like he didn't know what it was capable of. "What?" he asked. "I hurt you?"

"No, it's my shoulder . . . I don't know . . ." And I pressed myself farther into the wall.

He leaned closer, put his fingers on the collar of my shirt, like he was waiting for some sign from me before he pulled it aside. And I felt hot and cold at once, yes and no, trapping me in indecision.

"Ho-ly shit."

Reid dropped his hand and I stepped back.

Jason stood in the middle of the hall, half a grin on his

face. He stood too close to Bree, but Bree didn't seem to mind. And Krista just looked, unblinking. Jason shook his head and smirked. "Always with the rebounds, Reid." Then he looked to me. "It's his thing. Go for the girl when she's down. Makes you feel special, doesn't it?"

I looked to Reid for explanation, but I couldn't see anything under the anger. But before Reid could even open his mouth, Krista put her hands up, palm out. "Well, boys, this sure has been enlightening. But I believe we're all late for class."

The overhead speakers buzzed and Krista and Bree slipped into the classroom.

Jason smirked again and took off running for the end of the hall. And I stood there, feeling like I was missing the pieces to some puzzle—like I could only see the upper corner and had no idea what pieces I even needed to complete the rest of the picture.

"I'm late," Reid said.

"Me too." I stepped toward the doorway of the classroom and heard Reid's footsteps echo down the hall. My shoulder throbbed every time I moved it.

"Ms. Murphy." Dr. Arnold raised her pen into the air and jabbed it in my direction. "Are you planning to join us this morning?"

I felt the throb in my shoulder again, and the blood draining from my face. "Mallory? Are you okay?"

"I'm going to be sick," I said, bracing myself against the door frame.

"Go," she said.

I backed out of the doorway and ran down the hall toward the bathroom. I leaned over the sink and pulled my shirt down over my left shoulder, where Reid had touched me. Underneath, the faint red marks had turned dark. Bruised. I turned around and looked at my back. There was another bruise, like from a thumb.

I squeezed my eyes shut and thought *it's only real if I let it be.*

I opened my eyes, but the marks were still there. I really was going to be sick. Air. I needed air. I ran down the empty hallway, out into the bright late-morning sun, and took a deep breath. Two teachers were walking up the path from the other direction—they'd see me any second, so I kept moving. I ran through campus, out the side gate, across the street, down the path. To the old student center, where there was nothing but the remains of what used to be.

I sat on a half-wall, trying to think of nothing, and listened to the wind. I watched the leaves move with the breeze.

Everything shifted a little to the left with a strong gust. And I saw something past the student center, farther into the woods. A path. This wasn't the end of campus. I stood, brushed the dirt from my khaki pants, and crept over the bricks to the far corner. The path was narrow, but it was a definite path. It wound through the trunks, and as I followed, it narrowed.

A pile of rocks stood just off the side of the path with a small wooden cross standing in the middle, nearly overgrown with weeds now. There was something carved into the wood, in boxy letters. I pushed the weeds down. DANVERS JACK. GONE BUT NOT FORGOTTEN. The cross split under the weight of my hands, bringing ruin, like usual. I tried to prop it back up, and I felt an engraving on the other side. I flipped the piece over and read the other side, jagged letters etched into the rotting wood. FORGOTTEN BUT NOT GONE.

Wind rustled the leaves, and a few scattered down to the ground, a burnt orange, turning early. I wondered if Jack Danvers or Danvers Jack or whatever his name was haunted these woods. If he was tied to them now. If others could feel him, if they believed he wasn't truly gone.

I stood up and walked farther down the path, weeds popping up with more frequency, until I wasn't sure I was on the path anymore.

I spun around, and all I saw were trees. My breath caught, and I spun around in a full circle. The ground all looked the same, clusters of weeds breaking up the rocks and dirt. Trees everywhere. I put my hand on the nearest trunk, the one I had stopped at, and oriented myself in the direction I had been walking, then took two huge, deliberate steps backward.

I looked down and saw the difference. A faint path, a little more worn than where I had just been. I stepped backward again. Then I turned around, kept my eyes down on the ground, and started moving, following the weeds as they became sparser and sparser and I was back on the path again. Until I was next to the broken cross.

My heart beat fast. I had almost gotten lost. I saw how the woods could've swallowed him up so easily. They could've swallowed me up like that. I wondered how long it would be before someone would've noticed I was missing and come looking. How long it would take for me to go from *Gone but not forgotten* to *Forgotten but not gone.*

CHAPTER 8

I returned to campus for the rest of classes, stopping by Dr. Arnold's classroom beforehand to pick up my work. "Did you see the nurse?" she asked.

"Oh no, I think it was just something I ate."

"Usually you can only be excused by a note from the nurse. I'll let it slide this time, but you need to make up the lab. I'll be here this afternoon, if you're feeling up to it."

"Sure," I said. Not like I had any other plans. There was a pep rally tonight, but I wasn't exactly feeling peppy, or like rallying.

That afternoon, Dr. Arnold stayed in the room with me while I completed the experiment. I had to build a list of circuits and answer some math questions that went along with it. Dr. Arnold looked over my shoulder at the completed circuits, and I stopped writing. "Nice work, Mallory. You're a natural."

I wondered if I would've been a natural at chemistry, too, if I had actually done my homework at night and not with Dylan during study hall. If I had paid more attention to the book and less attention to him. Or if I hadn't been watching him instead of the beakers during class. If I would've given Brian a second glance if Dylan hadn't been my lab partner. If he would've caught me staring on the boardwalk.

A long line of ifs that didn't matter anyway because it was done.

That evening, I could hear the pep rally cheers all the way across campus. But there were no sounds coming from the dorm itself. I lay on my bed catching up on the rest of the summer reading, even though I'd already read the basic plot in Chloe's study books. Turns out I wasn't half bad as a student after all. I flipped the page and something caught my eye outside.

Smoke rose up from below my window. My stomach knotted, and I debated just running out the door, calling for help, something. But I didn't need any more rumors about me circulating campus. I kept the window closed but placed my forehead against it, looking down. Expecting the worst. I let out my breath and watched as it fogged the window.

Bree was down there, leaning against the bricks, sucking

on a cigarette and blowing smoke toward the trees. I thought about opening the window, telling her to go somewhere else, leave her discarded cigarette butts under her own window, but I didn't. Her left hand was shaking, just the slightest tremor. Someone called her name—I could hear it through my window pane. A girl's voice. Krista, I thought. Bree looked in the direction of the voice, and very slowly pressed herself farther against the bricks.

Apparently, soccer was big here. Like, really big. Saturday after lunch, the whole student body abandoned center campus and swarmed past the athletic center to the biggest of three soccer fields. I heard the buzz at the cafeteria as I grabbed a bagel to go—apparently, this was a big rivalry. Us versus some prep school from Vermont. I pushed back to my dorm as a sea of red T-shirts flew by me.

The dorm was nearly empty by the time I got back. Except for some guy I didn't know sneaking into the room of some girl I didn't know, taking advantage of the fact that no one was around. I fed dollar bills into the coin machine in the basement, went back upstairs to the pay phone, and tried calling Colleen. Her cell went straight to voice mail, and I lost the money. I tried her home phone, even though I knew the chances of her picking up were nearly zero, but I was desperate. It just rang and rang and rang. It didn't go to the answering machine, which meant someone was on the phone. Her mom, probably. Maybe she saw our New Hampshire number on the Caller ID and chose not to pick up. I was sure she was glad I was gone. Gone, and hopefully forgotten.

I hung up and my coins came pouring back out, overflowing the coin dispenser and scattering along the floor. The giggling in the room down the hall stopped, like they thought I was a teacher or something.

And I hated silence.

So I called that stupid 800 number my dad had set up for me.

"Mallory!" Mom said as soon as she picked up. "And it's not even Sunday!"

Sunday being the day I was supposed to call.

Then, after processing the information—daughter calling when daughter did not need to call—she added, "Is everything okay?"

"Sure, Mom. Just calling to say hi."

After a beat of silence: "I'm so glad you did! I've missed you. I miss you."

"Me too," I said, because that's what you say when someone says it first. Except as soon as the words escaped my mouth, I realized they were true. I sunk into the plastic chair beside the pay phone.

"Well, tell me what you've been up to, love. Tell me everything."

But her voice through the phone had this effect, tightening my airway, so I couldn't get any words out without everything coming pouring out, like the coins. "I'm good," I whispered.

Mom's voice dropped lower as she said, "Do you want to come home?"

Yes. "No," I said. Because it wasn't just my mom at home. It was a whole life, a whole horrifying mistake, and it was terrible. And she sounded so much better with me gone. She sounded like her old self again. Like the mom I missed. She hadn't been that person since the night Brian bled out on our kitchen floor. "I was just calling to say hi," I said again. "But I gotta go."

"All right," she said. "Tomorrow, then?"

"Tomorrow."

The silence was back. I walked to my room and opened the door, and as it squeaked open, I felt that fullness to the room, like my kitchen at home. The room felt charged, like it was waiting for some spark. Like it was waiting for *me*. And it craved. Oh, how I could feel it, deep in my bones, wanting me.

I pulled the door closed again, turned my key in the lock, and ran out the lounge door. I ran to that soccer game like I was the biggest fan this school had ever seen.

The alley had been dark as I walked home from Brian's house. And Colleen had the pepper spray, back at the party. I heard these footsteps, faintly, over the sound of my breathing, and I started moving faster.

I kept my eyes on the light at the other end. The moon was low in the sky, and there was this halo around it, from the clouds. The air was thick, about to burst. Humidity and something else crawled along my skin.

"Mallory," I heard.

And I started to run.

I dug my fingernails into my clenched fists and pumped my arms harder as I sprinted through the grass toward the roar of the crowd. To the sea of red. Where I joined the mob.

I found a spot on the top row of the bleachers, near the very edge. I stood when they stood. And clapped when they clapped. And watched what they watched. Which was Reid. Because he was good. Like, really, really good. He weaved between people, glancing up and to the side and down the field and moving his feet like he knew where the ball was at all times even though he wasn't looking. Like he could sense it.

Like I could sense that thing, even without looking, the way I could feel it in my room, picture it in semisolid form, hovering. I never had to look. Just like Reid.

Reid kept his eyes on the open field as he dribbled around people. He took a shot on goal, and of course he scored. His mouth turned into this giant smile, and I felt the corners of my mouth turning up with his.

He scanned the crowd, which was on its feet. They sat as one, a rogue clap or cheer escaping, but I couldn't tear my eyes away from his smile. So when he scanned a second time, he saw me, because I was the only one still standing. And then it occurred to me that I was the only one still standing, and I ached to sit, but I worried I was just doing it because everyone else was doing it, and I didn't want to be like everyone else.

Reid's smile, if possible, stretched wider, and then I had this horrifying thought. I shook my head, just a bit, and I thought, *Please don't wave.* Then Reid raised his hand and waved. I quickly sat down. But people had noticed. People on the field followed his eyes into the sea of red, and they saw me. I knew they saw me, because I knew what the weight of eyes felt like.

It felt like knives.

At the sound of the final whistle, I ran down the steps of the bleachers, the sound of my feet hidden under the sound of everyone else's feet. Reid was talking to the coach on the sideline, a bunch of players huddled around them. He was smiling. He caught my eye as I passed, and he smiled some more. I kept moving, but a soccer player in a scarlet shirt skipped off the field and ran up to me. Jason.

"Got yourself a boyfriend, Mallory?" Jason leaned close; warm smile, but his voice was ice.

"I don't do boyfriends." I yanked my arm back.

Jason reached his hand out and ran his fingers through the hair framing my face. "I'm a pretty good nonboyfriend."

I swatted his arm away and jerked my neck back. Now others were noticing. The people surrounding us fell silent. "Don't touch me," I said.

Jason laughed, like we were joking around, even though I wasn't and he knew it. He chucked me under the chin, like he thought I was cute. "I can't help it."

"Where's your girlfriend?" I asked, scanning the crowd for Bree.

Jason laughed. "I don't do girlfriends."

Reid was walking toward us, his smile completely gone. Last thing I needed was a scene with the two of them. Again. Jason reached for my shoulder, the one with the bruises, and I jerked back. "Don't fucking touch me." I took off across the fields.

I saw Bree as I passed the baseball field behind the main building, sitting under the bleachers, not doing a very good job of hiding if that was her purpose. As I got closer, I noticed she wasn't smoking or anything, she was laying on the ground, staring up through the slats of the bleachers, twirling a blade of grass above her face. Then I realized she was probably waiting for Jason. And I remembered the girl under my window the night before.

So I slowed down and walked toward her until she noticed me and propped herself onto her elbows. Her head was cocked to the side like she was trying to play it cool, but her hands were clenched, ripping up grass by her sides.

I stopped at the edge of the bleachers and said, "Jason's a scumbag."

She didn't do anything for a long pause, then she let out an extra-loud laugh. She said "Jealous much?" and leaned back into the grass.

Someone had been in my room. The door was unlocked. Nothing inside was out of place, but there was a feeling that only a person could leave. Nothing specific, but something. Like when Bree left the sticky tack behind, or the scent of my grandma's perfume, a reminder of what used to be. We leave footprints. When we leave.

When we die.

I sat on my desk chair and swiveled back and forth, the chair creaking under my movement. I was looking for anything out of place. Then I jumped up and stared back at my chair. It was warm. Worn. Someone had sat in it recently.

I sat back down and opened my desk drawers, and sure enough, everything was a little off. Papers were stacked too precisely. Pens were lined too neatly, where they had been scattered before.

My heart beat in my ears, like it was filling the room. Like when the feeling came at night. But underneath that, there was another noise. I strained to separate the two.

Knocking. Someone was knocking on my door.

I didn't open it. "Who is it?" I called.

"Reid. Hurry up or I'm gonna get in trouble."

I raced for the door and swung it open. Reid slipped inside and eased it quickly shut behind him. He hadn't showered since the game. I took a step back.

"Sorry," he said. "I know I reek. But I had to check on you."

"Check on me?" I breathed through my mouth.

"Yeah. I saw you with . . . is Jason bothering you?"

I sucked in a long breath through my nose and looked up at Reid, who had creases in his forehead from worrying. Then I realized that feeling in my room when I first came in, it was gone. I couldn't sense it, not even a little. All I could feel was Reid, and okay, he was kind of gross at the moment, but the room was just so decidedly him and nothing else, and it felt safe.

My eyes drifted back to my desk, to the papers stacked too neatly. I stepped closer to Reid, whose forehead creased even further.

"Someone was here," I whispered.

"Who?" He looked around the room quickly, from the closed window to the closed door. "Who was here?"

"I don't know. Everything's just a little . . . off."

Reid's shoulders relaxed. "Happened to me when I first

moved here. Every time I'd walk into my room it felt like someplace new. It'll grow on you."

"No. My door was open. Someone was in here. Who has keys?"

"Bree?" he said, looking at her empty bed.

But I had just seen her, and she'd clutched at the grass beside her when I passed. She was terrified of me. "Who else?"

Reid stepped closer and everything that wasn't right about the room faded away. "The deans, I guess. And the housemaster for emergencies, I think."

"I don't think Ms. Perkins likes me."

"She'd be risking her job. And for what? Why would she care? I mean, yeah, *I'm* nosy like that . . ." He grinned, like he thought he was making me feel better. He didn't know about the red paint. Or Brian's mom.

"And how else would you increase your social standing than with more secrets?"

He pressed his lips together. "I'm not like that."

And then he was even closer and I meant to say something like *everyone's like that*, or maybe roll my eyes at him, but I wondered how he had changed since his dad's death—he had to be different, and not just his hair. So I moved my hand to his arm, which was hot and damp, and I said, "What are you like?" Bold, like he remembered me.

He looked down at my hand on his arm, and I was frozen again. Indecisive. And so was he because he left his arm exactly where it was. Neither of us pulling back, but neither moving closer.

"Come to breakfast with me tomorrow morning and you can see."

"You can't just tell me how you like your eggs cooked?"

"No, I mean off campus."

And I realized he meant on a date. I didn't respond, but he didn't seem to notice, because that arm I'd been touching made its way to my side, and I didn't think we were any closer, but we must've been because I swear I could feel his heart, beating hard, like he was still recovering from his game.

"The door," I said, and I backed away, until all I felt was the empty space where he used to be.

Reid looked stunned, and he shook his head to get his bearings again. "What door?"

"The closet door. I left it closed." And now it wasn't. Now it was cracked, just enough to see a wedge of blackness. To feel that someone could be in, looking out. To know it could swing open or slam shut, just something, full of possibility. Undecided.

Reid ran his fingers through his hair, which was a little bit matted to his head from sweat. "All right, I'll check." Though I could tell from the way he walked across the room that he didn't believe me. He pulled the door open and his knuckles turned white on the door frame.

"What? What is it?" I rushed across the floor and pushed past him and saw.

No one was there.

But someone had been.

Everything hanging in my closet, including all my scarlet shirts, had been slashed, leaving scraps of fabric hanging from each other by threads. Jagged edging. A mess of strips and string covering the dresser and the floor.

Not like a joke.

Like hate.

CHAPTER 9

"What the fuck?" Reid asked. Then he whispered in my ear but I couldn't hear him because there was a buzzing, white noise, my memories short-circuiting. Everything about him fell away.

All I saw was Brian's mouth screaming "What the fuck?" and his mouth moving, shouting at me, not making any sense. And then I heard that buzzing again, where I couldn't make sense of anything else. I reeled backward and I was completely disoriented, like I wasn't sure whether it was then or now, or now or then, or whether it mattered at all.

And the next thing I knew I was in the lounge and Reid was pacing in front of me and the campus police came through the double doors.

"It was Jason Dorchester," I heard him say. "He's been bothering her. He harassed her at the game. Everyone saw it."

I shook my head. It wasn't Jason. He was still at the game. He didn't have time to beat me back here, slice my clothes up, and leave again.

"Okay," said a man with a blue button-down shirt. "Mallory, tell me what happened with Mr. Dorchester."

"Nothing. I told him to leave me alone and then I came back here."

"So you came straight back?"

"Yes."

I could see him thinking. "Is there anyone else who may be upset with you?"

Oh, just the mother of the boy I killed. No big deal. That was a thing that was not fixable. Not with a restraining order, and not with an *I'm sorry*. This was a punishment that was forever.

I didn't answer at first, even though the pseudo cop was still holding his pen over a pad of paper. Reid was pacing the lounge, running his hands through his hair, over and over and over again. Something settled in my stomach, some sort of resolution. Because I realized right then that Reid, with his way-too-concerned look, didn't really understand what I had done.

I realized something else in that moment too: I didn't want him to know. "You should go," I said.

"Yeah, I don't think so."

I looked away. "Please."

"I'm not leaving—"

The security guard held his hand up. "She asked you to leave. Now please do."

I looked at the wood-paneled wall until I heard the lounge door slam shut.

The guard cleared his throat. "All right, let's hear it. Cheating on the boyfriend? Or did you steal him from someone?"

My mouth fell open. "No . . . he's not . . . I didn't . . ."

"Okay, so what is it then?" And then I felt sick—that same hot and cold and then only hot that I felt at the funeral. I couldn't force the words. Couldn't even think them.

"My roommate moved out," I said, even though I didn't think she was involved. "She could still have a key."

He stood up and closed his pad of paper. "We'll see about getting your lock changed. But can I give you a piece of advice? Try keeping your enemies here to a minimum."

I didn't take a sleeping pill that night. Someone had a key. Someone was out there. Someone wanted me to fear, to regret, to know that they could get in. That they could hurt me. I took my desk chair and wedged it under the handle of the door, but that was kind of useless because the chair swiveled. At least it was a warning. It would wake me up, which was kind of ridiculous because it's not like I could sleep.

So I heard it coming for me, clear as anything.

Boom, boom, boom.

And then it was here. My room was throbbing, but I tried to ignore it. I shook my head and kept my eyes on the ground and pushed through the door out into the hallway. I squinted from the sudden change to light, but it didn't matter. The whole hallway was pulsating. *Mallory*, it whispered. I sucked in a deep breath and turned back to my door.

Wait.

I felt the hand on my shoulder, holding me in place, digging through my skin, directly to the bone.

I cried out, louder than I meant to, and a door opened down the hall. The hallway stopped throbbing. The hand was gone. Taryn rubbed at her eyes with her closed fists. "Are you okay?" she asked.

I scanned the hall and the room behind me and swallowed the lump in my throat. "Twisted my ankle," I said as I backed into my room and shut the door.

Back in my room, I turned on the light and stretched my shirt down over my shoulder. "Shit," I whispered. The marks were turning a deep purple, nearly black. And they hurt.

I paced back and forth across the room, and in my head I repeated *it's only real if you let it be, it's only real if you let it be.* I shook the thoughts from my head, deciding to clear my head of even that. I booted up my laptop. I wrote to Colleen. Nothing of consequence, nothing important. Just something real.

Hey, you up? *pretend there's something important here so you'll write back.*

When I hit send, I had a message from Reid. Getting you out of here in the morning. 9?

Reid thought getting me out of here might help, but it wouldn't. Colleen did that too. Thought distance could fix things. Hoped distance could fix things.

"Stand up," she'd said, disentangling herself from me under the boardwalk. "Stand up," she said again, with less authority, but with more urgency. "Mallory, we have to go."

My hands skimmed the sandy bottom, under the water, pieces of shells and trash digging into my palms. I pushed myself onto my knees, and the water seemed to churn all around me. Colleen bent over and gripped my upper arm. "I have some money," she said, rapid and nonsensically. What did money have to do with Brian bleeding on my kitchen floor? "At my house. But we have to hurry."

I sunk back down. Because I realized, right then, that Brian was dead.

I looked up at Colleen, who was staring across the expanse of ocean, the rain slowing as it fell around us, around everything. The white moon reflected off the ripples. They looked so small in the distance. But we both knew, out there, the undertow could pull you under, claim you for the sea.

"We can do it," she said to the sea. Her gaze went across the ocean

and back again, like her laughter earlier that night. She crouched down next to me and whispered, "Please. We have to move. Now."

My computer pinged again. Message from Colleen:

Wallowing in self-pity. Cody Parker is a prick.

I smiled.

What happened?

Alicia Maloney happened.

He's so not worth it. And, ew, you're twenty times hotter than her.

I know, right? Boys blow. Thank God I have you.

Turned out that distance never really changed anything.

Reid tapped on my window a few minutes before nine. I pulled up the blinds and blinked at his smile. "Getting ready?" he asked, which sounded all muffled through the window.

I hadn't responded to his message last night. Brian never would've done something like this. Of all the times I made excuses why I couldn't hang out with him alone, he never called or showed up or anything. He never acted like he cared either way.

"Don't I look ready?" I was in ratty sweatpants and an oversized T-shirt, and I could only imagine what my hair looked like.

His eyes drifted to my hair, and he tried not to grin. "The diner has a rule about bringing animals inside."

"Hey!" I said. He raised his eyebrows. "Five minutes," I mumbled.

I looked down at my pajamas and ran my tongue along my top teeth. I threw my hair in a ponytail and slid on jeans to keep out the morning chill. I looked like I hadn't slept, which wasn't surprising, but at least I brushed my teeth.

I was almost smiling when I pushed through the door to the lounge, but I quickly stopped. Because Jason was the closest person to me. And second closest was Krista. They sat in adjacent cushioned chairs, leaning forward, their heads bent toward each other. Whispering secrets. Their worth skyrocketing.

Jason looked up first. Then Krista. Then they looked to the front door, where Reid stood in the entrance, walking toward me, in jeans and a black T-shirt.

"Careful, Reid," said Jason, with his big cocky smile.

I froze.

"Come on, Mallory," Reid said, acting like he didn't hear Jason at all.

I didn't move.

"You know I didn't get to her room." Jason was standing now, and Krista had that hideous grin. "Everyone was at the game. Everyone. You know who had time to do it?" He extended his arm outward and pointed his finger and smiled. "Her."

My mouth dropped open. I know it's ridiculous, and I'd never believed it actually happened in real life, but there it was. My mouth just dropped. And Jason didn't stop then. He seemed really pleased by my reaction. "For the attention. Even the security guard thinks it."

I looked to Reid, but he was looking out the window, and his forehead was creased like he was thinking really hard. Probably doing math calculations or something. Time for me to get back to my room. Time for him to get back. Time enough for me to slash my own shirts.

Shit.

Reid held the door for me as we left, but I kept my distance, arms crossed over my stomach. It was colder than I thought. September mornings have a chill in New Jersey on the shore, but it was even worse here. Too many trees. Not enough sunlight getting through.

We walked to the lot behind the student center, and he led me to a black Honda.

We drove out of campus in silence. We got closer to civilization a mile or so down the windy road—a pharmacy and a gas station, potentially the ghetto one, but it didn't look so bad—and then a diner. In a tin box on wheels. For real.

He pulled onto the grass next to a blue BMW, downtrodden weeds as parking spots, and turned toward me. "I know you didn't do it."

I cocked my head to the side. "How do you know?" I was hoping the security guard would come to the same conclusion.

"Because I know you. I know you were scared. I know you *are* scared." I opened my mouth in protest but he waved me away and continued. "I know you're not faking it."

He was remembering the old version of me again. He couldn't possibly know what I was capable of. I was betting he didn't even know the things he was capable of. There was a time when I didn't know what I was capable of either. But I knew now. I knew I was capable of anything. Anything.

"You don't know that," I said.

He shrugged. "Fine. Then I am choosing to believe you. See? It's not so hard." Except from the way he slammed his car door, it looked like it was exactly that hard.

Taryn and Bree were huddled in the back booth, leaning over the center. Taryn was nibbling the end of a piece of toast. Bree had scrambled eggs, but she was just moving the pieces around the plate.

Reid and I slid into a booth at the opposite end, and I read over the menu. Reid took it from my hands and shook his head. "Don't bother. Only thing worth eating here is the burger. Cheese at your own risk."

"Um, it's breakfast time. And why are we here if it sucks?"

"I like it because it's away. And, like I said, good burgers."

I pointed behind us, to Taryn and Bree. "She got eggs."

"Bet she's not eating it."

I craned my neck. He was right. Taryn was still holding a barely eaten piece of toast, whispering across the table, and then Bree backed up against the booth and hissed, "Why didn't you tell me before?"

Then Taryn reached out her hand and Bree ignored it. I heard another car pull up, but the engine idled as a car door opened and slammed shut, and then drove away. Krista walked in and slid into the booth beside Bree. She pushed Bree's untouched plate to the side and started using her pointer finger to trace something out on the table, or make a point, or clean up crumbs. Unclear which.

The waitress arrived, too skinny for her uniform, her black hair in a tight bun. "What'll it be?" she said.

"Two burgers," I answered. "No cheese."

Krista walked past us to the napkin dispenser and pulled out a thick stack. The corners of her mouth were turned down, and she looked painfully bored.

"What's up with her?" I asked.

"Don't know. Don't care. She and Jason share the same DNA for sure."

"They seem like more than cousins, if you get what I'm saying."

"Yeah. They're close. In a weird way. But I don't think it's like that. I don't know. Maybe it is. I don't really get her. She's . . . she's from someplace else."

"Someplace else?"

"I think the Dorchesters adopted her, but it was kinda recent. So wherever she's from, it probably wasn't good. And that's a secret that surprisingly hasn't made it into circulation, so it must be worth something to Jason."

I watched her walk back to her booth and hand Bree the stack of napkins. She dabbed at her eyes, and Krista rubbed her upper back, whispering into her ear.

I ate all the burger I could, then pushed the rest to Reid. As he finished off my leftovers, I drummed my fingers on the table and said, "What did Jason mean? When he said you go for girls when they're down?"

Reid swallowed whatever was left in his mouth and coughed into his closed fist. "What he *means* is that he's jealous."

I could feel the rest of the answer hovering in the air, waiting for Reid. He rolled his head around and cut his eyes to the table of girls behind us. "And he meant Taryn," he whispered.

Not the answer I expected. "You were with Taryn?" I whispered back.

"Kind of. Not exactly. Almost. Jason and I were roommates last year, and they were together, and then they weren't, and . . . it's complicated."

I knew there was a bunch of information left out of that sentence, skipped over in the long pause, replaced with the word *complicated*.

But I was stuck on one thing. "Taryn?" I asked again.

Reid set his jaw and leaned forward. "She wasn't always like that. She never even talked to Krista until . . ."

I was shaking my head to myself. If he liked girls like her, how could he possibly like girls like me? When I looked back at Reid, he was watching their table.

"You still like her," I said.

Reid looked at me and shook his head. "No. And I don't think I ever really did. It was just the situation, you know?"

"Yeah," I said, but I also decided right then that I definitely did not like Taryn.

Reid grinned and said, "So don't be jealous."

"I'm not jealous," I said. Which made him smile. Which made me furious. "I'm *not*."

He smiled, and I couldn't help smiling back. He said, "Can

we get the check?" but he was still looking at me. I knew exactly what was about to happen. We'd leave and walk to the car and I'd stop beside the door and he'd kiss me. An inevitable string of events, set in motion right now.

"Be right back," I said, off to the bathroom to check for sesame seeds in my teeth.

I walked to the back of the diner, past the front counter where people sat on barstools. Back toward the kitchen. And then I paused. Because right there, right past the bathroom, was a chopping board. A chopping board covered in sliced tomatoes, one left mid-cut. And a knife. Not a big one. Not like the one missing from my kitchen. But big enough. Big enough to scare someone off. Big enough to protect myself.

Everything else faded away. The promise of Reid kissing me. The smell of ground beef, the sound of bacon sizzling. The smoke from the barstools. Just me, two feet of emptiness, and the knife.

I took it.

CHAPTER 10

I grabbed the black handle, the blade still dripping with tomato juice, and shoved it deep into my bag. I spun around, back to the bathroom. And Krista stood there. In front of the bathroom door, which was still swinging behind her. Her mouth was pressed tightly together. I didn't know how long she'd been standing there.

So I readjusted my ponytail to keep my hands busy and said, "What's wrong with Bree?"

She didn't blink. "Something of very little consequence, I'm sure."

"Doesn't look like it."

She plastered her fake, preppy smile on and said, "But it is."

Reid didn't kiss me outside the diner. I didn't give him a chance. I pulled on the door handle over and over until he gave in and pressed the unlock button on his keychain. Then I stared out the window.

Reid kept glancing at me on the way home. He drove with one hand on the wheel and one on the center console, like he was thinking of reaching out and taking my hand, but wasn't sure how I'd react. To be honest, I wasn't sure how I'd react either. I was too preoccupied with the fact that I could feel the blade through the fabric of my bag, wedged between my body and the car door.

Reid flipped the headlights on, even though it was late morning, bordering on early afternoon. The sky had grayed, and the air had that heavy feeling, like it was about to bust. Like something big was coming.

The way it feels before a storm. Just like it felt when I was racing through the alleys that night. I was walking and I heard footsteps and then my name . . .

"Mallory?" Reid said.

"Hmm?"

"Did you hear me?"

"Sorry, what?"

"Remember after the funeral, when you came in my room—"

"Yes, Reid. Seriously, you can stop asking that. I remember.

And, unlike you, I remember *all* of it." I didn't know why I was acting so angry, but I couldn't stop the way the words came out with bite.

"No," he said quietly. "I remember too." A fat drop fell on the windshield, and then another. "That's what I wanted to tell you. It was my dad's funeral, you know? I wasn't supposed to be smiling. I wasn't supposed to feel . . . I wasn't supposed to feel *anything*. Just hollow."

And then the sky burst open, and Reid turned on the windshield wipers. He pulled into campus and parked behind the student center. I couldn't see anything, and the car was still running, like we could go anywhere still. Like we were unfinished.

I heard Reid unbuckle his seat belt, so I unhooked mine. But he didn't move, and neither did I, because everything still felt unfinished. An inevitable, unalterable sequence of events. I turned to look at Reid, and he was looking back at me, like he was thinking the exact same thing.

Light off, light on.

I met him halfway, twisting unnaturally in my seat to get there, and my mouth found his before his arms pulled me tighter. And the rain pelting down outside made it seem like we were the only people in the world, and the thickness in the air made it feel like what we were doing was not at all dangerous, like we were being pushed together, like it was the only decision, like it was logical.

I kissed him without thinking. Of all the reasons I shouldn't, of all the reasons I couldn't. And it felt like he was doing the same thing. So I crawled across the center console, and Reid seemed surprised but not at all upset, because I felt the corners of his mouth turn up.

And Colleen's voice in my head was saying *Do what you want to do.*

And it turns out what I wanted to do at that very moment was smile. So that's exactly what I did. And Reid was doing the exact same thing.

A blue car pulled up beside us, and doors slammed. Someone giggled outside our window—it sounded like Taryn. And then that someone tapped on our window, which made me think it wasn't Taryn, because Taryn didn't seem like the type to do anything.

I slid off Reid's lap and sat on my side again, and we both stared out the front windshield. He turned the engine off, and the voices faded into the distance, swallowed up by the rain.

He left his hand on the key, like he was wondering what to do next. "I can drive you around the back entrance. It's closer to your dorm," Reid said.

"No," I said, grabbing my bag. "I'll run."

I backed out of the car, gripping the blade through my bag. I wiped the rain from my face, smiling, as I raced across campus. I wasn't sure if was supposed to be smiling, if I was supposed to feel anything at all—other than hollow.

Three days after Brian died, I heard a scraping sound out back. Through the kitchen. Which I had been avoiding. But I thought maybe it was Colleen sneaking over to see me.

But when I opened the back door, I saw Brian's mom standing on a garbage can, looking through the kitchen window. She saw me and stumbled—the garbage spilling around the patio. She crawled out of the middle of it, her fingers digging into old food and paper and dirt. She looked up at me and she screamed, "You!" I froze. My legs wouldn't move.

She stood up and pieces of trash clung to her—a napkin on her leg, yesterday's dinner on her elbow. I cringed. I was embarrassed for her—no, I wanted *her to be embarrassed. But she didn't notice. And that was terrifying. She didn't notice anything but me. She walked toward the back door. Toward me. I focused on the napkin clinging to her leg.*

"You took him from me! You took him!"

I could see the blood flowing under the surface of her skin through her neck. And I just stood there, shaking my head. I walked backward and she walked forward until she was at the back entrance of the kitchen, and finally she yelled, half delusional, "Where is he?"

Then my dad was there, pulling me back. He was talking real low to Brian's mom, and then he was yelling for my mom. Then my mom was there, but she was just shaking, staring past me at Brian's mom, who wasn't making any sense. "Where is he?" she yelled again. Dad let go of me and placed his hands on her arms. He kept talking real low and calm, even though nothing about this felt low or calm. He eased her back through the door and turned the lock, and then he called the cops. That's how we got the restraining order.

Right then, with Brian's mom in the backyard and Dad on the phone and Mom shaking behind me, that was the first time the kitchen started pulsating.

And I knew she had come to the right place after all. Because he was *here.*

In my dorm room, I changed out of my dripping-wet clothes. Then I took out the knife. I wiped the blade with a tissue, careful not to snag my fingers. I cleaned off the leftover flesh from the tomato. And then I pushed it into the back of my bottom drawer. Behind my binders and office supplies. I slammed the drawer shut.

I booted up my computer, prepared to write this *Lord of the Flies* essay, but I couldn't concentrate. The cursor blinked on the Word document until the screen went to sleep. I stared at the bottom drawer, imagining the knife laying idle inside. So close. Too close.

I retreated to my bed, but I could smell it still. I could. Ripe and acidic. Full of possibility. Good and evil and offense and defense and life and death.

Lights out. The whole room was beating, and I stood in the middle of it, willing it away. *Mallory*, it whispered. I turned toward my bed, where I thought I'd heard it. No, I saw it out of the corner of my eye, by the desk. The dark shape. I whipped my head toward it, but it shifted again, to the closet, just at the edge of my vision. And then the room started to blur, like my vision couldn't keep up with what I was trying to see.

Wait, it said, like it was right behind me.

"No, no, no," I mumbled. Because I knew what was coming next. The hand, pressing down on me. *It's only real if you let it be*, I thought.

Two hands pressed down on my shoulders. I shrugged them off violently and yelled, "Get away!"

"Whoa, sorry."

I turned around, the beating of the room now only in my own head, in my own chest. I tried to slow my breathing. Reid had his hands held up in the air. I looked around my empty room, then at him. I took slow breaths, and I heard the beating of my heart return to normal.

"You scared me," I said, once I trusted myself to speak again.

Reid tilted his head to the side. "Who were you talking to?"

My face was hot, and I willed my eyes to stay on his. "No one."

"You look terrified."

I looked away—at the closed door and the open window, at the shades hanging in front of the window, alternately blowing inward and slapping back against the window frame. "How the hell did you get in my room?"

"Your window. Sorry, I knocked first. You didn't hear. And you . . . you were . . ."

"I locked it."

"No, it was open."

I couldn't keep my eyes still. They searched the corners of the room, the space behind me. I'd locked the window, I was sure of it. Almost sure of it. "I thought something was wrong," he said.

"I thought I saw . . . I thought I felt . . ." I glanced down to my shoulder and back at Reid and shook my head. "Never mind."

"You thought you felt what?"

Things I didn't want Reid to know about. My shoulder burned where Reid had touched the bruises. I pulled on the collar of my pajamas to make sure they remained covered.

Then I realized I was still in my pajamas, and Reid was in

dark sweats. The carpet felt cold under the soles of my feet. "What are you doing here?"

He pointed to my laptop. "I sent you a bunch of e-mails. Like, a ton. But you never responded."

I kept my eyes on him as I backed toward my desk, unsure why I didn't trust him. Why couldn't I just choose to trust him, like he chose to trust me at the diner? He didn't move, didn't say anything at my lack of trust. Instead he watched as I booted up the computer and scanned my e-mail. Reid Carlson: we good? Reid Carlson: hey, can you just write back? Reid Carlson. Reid Carlson.

"I didn't want to just . . . leave things. Again."

I instinctively put my fingers to my lips, remembering. Watched as his eyes followed my hand. Watched as his eyes stayed there, even after I pulled my hand away.

Now I didn't know what he expected from me. And he needed to know why he shouldn't expect anything, really, at all.

"Sometimes I think I can feel him," I said. "Hear him, even. I mean, I *do*. I do feel him. I do hear him. Like he's right here . . ." I shuddered, imagining him watching me even now.

Reid sat on my bed, ran his hand across my blue comforter, like an invitation. I wondered if he knew where he was sitting—what he was doing. "I guess things . . . happen after a trauma," he said, looking somewhere beyond me.

"Things like this?" I waved my arms around the air, like Brian was somewhere in the emptiness.

"I don't know. Maybe." He shrugged and scooted farther onto my bed. I stayed where I was, my back against my desk. "When my dad died—I mean, after we found him, my mom completely lost her vision. She couldn't see anything. But it was all psychological. There wasn't anything physically wrong with her."

"You mean like hysterical blindness?" We'd watched a movie in history class last year about World War II, and some guy who just stopped seeing, for no real reason at all. I mean, other than the fact that everyone was dying around him.

"Yeah, like that. The real term is 'conversion disorder.' I guess so it doesn't sound so . . . hysterical. Therapy veteran," he confessed.

"She couldn't see because she was *upset*," I said, like an accusation. Because I could see just fine. Not the same type of thing.

"But that's not how she explained it. It was more like she couldn't *not* see. Like she couldn't see anything *but* my dad . . ." I imagined what Reid was seeing in that pause. His father, on the ground? In the snow? Or did he see his mother first, see her face, as she saw her husband? Which was worse? He ran his hand through his hair one, two, three times. And on the third time I crossed the room and took his hand and sat beside him on my bed.

"It's like she was stuck," he said.

"For how long?" I whispered.

"I'm not sure. I had to go stay with my grandparents, but by the time we got home for the funeral, she took one look at me and told me to change my tie. Two or three days, I guess."

"Brian's been dead for two *months*," I said.

"Brian," he said. And I realized he'd never heard his name before. I wondered if it made it more real. If he understood that he used to be a person and now he wasn't—because of me.

And just in case he didn't understand, I said, "He was my boyfriend."

His hand slipped away, and mine immediately felt cold. "Mallory," he said. "I'm so sorry."

Then I stood up because I couldn't breathe. And he pretended not to notice that my breath shook each time I exhaled. Instead, he slid down onto my bed, against the concrete wall, and said, "Do you want me to leave?"

I thought of what Colleen would tell me. *Say yes,* she'd say. Or maybe, *Say no.* Maybe something else. I didn't know anymore.

Reid was looking at the ceiling, like he didn't care either way. But he was holding his breath, I could tell. Which made my decision for me. I slid into bed beside him, hovering near the edge, and miraculously, given the width of the bed, we did not touch. I closed my eyes, found his hand again, and laced my fingers together with his.

And when I squeezed his hand, his grip tightened around mine as well. I stared at my desk, thinking I could probably take a sleeping pill now. I could sleep without worrying about someone sneaking into my room. Slashing my shirts. Coming for me.

The tension left Reid's hand, but his fingers still lay between mine. I shifted so I was on my back, a little closer to him. I ignored the vial of pills in the drawer. I didn't want to take them.

Turns out, I didn't want to miss this feeling.

I slept.

Somewhere in the night, I must've slept, because I woke. And you can't wake without sleeping first.

The sound of Reid's light snoring woke me early. My arm was hanging off the bed, and I didn't know if I should just lay there, hovering near the edge, or move closer to Reid.

So instead I got up.

I turned on my computer and typed *conversion disorder* into a search engine and began to read.

Loss of hearing, loss of speech, paralysis, numbness with no physical cause. Hallucinations.

Hysterical blindness: Loss of sight of a psychological nature.

Hysterical pregnancy: Clinical pregnancy symptoms when the person is not pregnant; most often mental in nature.

See also: Somatoform disorder. Hysteria.

Reid slept on while the words seared themselves into my brain. Psychological. Hallucinations. Hysteria.

I walked to the mirror hanging from the back of my closet door and tugged the collar of my shirt down. Maybe I was doing it to myself, in my sleep, in some other plane of existence. I raised my right arm across my chest and tried to line up the fingerprints. But my thumb was in the front, and the thumbprint was on my back. No matter how much I twisted, I couldn't get the prints to line up. I tried my left hand instead, bringing it up to the same shoulder. I could line it up—sort of—but couldn't get enough force to leave a mark. Not these deep bruises, which were now so black they'd started to look purple again.

"Hey." Reid stretched his arms over his head and violently rubbed at his hair, which then miraculously fell into place. Stupid hair. "Been up long?"

I spun so my back was to the mirror, making sure my shirt was covering the marks. "Not too long. You snore," I said.

He paused at the edge of the bed and hopped down. "What time is it?"

"Six." I didn't look at him when I answered. Because now there was light, and I was too nervous to look at his face. To see if he regretted knowing about me. If he thought I was crazy.

"I need to get back before Durham's morning run."

"That's how it works? You have a whole routine about sneaking into people's rooms?"

"Hey. It's just common knowledge. Go after Perkins' light goes off, which, by the way, is not an exact science. Be back before Durham's run. It's just things you know after a while. This isn't something I do a lot." Which meant it was something he had at least done a few times before. I hated that I felt jealous. *Hated* it. It's not like I'd been on my own waiting for him, just like he hadn't been waiting alone for me. We had lived, for two years. Made choices and mistakes, had good days and bad days.

And then he was taking these long strides to my window. One, two, three. Changed his mind, walked back to me. Didn't even slow down when he reached me—he walked me back until I was against the wall, and he kissed me. Like he'd been waiting all night to do it. Then he rested his forehead against mine for a second before walking away. He straddled the sill. "Mallory," he said, like he meant something more, but then he was gone. The absence of him felt like a tangible thing.

That morning I realized I didn't have any red polos to wear. Just the one shirt from Friday that was still in the hamper, and

I hadn't done laundry. I'd have to make a trip to the school store after class. In the meantime, I found a reddish T-shirt that I thought might blend in a little.

I was wrong.

"Ms. Murphy," Mr. Durham said as I slid into my seat for English. "You cannot be in class like this."

"Oh," I said. I kind of figured people would know about the slashed shirts. "I don't have any clean uniform shirts."

"Monroe takes student responsibility quite seriously." Apparently, Mr. Durham *did* know. And, apparently, Jason's rumor had also reached him. "You are welcome to return when you manage to find some appropriate attire. Perhaps a friend will lend you a shirt?"

I scanned the room, and everyone who had been looking at me was suddenly looking down. Even the ones who used to smile at me. Like the social stigma of *girl who slashed own shirts for attention* was contagious. The only one not looking down was Bree. She was staring out the window. Thankfully Krista wasn't in class yet. Eventually Chloe held her room keys in her outstretched hand. But I didn't want to take her down with me.

"Thanks," I said, "but I'll manage." I snatched up my books and hurried out of the room just as the bell rang.

My neck felt hot, even though the hall was cool. Heat crept upward, and I thought I might be sick. I slid into the nearest restroom, splashed water on my face and across the back of my neck. Then I stared at the mirror and took several deep breaths.

I heard voices in the hall.

"I can't stop her," someone hissed.

"Sure you can." The voice, not even hushed, belonged to Jason.

"I can't." The whisper was pleading this time.

There was a beat of silence, then a squeak, a sharp sound emitted from a throat, and the lowered voice. "Fix it, Krista. Lovely, lovely Krista."

I froze. Soundless. Noiseless. And waited.

I heard a throat being cleared once, twice. And then footsteps racing down the hall. Then there was silence. I tiptoed out of the restroom, and Jason was standing across the hall, staring at me.

He looked irate. Furious.

Hysterical.

Like Brian had.

CHAPTER 11

Brian stood under the living-room window, the screen lying beside him on the tiled floor. His mouth was moving and he was screaming, but he wasn't making any sense. I stared at the floor, at the pieces of the white vase with the blue flowers. A petal lay at my feet.

Then I looked back at Brian, and this chill ran up the base of my spine, like I could feel the wrongness of the situation.

"What the hell are you doing here?" I shouted back. Finally.

Brian shook his head, like he was clearing his own words. He looked at the floor, and looked at me with this odd expression, like he wasn't really sure why he was there either. He seemed to register the wrongness of the situation too.

Then Brian was just breathing hard, thinking. And I was thinking too. Thinking Brian wouldn't hurt me, wouldn't try to hurt me, because people are generally good. But then I had believed that Brian wouldn't break into my house either, because good people don't do that. Yet here he was. And I was thinking about that guy on the skateboard, the one he beat the crap out of for no real reason at all. So while he stood there thinking, I sprinted for the phone on the side table.

And that seemed to make Brian's mind up for him, because he sprinted too.

My hands shook as I pressed power, and Brian was right in front of me, but he wasn't doing anything. "Mallory, wait," he said. His amber eyes were pleading, but there was something off about them.

He was so close, and he was so much stronger than me, so all I could punch was the 9 before he slapped the phone out of my hand. It shattered on the floor, the battery pack shooting out across the tile. "Shit," he said, gripping my wrist. "Just . . . wait."

"Let go," I said, only it came out all high-pitched and tiny, like the fear was gripping me around the neck. Or like my body was trying to hold on to all the oxygen, just in case.

But he didn't let go. His grip tightened around my arm and he shook me and said, "Listen."

Up close I could tell that his pupils were dilated unnaturally, and when he spoke, his breath smelled like cigarettes and liquor. So I wrenched my arm as hard as I could and backpedaled into the dining room. Then my foot caught—slipped on the phone's battery pack.

I fell, back, back, into Mom's china cabinet. It gave out with barely any resistance, shards of glass cascading around me as I slid to the floor. Tiny specks of red bloomed on my arms as Brian's footsteps crunched the glass, coming closer.

There was a part of me that wanted to run from the way Jason was looking at me. Like I had witnessed something I shouldn't have. Like he wanted to take his anger out on something, and I was the closest thing. But there was another part of me that didn't want to run at all, something I tried to ignore, fighting its way to the surface.

I shoved it back down. "You're disgusting," I said.

He blinked in surprise and said, "You're one to talk."

"You make a habit of bullying girls?" And I felt that thing rising up in me, but I shook it away again.

Jason laughed. "Her? You think she's a girl? She's *nothing*. What's it called when something can't live without a host? A parasite, right? That's Krista. She's a parasite. And she's *nothing* without me."

I didn't like Krista, I didn't like anything about Krista. But this feeling kept rising until I could feel it in my arms, making me jittery. I wanted to hurt him. I wanted to smack the smile off his face, push his skull into the concrete wall, feel his weight give out as he sank to the floor.

I was breathing heavily, filled with terror over what I wanted to do to him, so I turned and ran down the hall.

"Run along, Mallory," Jason called after me. "Run along."

I found a place in the quad to work so I wouldn't have to go back to my room. So I wouldn't have to think about the feeling that was fighting to get out. I had to pass the time until noon when the school store was open anyway. I sat under the giant oak where I'd first seen Reid, opened my laptop, and stared at the blank document for my *Lord of the Flies* essay again.

I couldn't figure out how to write what was so obvious to me. How you can look at little pieces of someone's life and tell the type of person he is. In flashes. Only you don't know what you're looking for until much later—like when the news crews show up to interview you and you say, "Yeah, there was always something not right about him . . ."

I wondered if people said that about me.

Like anything, there are always signs.

The summer before I met Brian, before sophomore year, we had a bonfire on the shore. It was just me and Colleen and our friends and our sort-of friends. Cheap cans of beer, people from our class, Dylan, before I knew him all that well, and Danielle, his girlfriend.

We were supposed to camp out there, only Danielle started complaining about the cold. And she was right. The sand got cold, and it was kind of gross to lie in. And there weren't enough blankets to go around.

So Dylan led us down the beach to the shed where the lifeguards kept their gear and the chairs and umbrellas for rent. Dylan pulled a Swiss Army knife from his back pocket and fiddled with it inside the padlock until it clicked open. We'd marched in single file behind him.

Colleen swayed across the room and swung her arm over Dylan. "My hero," she'd said.

And then Danielle pushed her in the back.

"What the hell?" Colleen asked.

"Hands off my boyfriend," Danielle said.

"Him? Don't worry. Not my type. Too skinny."

"I'm not too skinny," Dylan said. Even though back then he was.

And Danielle said, "Right. Is there anyone in this room besides him that you haven't *been with?" Colleen's mouth fell open, but nothing came out. Danielle smirked and said, "Like you have a type, you fucking slut."*

And I felt this thing start to rise. It started in my gut and moved up through my chest, and it clenched my fists and shot through my legs. I ran at Danielle and pushed her into the back wall.

She scratched at my arm with her sharp, manicured nails. I pushed her again and heard her head thump against the wood, and it felt good. Someone screamed, "Girl fight!" But then someone pulled me off, pulled me outside, and Colleen had her arms around me. She turned me around and looked at my arm. "Crazy bitch cut you."

I touched my right hand to the scratch on my left arm, raised my fingers up, and looked at the blood. Then Colleen and I started laughing. Uncontrollable laughter. We stumbled back down the beach and found a place to camp out, behind a dune.

We lay shivering from the cold sand beneath us. And Colleen said, "You know, I didn't really have a comeback for that."

And I'd said, "Yeah, well, you're my *fucking slut."*

She rolled onto her side and curled her body around mine, trying to keep us both warm, and then she started laughing again. She whispered into my ear, "Those boys don't know what they're missing right now."

The prosecutors didn't know about that night on the beach. I was sure of it. Because if they did, it probably would've canceled out what they knew about Brian. Brian liked to fight. He went looking for it. That guy on the skateboard wasn't an isolated incident. Even Joe's crooked nose was because of Brian. But I had a history too.

And now I was wondering why Dylan didn't tell the cops about that night when I shoved his girlfriend into the wall so hard the sound from her head hitting wood echoed through the shed. He didn't tell. Otherwise, Brian's history of violence would've meant less.

So I wrote that *Lord of the Flies* essay about everything we didn't see. About the boys at their boarding school. About who they were beforehand. About how they were always those people, if only William Golding would've showed us their history. It wouldn't have been so shocking.

At noon I went to the school store and used the account Dad had set up to replenish my supply of Monroe polo shirts. I changed in the bathroom and went to the rest of my afternoon classes. By the time classes were over, a fog had settled, low and heavy, over campus. People kept jumping out at each other, I guessed, because there was lots of squealing and laughter. Like it was funny not knowing what was two feet behind you.

I left my books in my room, but I couldn't stay there. Everything in it felt like limbo. The cracked closet door. The shades on the window, halfway up. The unmade bed. The knife in the bottom drawer.

The great thing about the fog is that it works two ways. I couldn't see if someone was lurking behind me, but nobody could see me through the fog either. I saw muted red moving in the distance, students walking across campus, but I couldn't tell who they were. Which meant they couldn't tell who I was either.

It felt safe.

I walked off campus, toward the old student center, where nobody would be. Just me and forgotten buildings and a sign for a forgotten boy. But at the road I heard an engine. A low rumble, slipping through the fog. I stepped into the street, and a green shape came into focus. All soft around the edges, muted by the white, like a dream.

I stopped breathing. Underneath the fog, the car drifted in and out of focus, like a memory I was trying to grasp onto. Like something I was forgetting, just beyond my reach. The engine turned off. A door clicked open. A step. Two steps. A door slamming shut. I backed up, silently, until I couldn't see the green anymore, letting the fog hide me as well. Then I turned around and ran back toward campus. I stared at the two feet in front of me, which was all I could really see, until I tripped over the front steps of my dorm. But I didn't even pause before pushing myself back up and racing down the hall.

My fingers shook as I dialed the 800 number for home.

"Mallory?" Dad answered the phone. Which was odd. Since it was Monday, and only late afternoon.

"What are you doing home?" I asked.

"I took off. There were a few things I needed to help out with around here."

My stomach flipped. "Is Mom okay?"

"Of course," he said, like he was annoyed I'd even suggested she might not be. "But she's resting right now, so maybe if you call back tomorrow you can catch her—"

"Dad. It's Brian's mom," I said. "She's here." My voice broke and I cupped my hand over my mouth.

And then there was silence. I could hear him breathing and, beyond that, I could hear the swish of fabric as he moved to another room.

"No, Mallory, she's not."

"I saw—"

"Mallory. Brian's mother. She was admitted to the hospital yesterday. She's not in New Hampshire. She's here. At a hospital. She's not going anywhere."

"What happened?" I asked. But underneath that I thought of the vision in the fog, drifting in and out of focus.

"She had a breakdown. She was here," he said, hushed. "At the back door. Looking for Brian."

"Like—?"

"Yes," he said, probably remembering the same thing.

"Gotta go," I said, just a whisper, picturing her screaming for her son as she stood in the doorway to my kitchen.

I paced the hall with my hands resting on top of my head, like I used to do after the required mile run in gym class, trying to catch my breath. I stared at the entrance to my room, but I didn't go in.

I was scared of what else I might see. Like when I was

seven and I'd wake up and still see the people from my dream, moving like a fragmented video. At the door. Blink. At the foot of my bed. Blink. At my side.

Here and not here.

And then they'd fade away as the fog lifted and the dream remained a dream and the real remained real. As I got older, the boundary grew stronger, and the things that weren't real remained on one side, and the things that were remained on the other.

Until now.

I kept pacing that hall. People ignored me, on their way to dinner and back again. I needed to know that something was real. I needed to feel something real.

So I left. I sprinted down the hall and across the quad as dusk settled in like a long shadow, clinging to the fog. I raced to Danvers West and busted into the lounge, breathing heavily. Jason and a bunch of guys from the soccer team stared at me. Stared and smirked.

"To what do we owe this pleasure?" Jason asked.

I looked from couch to couch, looking for Reid's face. I swallowed the thick air, along with my pride. "Can someone get Reid?"

Jason bared all his teeth when he smiled this time. "Get him yourself, Mallory."

When I turned for the hall, someone whistled at me. The

hallway was empty, and so was the stairwell. Then I wondered how Reid had snuck out of his room from the second floor the night before. Not through the door, that's for sure. They're alarmed at night. Through someone else's room. Great. Another secret for distribution.

Music came from room 203. I knocked gently.

"Come in," he called.

I opened the door and pulled it shut behind me, leaning against it. Reid had his back to me, his bare back actually, since he was half dressed, postshower.

"Oh," I said. And then I looked away. At anywhere but at his bare back. At the walls, with the posters of bands I'd never heard of. At his desk, with books I'd never read. At his bed, with the black-and-gray stripes.

"Oh," he said back. He pulled a gray T-shirt over his head. "How did you . . ."

"Jason," I said. "I had to see you, but they wouldn't get you, so I came up . . . Sorry you didn't know it was me."

"Yeah, because obviously I'd never want you to see me without a shirt. God forbid."

I almost said *you wish* or something else coy or flirty or meaningless. That's what I'd say if it was Dylan, or Brian—I'd say something not serious. Because I hadn't been.

"Okay, so what's up? You had to see me?"

But now, in his room, the whole thing felt ridiculous. To

say that I saw something that couldn't be real. That I saw it and heard it. To say I didn't know what was real anymore.

To say that I wanted to feel something real.

"I was just thinking how different things would be if I'd come here freshman year."

Say something real.

"If I was how you remembered me instead." But the words I didn't say felt stronger.

Am I even real anymore? Am I here, standing in front of you, or am I still under the boardwalk somewhere, covered in blood?

Reid looked like he didn't know what to say. "You're not exactly how I remembered you," he said. And this buzzing filled my ears. "Mostly, you're more than I remember. But in some ways, you're the same. Like you still hold your breath when you're nervous." He grinned, and stepped closer. "You held your breath in your room this morning. And you're holding your breath now. Why are you nervous, Mallory?"

Because this wasn't in his car, where it seemed like we were finishing something we'd started two years earlier, like it was the only choice, like everything had been leading up to that moment. Because last night, when he asked to stay, he had held his breath too. Because I had come here, on my own, and now he was standing halfway across the room, daring me to close it. And I was closing it.

"I'm not nervous," I said, except I was. Because it felt like we were starting right now. Then I was so close I could feel his breath, coming a little too fast. And my hands were on his chest, like I could push him away any minute, but I didn't. I spread my palms flat and tried to feel his heartbeat.

It was racing.

And then there was knocking. "Open up. Now."

Reid winced and I looked around the room for some place to hide. But Reid just shook his head and put a finger to my lips.

"Mr. Carlson. Open this door, or I'll open it for you."

He jabbed his finger at his desk chair, and he backed up toward his bed. I guess so it would look like we were having an innocent study session or something. And then Mr. Durham turned the handle and was in the room, trying to look disappointed, but he had looked at me, and now he only looked confused.

"Out," he said.

I didn't look at Reid as I left. And I didn't look at Jason as I walked through the lounge. But I could feel him smiling.

I started taking sleeping pills again that night. Because it turned out the things I was most scared of didn't really exist. *It's only real if you let it be,* I thought as I drifted off to sleep to the *boom, boom, boom* coming closer.

But in the morning, there was something dried and stiff across my shoulder. Drops of blood, sticking my skin to my shirt. I ran to the bathroom and looked in the mirror. I hissed and shivered. Because underneath the dried blood, a blister had formed and burst along one of the finger marks on my shoulder.

I ran my finger along my skin and brought a dark drop of blood close to my face.

Then I smeared it across the mirror, just to make sure it was real.

CHAPTER 12

I ran the faucet full blast, scooped up handfuls of water, and splashed them over my shoulder repeatedly, soaking my shirt, my arm, and the ends of my hair. I dabbed at the broken skin with paper towels and glanced in the mirror again.

There were eyes over my shoulder. Blue, and curious. Bree stood too close, staring at the handprint on my shoulder—at the blood. Then she slowly raised her eyes to meet mine in the mirror. I jerked the wet shirt back over my shoulder. "It was an accident," I said, and the words echoed around the bathroom.

"Did she tell you to say that?" Bree whispered.

"Did *who* tell me to say that?" I asked, spinning to face her.

She shook her head quickly. "Never mind."

"No, Bree," I said, because she was squeezing her eyes shut, which is what I did when I was thinking of something I didn't want to think about. "Who?"

She laughed quietly to herself. "Nobody. God, it's this place, you know? I can't sleep here. And now I'm losing my mind." She laughed again. And then she seemed to realize she was alone. In the bathroom. With me. She cleared her throat and took a step back.

"I get it," I said, to make her stop moving away. "I can't sleep here either. Not without sleeping pills."

Her cheeks tensed, like maybe she was trying to smile, but didn't quite remember how. She left the room first. I followed as quickly as I could, but the door across the hall had already latched behind her.

I stepped on a pink paper just inside my room. I unfolded it and swore under my breath. A violation form for unauthorized visitation. A revocation of all visitation privileges for two weeks. At least I could still see Reid during study hall. I was more concerned with the carbon copy obviously missing below. I cringed, thinking about it making its way to my parents.

I had an e-mail from Reid, trying to find overlapping free time, since he also lost visitation *and* study hall privileges.

I wrote back: I didn't lose study hall.

He responded: second violation.

I didn't respond to that. I got a knot in my stomach, thinking of another girl in his room. Which I knew was ridiculous.

But still. I wondered if it was Taryn. And what they were caught doing. It reminded me that there was all this history here that I didn't know anything about.

I heard my name in the whispers throughout the classroom. Mr. Durham walked around the U-shaped tables, collecting our *Lord of the Flies* essays. He took my paper with the tips of his fingers, not even looking at me. But everyone else was looking, even more than usual. Like the new rumor circulating around school, making its way from wallet to wallet, was that I'd been caught in Reid's room.

"Slut." I heard from somewhere across the room, followed by a few snickers. Okay, apparently not. Apparently the rumor was that I'd been caught screwing Reid Carlson in his room. Good to know.

"Don't listen," Chloe said. She leaned toward me. "Next week, it'll be something else."

Of course. Because here at Monroe, you could transform in a day. How quickly I had gone from *girl-who-escaped-the-roof* to *girl-who-slashes-own-shirts-for-attention* to *slut.*

And then I started laughing. Horrible, really. But I was laughing. Because of all the things they could say about me, equal parts horrible and true, this was so far from the mark it was funny.

We were treading water in the ocean, Colleen and I, Brian and Dylan, Joe and Sammy, and Cody Parker. We were out past the spot where the waves broke, drifting with the surfboards, all pointed toward the horizon.

Colleen was hanging on Cody's back, trying to dunk him, but not really. They all had their surfboards, everyone but me, but nobody was trying to do any surfing. It was just an excuse for us to be out here, on the beach for the surfers and not for the swimmers, which was full of tourists.

Brian had one hand on his board and one arm wrapped around me, holding me up. I couldn't tread water on my own with his arm around me anyway. His legs kept getting in the way. "Chill out, Mallory," he'd said. "I'm not gonna let you drown."

But I couldn't stop my legs from kicking, or my free arm from making small circles in the water. So eventually he hauled me onto his surfboard, so I was less annoying, I guess. But I guess that got pretty boring pretty damn fast, because, while Joe was still in the middle of a sentence, Brian untied the back of my bathing suit.

"Jesus, Brian," I'd said, trying to grab onto the back and tie it together again. But then Brian flipped the surfboard, and I didn't even have time to take a breath. I swallowed salt water and broke through the surface, still choking on water, trying to stay afloat while simultaneously holding the back of my suit together.

Brian laughed and pulled me toward him. And since I needed one hand to hold my top on, I couldn't let go of him without falling under again. I held on tightly to his neck. Brian was laughing, but he was looking at everyone else.

And Joe said, "Get a room already."

Brian said, "You're coming tonight, right?"

"Coming where?" I asked. And then I turned away and coughed again.

"Party at my place," he said, like I should've known. But I didn't.

And then Colleen said, "Still grounded."

"What about you? Are you grounded too?" Brian asked, never taking his eyes off me.

I was still pressed up against him, and I could see Dylan out of the corner of my eye, watching us. So I said, "No. And my parents will be out anyway." And then Brian kissed me on the mouth in front of everyone, and I didn't pull away because I was still trying to figure out how to tie my bathing suit back on.

"Let's surf," Dylan said. He paddled past me without a glance in my direction. Brian backed away, smiling, as I struggled to stay both clothed and above water at the same time. Colleen grabbed me by the arm and pulled me toward her board. She didn't surf. Never had. But she'd had that board for years, for situations exactly like this. The rest of them paddled closer to shore, sitting on their boards. Not quite surfing yet. Pre-surfing, maybe.

Colleen turned me around and leaned down toward the water. She tied the knot, extra tight. "Asshole," she said.

I spun around, treading water a few inches away from her. "What's your problem with him?"

"What's my *problem? What's* his *problem? You should be with someone else."*

I looked at the guys, straddling their boards, waiting for a wave. "Like who, Dylan?"

Colleen watched them as well. "No, not Dylan." Then she dipped off her board into the water, level with me, looked directly in my eyes, and said, "Brian isn't right for you."

"You mean because he's older? You think I don't know how to act? What to do? You think you're the only one who can get an older guy?"

"Don't be stupid, Mallory."

"You're telling me *not to be stupid? Seriously?"*

Colleen had stared at me, like she was waiting for me to say what she knew I was going to say. I didn't. But it didn't matter. She knew I was thinking it. But she didn't yell. She said, "You're not like me." Which did something to the inside of me, because suddenly I couldn't stay above water. Not while I was facing her.

I started swimming away before she could see my face, but she grabbed onto my ankle as I swam. "Don't," she said, even though I still wasn't looking at her. I kicked her off and swam for the surfboards. But she said it anyway. "I didn't mean it like that."

Brian smiled as he saw me approaching. He pulled me onto his board, and we sat, facing each other, while people caught waves around us. But his smile made me nervous, the way he was kind of seeing me, but kind of not, and now Colleen's words had settled into my head.

"Sorry," I said. "I forgot that I promised to help Colleen with something tonight."

Brian groaned and said, "You're killing me, Mallory. Absolutely killing me."

I knew how I was supposed to feel when I was with him. Well, I knew what I was not supposed to feel. I wasn't supposed to feel anxious. Not tense either. Or maybe I was. Maybe this was normal. I didn't know. So I let him whisper in my ear and put his hands on my hips. And I listened to him list all the ways in which I was slowly killing him.

None of which turned out to be the actual way that I killed him.

It was funny. In a very unfunny way. But I couldn't stop laughing. "Ms. Murphy," Mr. Durham seethed. "Do you find William Golding humorous? Does he make you laugh?"

"No, sir," I said, trying to suppress a smile. And then I thought, *Well I am hysterical*, and I laughed some more.

"Please, enlighten us. What is so funny today?"

"This place," I said, choking on my laughter. "And everyone in it."

"You're excused, Ms. Murphy."

I wasn't sure where I was being excused to, but the message

was clear: get out. So I did. It was raining again. Misting, really. Like you didn't even notice it was raining until you realized you were dripping wet.

I went back to the dorm and dialed home. Mom answered on the first ring.

"So," I began, "there was a misunderstanding. It's not a big deal, but there's probably a form being sent home to you."

"What kind of misunderstanding?" Mom slowed her voice, and I could imagine her sitting down.

"Well, I was doing some homework with a guy—Reid Carlson, actually—remember him?" Because I thought it might go over better if she did. "But I forgot to check in."

"I don't understand. Check in where?"

"His room. Like I said, it was a misunderstanding. It's all straightened up now, but I lost visitation rights for two weeks. No big deal."

"No big deal?" she said. "Mallory, honey, I don't think it's such a good idea for you to become involved with anyone right now."

"I'm not *involved,* Mom. We were working." My voice turned sharp, because I knew she didn't want me in a boy's room because she was worried about what I might do, not what he might do.

"Please, Mallory. Please be careful."

I thought of the knife in my room. "Yes, Mother." And I hung up the phone.

I remained in the lounge until next period and endured the looks and whispers for the rest of my classes without making a scene.

But after class, I had nowhere to go. Kind of ridiculous that I had been watching the second hand crawl along, mentally trying to push it around, when, really, I didn't know what I was rushing toward. It was still kind of raining out, and I was in no hurry to return to my dorm room. Not when I'd be stuck there all night, by myself, with whatever was coming for me.

I walked down the stairs after last period, and kept going after the first floor, until I was in the basement with the student store and, beyond that, the health center. Which was kind of a comical name, since it was just one nurse, and she only worked during school hours.

I guess that's why she was already packing up for the day. She paused when she saw me standing in her doorway.

"Can I help you?" she asked.

"Do you have any Band-Aids? The big kind?"

She put her bag back down and walked to a cabinet over the sink. "I do," she said. "How big are we talking? Let me take a look at the cut."

I instinctively turned my left shoulder so it was facing away from her. "Oh no, that's okay." And then, when she made no move to come closer, I added, "It's just a blister."

"A very large blister," she said, handing me a stack of

Band-Aids. She went back to gathering up her papers and purse, and she slung a raincoat over her arm. "You know," she said, filing papers into her bag, "there are avenues to report things here so you don't have to go through the school administration. I am one of them."

My first instinct was that she was threatening me, that I was being reported for something by someone, but her words were too soft. Too careful. Like she was trying to tell me something. Like she knew something. Or thought I knew something. She cleared her throat and said, "I was on duty at the soccer game last week. Mallory, right?"

I nodded. Then I realized she was saying she witnessed the fight with Jason, and I felt my face turning color. "It's just a blister," I repeated.

She put a hand on the small of my back and guided me out of the room, locking the door behind her. "Okay," she said. "But if it's ever more than a blister, you know where to find me." She stared into my eyes, and hers were this bright hazel, the type that could turn kind or mean or harsh or compassionate in a blink. "Somebody has to say something."

Her eyes were something in between at the moment.

The mist had stopped, and people were back outside. I planned to drop my stuff in my room and see if I could run into Reid, who'd probably be heading back from practice soon. Or maybe he was already back. Because Jason was in our lounge. He was still in his practice clothes, socks pulled high over shin guards. His cleats had tracked mud and grass across the floor.

His head was back on the couch, and Krista was hovering over him. She had a bunch of wet paper towels pressed to his cheek. "Get me something. It hurts."

"Go to the nurse," she said.

"She doesn't like me. And besides, I have you. Family first, right?"

Krista froze when she saw me. Jason tried to smile at me, but his lower lip was swollen and the top of his cheek was reddish purple, and he winced from the pain. "Your boyfriend fights dirty," he said. Then a sound that must have been laughter escaped from his throat.

I backed out the front entrance, my heart in my throat, and headed away from center campus. Away from the cafeteria. Away from anywhere Reid might be. Because I pictured Brian, using his fists, taking that kid on the skateboard down. And my lawyer saying *history of violence*.

And me, pushing Danielle into the wall. And imagining doing the same to Jason. Wanting to do the same to Jason. And Reid, actually doing it.

Not right for you.

The irony was, he was entirely right for me. I understood

exactly why he did it. Which is why I shouldn't be with him. I shouldn't.

The ground was wet, and the mist hovered a little, just above the grass, but I saw the shape of a guy moving toward me, calling my name. Reid. I sprinted toward the gate, heading toward the old student center.

But Reid ran too. The fog drifted up, above the grass, along the road.

His hands gripped my shoulders, spinning me around. "Hey, I was calling you." He didn't know how much he was hurting me. I pushed his hands off.

He was staring at me, breathing heavily from the run, and then I saw a flash behind him. Green, through the fog, moving along the road past the gate. Slowly, without stopping.

Not real, not real, not real.

Reid turned and stared at the spot where Brian's mom could not possibly be, and when he turned back, his forehead was creased and he put his hand on my shoulder again.

"What? What is it?"

I jerked away.

Reid pulled his hand back, and all the color drained from his face. He was still staring at the spot where his hand had just been. I looked down and saw the dark red spreading on the scarlet shirt. "What's wrong with your shoulder?" he asked. "Did Jason do this?"

I stepped back, my right hand over my shoulder. “Nobody did this. You beat him up.”

“What? Jason?” Reid shook his head, then stopped and nodded. “He told on you—on us. I paid him back for it. Forget about him. Let me see your shoulder.”

“You paid him back for it? You mean you punched him in the face.”

“What the hell, Mallory? So I hit him. I was angry and I hit him. You’re really going to give me a hard time about this? You, of all people?” His clenched hand flew to his mouth, like he was trying to push the words back inside. And then he opened his mouth to say something, come up with some excuse, but nothing could undo that.

“I didn’t mean because . . .”

I waved my arm in front of my face, trying to stop the words before they arrived.

“I meant because we’re . . .”

“Just stop talking, Reid.”

I stepped back, hands palm out toward him, shaking my head. The fog making its way inside, swirling and churning until all I heard was Reid, all I saw was the inside of Reid, and what he really thought.

The mist was forming back into fog, like everything was happening in reverse. Death to life, rain to cloud, thickening around me. I felt the blood seeping out of me, and I waited for a moment, thinking it might reverse course or something, like everything else. But the drops kept running down the length of my arm, like tears.

That night, the *boom, boom, boom* sounded hollow. Closer. Faster. Not so much like the beating of his heart. As my mind started to drift, I heard something else. The *boom, boom, boom* and then a scratching at my door, like an animal trying to get in.

And a voice. "Please," it cried. "Please let me in."

Not at all like the usual whisper I'd hear calling my name, asking me to wait.

This was a girl. I worried it was another attempt at initiation—worried that I'd get dragged out of my room and abandoned on some roof while half unconscious.

"Please," she cried again, and then she gulped back a sob—real fear, hard to fake.

I swung my legs out of bed, and my head felt funny from the sleeping pill—too full, too slow—but there was another cry on the other side of the door, and I had to get there. *Step,* I instructed my leg. *Move.* Again. And again. But everything was so painstakingly slow. I unlocked the door, and the handle quickly turned from the other side. And then Bree was in my room, gripping on to my arms, leaning into me. Her eyes were wild.

I stumbled back, into my desk. "Help me," she whispered.

I nodded, because that's really all I was capable of doing. And even that was a stretch. I was still fading, fading—fighting it, but fading still.

"Can I stay?" she asked. She was looking at her empty bed. Like she meant longer than just that moment. Like she meant indefinitely.

I opened my mouth to say no, but the room felt different with her in it. I imagined her steady breathing across the room at night, and her clothes hanging in the closet, and everything felt crowded, but in a good way. Like sleeping bags lined up next to each other at a slumber party.

Bree looked over her shoulder at the open door. She ran and pushed it closed. "She's coming," she said. Or maybe it was *he's coming,* but she had whispered, and now the words were gone.

I tried to force my mouth to form the word, *Who?* But I had nothing. All I knew was that she was terrified. So terrified that she came to me, like I was the lesser of two evils. Or maybe because she knew I *could* help her.

And I could.

I fell to my knees, which was the easiest thing I'd done so far. And I pulled open the bottom drawer of the desk. I felt my breath slowing, slowing, even though it should've been speeding up from the adrenaline. *Look,* I willed her.

And she did. She looked down, and she looked at me, and I

saw her throat move as she swallowed. Then she looked at the door again. Back to me. The door. And I heard her name, sounding far, far away.

Take the . . . I started to think.

And I was gone.

Kind of.

But I had this hazy vision of a shadow looking down at me, head cocked to the side. And I heard voices. Whispers. Like static moving through my brain.

I woke up to my alarm. In my bed. I shook my head, trying to judge what was real and what wasn't. The room looked untouched. I was on my back, sheets pulled up to my neck. I turned off the alarm and tested the door. Locked.

I took a deep breath. A dream. Just a dream.

I got my shower caddy together and grabbed my bathrobe. And then, just to be sure, I pulled open the bottom drawer to my desk.

The knife was gone.

CHAPTER 13

Somebody took my knife. Not exactly something I could report. I pulled the brush through my hair, tearing at the knots. Tearing even after there were no knots left. Last night had happened. It had really happened. And something else had happened, between the time I opened the desk drawer and made it to my bed. But I couldn't remember.

I closed my eyes and ran through the events again and again: the knocking, Bree, the knife. I dropped the brush. Oh God, Bree. Had she taken it? Had she used it?

I ran out into the hall, toward her room. Bree was there. In the hall. Walking from the bathroom, in her robe, toward her room. Taryn moved in the opposite direction with a shower caddy in her hand. Neither looked up at me, though they must've noticed me, standing, *staring,* in the middle of the hall.

It happened and the knife was gone and Bree was fine. But now she wouldn't look at me.

A new feeling settled in my stomach. Fear. She must've reported me. Ran to Ms. Perkins, showing her the knife. Maybe the campus police were on their way. Or Dad, with his disapproving look, or Mom, with no look, really, at all. On their way to retrieve me because I wasn't welcome here any longer.

Except no one came. I got ready for class, like normal, and everyone acted like they normally acted around me now. Which was to say, they either looked too much or not at all.

But every time someone came to the classroom door, my heart leapt into my throat. Every time someone uttered a name that started with the letter *M*, I jumped. But the next few classes passed without incident.

At lunch, I saw Ms. Perkins in the quad. She glanced my way, just for a second, and then kept talking to the teacher next to her. I let out a long breath.

Nobody told.

But the knife was still gone.

I sat under the giant oak by myself. The ground was a little on the damp side, but the dirt up around the roots was dry. Added bonus: nobody else was out here.

Except Reid. Walking toward me, his hands deep in his pockets.

Reid skipped class. He had to, that was the only way he'd find me on my lunch period. "Mallory," he called as I gathered up my half-eaten lunch. I didn't have time to pack it all up and escape before he got here.

He looked at my shoulder first. Just a quick look, but I noticed, and I felt the scabs itching underneath the bandage.

Then he sat down beside me. "I'm sorry," he said, which I hated. But then he said, "I'm sorry you're upset. But I'm not sorry that I did it," which I loved. "And I'm sorry the words came out wrong . . ."

"Stop apologizing," I said.

"I like you." The air felt too warm suddenly. Because I realized that Brian had never said those words. So ridiculous. He'd said a lot of other things, which I'd thought amounted to the same thing.

But they didn't.

Reid kept talking. "I like you, but . . ." Ah, the famous *I like you, but . . .* "Does it have to be this hard?"

Everything's this hard. "If this is you breaking up with me, save it. You have to be together before you can break up."

"That's not what I'm saying. I'm saying . . . let's start over. Go back. I'm the guy you used to see three times a year and now we're here at school together. Let's go back."

Go back. A do-over. Like this was all a game. Like what you do doesn't count unless you want it to.

"Say yes," he said.

Reid of all people should know you can't go back. Can't start over. Can't call redo and play a better hand. But here he was, pretending we could. If you pretend something hard enough, could it become real?

I shifted so I was facing him, raised myself up on my knees. He pulled me closer, his arms around my back, and I rested my forehead against his chest. My hands gripped his shirt, like I was begging for something. Like I was kneeling at some altar. Like this whole thing was some kind of prayer.

That night, there was a shadow under my door. Just standing there. Waiting. Every few seconds it shifted a little. Then it went away. And then it came back. It was after lights out, but I hadn't taken the sleeping pill yet. I slowly eased the top drawer of my desk open and slid the scissors into the waistband of my pajama pants. And then I walked very cautiously, so I wouldn't cut myself.

I cracked the door, and as my eyes adjusted to the light, I saw Bree, with her eyes wide, like she'd been caught in my headlights. "What is it?" I asked.

"Sorry. I was about to knock."

"Um, about last night," I said.

"Oh God, I'm mortified," Bree said, throwing her hands into the air. Then she smiled, looking past me. "I mean, seriously. You must've thought I was crazy."

"I thought you were scared. But I'd taken a sleeping pill. And . . ."

"Right. You told me."

"What were you running from?"

"Oh. Nothing, really. It's just, I can't sleep. And Taryn snores. I know you wouldn't guess it by looking at her, but she does. And I'm having, like, nightmares or something. Except without really sleeping. Weird, huh?"

"Weird," I said. "So about the, uh . . ."

But Bree just stared at me, her head cocked to the side. Like she wasn't about to acknowledge what she and I both knew I'd showed her. "About the *what*?"

"The sleeping pill. I don't know if I said something, maybe? Or did something? I wasn't really thinking straight."

Bree was looking over my shoulder, into the room, and I realized I was holding my breath. And then I realized why. I was hoping she'd ask to move back in. Pathetic.

"Well, that's kind of why I'm here," Bree said, still looking into the room. "I was wondering if you could spare one."

I tried to look into her eyes, but she looked unfocused. Tired, I guessed. Was this the start of friendship? Or the restart? Maybe like Reid said, we could have do-overs. I didn't know. But I also didn't know what harm a single sleeping pill could do. So I went to the drawer and pulled out the vial, and all the while Bree stayed in the door frame, with her eyes too wide, watching.

She held out her palm, and I could see her veins running through it. I could see this faint tremor, too, like I saw under the window the other day. She really did need sleep. She needed my help. I tapped the lip of the vial on her open palm, and a single pill settled into the crease of her hand.

She closed her fist around it. "Okay," she whispered, backing away.

"Okay," I said, and I watched her walk down the hall like in a trance, absently fumbling with her doorknob, her fist still closed around that single pill. Like it was worth something.

Then I took one myself. And right after, I heard something outside my window. Someone was there. I was sure of it. Almost sure of it. I heard the resistance of the lock as it was pushed upward. I turned on the lights and threw open the shades, but I could only see my reflection. I darted across the room and turned off the lights—and I swear I saw a dark figure heading for the trees.

Long, lanky strides. Hair lit in the moonlight. Brian.

Hysteria, I thought. In my mind. Hallucinations. So I jerked the blinds closed and lay on the bed and took comfort in the familiarity of what would happen next.

The beating of his heart. My name, whispered. Begging me to wait. And his hand.

I let it come, and I felt some relief, finally. Like this was the consequence. And all I had to do was endure it.

The next day was full of a different kind of talk. Reid and Krista. Fighting.

"He called her a manipulative bitch," some girl whispered in math. Lisa? Lissa?

"No, he said she was a *pathetic*, manipulative bitch," the girl next to her said.

"Was that before or after she kissed him?"

My head slipped off my hand and nearly banged into the table. The girls looked at me, and they didn't look away, or stare too long, or anything. The one closest to me leaned over and grinned. She whispered, "Before she *tried* to kiss him."

I smiled quickly at her, and ran the image through my mind. Krista cornering him. Trying to kiss him. Reid pushing her back, calling her a manipulative bitch. No, a *pathetic*, manipulative bitch. Perfect. And then I thought of these two girls, and I thought that maybe there were a lot of people like that—normal, non-bitchy, non-crazy people, like Chloe—and

I just hadn't looked hard enough yet. I also thought I should probably start looking.

Reid found me after class—before his game. He was out of breath, and probably running late for warm-ups. "So," he said, "I should probably tell you that I got in a fight with Krista."

"So I heard," I said.

"Not, like, a physical one or anything."

"I know."

"She tried to kiss me," he said.

"I heard that too. Funny. I thought she didn't like you."

"She doesn't," he said.

"I don't get it."

"She was trying to mess with me. And you."

"Why does she hate us?"

"It's not us, don't you see? It's not even *her*. But I'm so freaking sick of it." He closed his eyes and shook his head, then refocused on me. "Oh, but in the interest of full disclosure, I should *also* tell you that Saturday is in two days."

"Good math, Reid."

"Thanks. Yeah. No school. No practice. I'm free. Available. You know, if you're going to be around . . ."

"Good to know," I said, and I couldn't stop the stupid smile from spreading across my face.

"But now I gotta go kick some soccer ass. See you soon?"

"See you soon," I promised.

And suddenly the next two days couldn't be over fast enough. I watched him race off to get ready for his game, and I sat under the giant oak, just staring off into the distance. Watching while the sky turned different shades of blue as the clouds moved across the sun. Like Colleen and I used to do on the summer evenings from the boardwalk.

I went back to my dorm to send her an e-mail. But as I walked through the lounge, I saw Krista sitting with Taryn and Bree, and I caught the end of Krista's sentence. "He won't get away with it," she said, bringing her fist down on the coffee table like a gavel.

I grinned, thinking how inconsequential they were. How Reid didn't give a crap what they said about him. How Reid was bigger than all this. And then they all followed me with their eyes as I walked across the room. Except for Bree. Bree didn't look up. Like we were arguing about something.

The afternoon of the party, after I argued with Colleen, after I left her in the water for Brian, and then after he had left me, I got a text from her. A peace offering, I guess: I'm still grounded. But you should go.

I wrote back: Lame without you anyway.

And she wrote: My life would be complete if you had a Y chromosome.

So when she showed up that night, catching fireflies on my back patio, I knew she was doing it for me. Not for her. Not for Cody Parker. Me.

I left the girls in the lounge, and I sent Colleen an e-mail. There might be stuff to tell you, I wrote, which I knew she'd interpret as boy stuff. But I felt like I was lying to her, by all the things I wasn't saying. Reid's name. The blood on my shoulder, the fingerprints on my skin, the knife I stole and lost, or possibly just misplaced in my psychosis. The things I saw that were not there. She sent an e-mail right back saying she'd be ungrounded Saturday.

For the first time in a long time, I was looking forward instead of backward. To what comes next.

Two more days.

CHAPTER 14

That night, like always, it started with the heartbeat. *Boom, boom, boom.*

And then my name. *Mallory. Wait.*

And then the hand. The fingers, digging in, grinding down through muscle and nerve. Shocks of pain radiating down my arm.

But then, there was a different dream.

First I saw Brian's mouth, saying, "Mallory, wait." Like always. And then Brian's mother appeared, reaching a hand out to me, garbage hanging from her clothes, asking me to wait. Then I was leaning in to kiss Reid, but his hands were on my shoulders, pushing me back, and he was saying, "Wait." And then Colleen was curled up behind me on the sand, whispering, "Wait," into my ear. And then I was walking into the fog, wandering away from campus, down that path past the cross, and a boy was running in front of me, getting farther and farther away, and I was the one chasing after him. I was the one screaming, "Wait!"

Click.

My door. Was it in my dream? Or was it from that place where things that did not exist whispered in my ear? It felt real as anything.

I jumped out of bed and my head swam like my blood was running in the wrong direction. I dove for the door, but it was locked.

Maybe it was the closet.

I took my scissors out and held them in front of me as I flung open the closet door, but nothing moved except the clothes, the hangers squeaking with the faintest motion.

I checked the window. This time I kept the light off. I pulled the shade up and placed my hands against the glass, peering out. The moon was bright, and the trees looked like tall shadows. Nothing moved.

Then I stepped back and saw a mark against the glass. A handprint. I flipped the lights on and saw that it was red, like blood. I went closer to inspect the handprint, hoping it was something other than blood. But it wasn't.

And it was on the inside.

It was mine.

The moon had been bright that night, even though it was raining. And I was running, sprinting, wheezing with each step. The alley moving by me in a blur. Feet on the wooden boardwalk. The moon was too bright. I *was too bright. Over the dunes. Down on the sand at high tide. The white light reflected off the water, reflected off me. There was so much blood.*

Too much blood. I didn't understand how there could possibly be that much blood on my hands, on my arms, on my chest. How did it get there? How did it get everywhere?

I raced toward the pier, where the boardwalk juts out. To the darkness. And I fell onto my knees in the water and dug my hands deep under the sand, trying to scrub it all off. I fell face-first, and I picked up fistfuls of sand and ground it into the front of my shirt. Over my arms. Everywhere.

The salt water stung my eyes. And it stung my arms, where the blood was my own. And then I sat back, while the water and Brian's blood lapped around me, and I waited. I waited. I waited.

In the light of my room, my hands came into focus. The right one was clean. The left was coated red. I wiped it on my pants, but the red had settled into the lines of my palm. There were no cuts. The blood was dripping from my shoulder, down my arm, to my hand. Blood fell from my middle finger onto the floor.

I balled up a shirt and wiped up the blood. Then I pressed it to my shoulder. I was scared to look, but I had to. The whole handprint was raw—blistered—like it had been faintly seared into my shoulder. And the blister where the pinky finger left a mark was weeping blood.

It was nearly dawn. I ran to the bathroom and dabbed at my shoulder, hissing with pain. I rinsed all the blood off before anyone woke up, and rebandaged it gently. I pressed my hand down on top of it, like I might somehow hold in all the blood, or make it clot or something.

Stop the blood.

Stop the blood. Stop the blood. The words echoed in my head, like they were mine, but I wasn't thinking it. *Stop the blood,* I heard it again.

My hand shook as I pressed down harder. By the time the blood stopped dripping from the wound, people were starting to come into the bathroom, half-awake, carrying shower caddies. I waited until they all went to class before stripping the sheets from my bed and running everything down to the laundry room.

Another unexcused absence would land me an additional

violation, according to the handbook. I wondered what the consequence would be this time. What could they possibly take away from me now?

After I remade the bed, my first instinct was to find Reid and show him my shoulder. Tell him what was happening. Ask if he knew what to do. Or maybe ask nothing. Maybe just seek some sort of comfort with him.

But we were starting over. He made me think I actually could. So when I saw him briefly after class, before practice, I tried to mirror the smile on his face.

"Good day?" he asked.

"Great day," I said. All these people were milling by us, smiling at Reid.

One of his teammates hooked an arm around his neck, dragging him down the hall, laughing. I turned around, toward the other exit, and then he was beside me again, spinning me around. Really close. His hands were on my upper arms, and he was staring at me, like he was willing me to say something. But I didn't. When he finally spoke, he said, "You know what tomorrow is?"

"Saturday," I said. He was smiling as he backed away, and was smiling still as the crowd swallowed him up. I turned and bumped directly into Bree.

"Hey," I said, but she tried to move around me without looking.

I stepped to the side, stood directly in her path, and said, "Bree."

She froze, and there was something not quite right about her. I realized she was holding her breath. Waiting.

"You okay? I mean, the sleep?"

Her shoulders relaxed and she let out her breath. She nodded rapidly, like she didn't want to really talk. "I'm good," she said.

I was so used to Colleen, who I could read. Most of the time, at least. But now I felt like I was squinting at Bree, trying to decipher the meaning. "You're good," I repeated slowly, almost to myself.

"That's what I said." Bree's eyes locked onto something over my shoulder, and she kept moving.

Friday night. Two hours until it was technically Saturday. Eight hours until I could say it was Saturday and mean it. Eleven hours until breakfast opened and I had a legitimate excuse to look for Reid. Eleven hours.

I could sleep through eight of them, easy. Then I could get ready. Maybe even call Colleen beforehand.

The room was pulsating. Just like the kitchen used to. Except my shoulder was throbbing along with it. Like I was a part of it now. Like it had claimed me, or claimed part of me, and it was yearning for the rest. Like it had its talons in and wasn't about to let go now.

Boom, boom, boom. I started to fade. I thought of Reid, telling me to go back. *Boom, boom, boom.* It was getting louder. Coming closer. Right outside my door. But I couldn't see anything.

Go back. *Think, think, think.* I heard my name, and the word "wait," and I thought *Wait.* And I felt that hand reaching for me, but instead it was hovering. In the moment before.

Think.

But I was fading.

Think.

But I felt someone—something?—no, someone, standing over me.

Think.

But I was gone.

Brian stood over me, as I lay in the remains of the china cabinet, tiny pinpricks of glass sticking out of my skin. He shook his head, like he was trying to undo it all. It was like he realized, even in his out-of-control state, how out of control the situation had gotten. But he didn't stop. He reached for me still. "Why are you doing this?" he screamed, which made no sense, like this was all somehow my fault. "How could you do this?" he yelled again, like this was his house and I was destroying it.

I crab-walked backward through the glass, and pieces pierced my skin again, this time into my palms. And I thought, No, no, no, *but he kept coming anyway, crunching the glass under his shoes.*

Then he stopped and looked around the room and he winced, paled. And he said, "Can you just wait *one goddamn second?"*

And in that pause, I righted myself, scrambled to my feet. Then I ran. I sprinted into the kitchen, and he ran behind me—I could feel him, right behind me. I looked to the door, and it felt important, that look, like I was willing something to happen, but I couldn't remember what. And when nothing happened, I made a choice. Because he was right *behind me and he wouldn't stop. So I darted left at the granite island and I grabbed a knife. "Mallory," he said.*

I spun around. So he would see the knife. So he would stop.

"Wait," he said.

Because he couldn't. But I couldn't, either. There was no time.

I turned my head away, toward the door, but I still felt the resistance. The pressure. The shock. I looked back at Brian, like maybe I was imagining it, but I wasn't. Brian was looking down. And then he looked up at me, and his mouth formed the word "no." A long exhale. Like the word was dying along with him.

I woke up choking. Like something was sitting on my chest, constricting my lungs. I stared at the ceiling, suffocating, trying to remember how to breathe. *Breathe.* And finally, I sucked in a horrific, wheezing breath. I squeezed my eyes shut and breathed deeply through my nose. And then I smelled it. Something faint, metallic, acidic.

I opened my eyes. The room felt full. I pushed myself up on my elbows.

There was a person on the floor. Face up. And there was blood. A lot of blood. Two static bloodred puddles, stretching out from the arms. Both wrists were slit halfway up the arm. And the knife, just beside the body. Taunting me.

"No." I scampered down from the bed. "No!" I yelled.

I couldn't see, even though I could look. And in a brief moment of clarity I thought, *Hysteria,* even while the rest of me refused to process. I couldn't see his face, just a blur. I could look, but I could not see.

And my brain whispered, *Brian, Brian, Brian.*

I stumbled past my desk, and my foot slipped in the stickiness, but I caught myself on the edge of the desk and kept moving for the door. My fingers scratched along the door and fumbled with the handle and then it flew open and there was light, there was so much light. I ran down the hall, and the word in my head fought its way out. "Brian!" I shouted.

And for a moment, all I could see was him, and I heard his name being shouted, but I couldn't tell whether it was then or now and it didn't matter anyway because this couldn't be real.

This was not real.

Brian was in the ground. I saw them lower the wooden box into the hole in the earth. I heard somebody wail for him as I cowered behind the pickets of a fence.

I spun in the hall, and there were footprints on the floor, made of blood, leading from my room, directly to me.

Crazy. I was crazy.

"Help!" I cried. And a door creaked open. And then another. Because I kept screaming for help. But nobody helped me. People crept along the path of bloody footprints, tracing it back to its source.

And I knew it was real when the screaming started.

There was too much screaming. So much. Until it didn't even sound like screaming anymore. More like that ringing I'd hear in my ears when there was nothing making a sound at all.

People came. People in authority. The screaming around me turned to crying, and there were questions, but I couldn't speak. I was still sitting, silently, in the middle of the hallway.

A name was being passed around, in whispers, underneath the crying, just out of earshot.

And then it reached me, the word. *Jason*, I heard. *Jason Dorchester. Jason Dorchester. Jason Dorchester.*

Then the cold hands came. Maybe the presence. Maybe a new one. Maybe something else.

Maybe this is how it ends. With a dead body and cold hands, reaching for me.

CHAPTER 15

There were fluorescent lights. Starchy sheets. White walls. And people in scrubs moving their mouths. My ears were ringing, then stopped. And then the voices came. Light off. Light on.

"Mallory." A woman with wisps of red hair falling into her face was leaning over me. She turned her head to the side and said, "Run a full tox screen." When she stepped back, I saw there were other types of uniforms in the room. The dark-blue kind, with gold shields. She cleared her throat and said, "You'll have to wait your turn."

A man started to protest but she raised her hand up, palm out. "First of all, we make sure she's lucid. Second of all, and you should know this already, you wait for her parents."

I started to feel sick, thinking of my parents. Then thinking of the cops. And then thinking of the body on the floor.

Jason. So I didn't even wince when the doctor slid a needle into the crook of my elbow, drawing the blood out.

I felt the pull as blood seeped out, drawing more along with it. Then she left, and I waited, alone.

Like before: I waited, I waited, I waited. I waited for hours, maybe even longer.

The door swung open and my parents barged in, the doctor with the red hair right behind them.

"What's going on?" Mom asked. She ran to my bed and put a hand on my side. "I don't understand. Is she hurt?" Then she turned to me. "Are you hurt?"

I stared back.

The doctor cleared her throat. "Your daughter was at the scene of a crime, and, apparently, she was unresponsive."

"Unresponsive?" Dad said. "You mean unconscious?"

"No," she said. "I mean unresponsive. She didn't respond to verbal questions, and she didn't seem to know where she was." She held up the clipboard in her hand. "Tox screen results are back. Everything normal, except—did you take a sleeping aid?"

"Yes," I said, which I guess was my first response since they brought me in.

"Okay, otherwise, she's clean."

I guess they couldn't detect the orange fire I felt inside, like nerves twitching on overdrive.

My parents stared at me. Dad was looking back and forth

between me and the doctor, like he was trying to put together the pieces to some puzzle. "I don't think I understand," he said. "Scene of a crime?"

The doctor looked toward the door and knocked twice, almost like she was asking to be let out. A man and a woman in police uniforms entered the room.

Mom sank into the seat beside the bed. "She's okay?" Dad asked.

The doctor smiled stiffly. "According to this," she said, jabbing a finger at her stack of papers. She left the room.

The two cops stood at the end of my bed. The woman licked her lips, like she was preparing to devour me. The man cleared his throat. "I'm Officer James, and this is Officer Dowle. Why don't you start by telling us the events of last night."

"I was sleeping," I whispered.

Officer Dowle bounced a little on her toes, like she was ready to pounce. I kept my eyes on Officer James when he spoke again. "Okay, before that, then. What is the nature of your relationship with Jason Dorchester?"

"I have no relationship with Jason Dorchester."

"You don't know him?"

I sighed. "I know him."

"Would you consider your encounters positive?"

"Not really," I said, and I felt Mom tense beside me.

"Care to elaborate?"

"He doesn't like me. Didn't. Well, he did at first. I wasn't interested, so now he hates me. Hated me. Hates me." The dead can still hate, I was sure of it.

"Interesting," said Officer Dowle, and I didn't know whether she was talking about my story or my shift in tenses.

"Okay, so last night," Officer James continued.

"I took a sleeping pill. Like every night."

"And why," Officer Dowle said, staring at my face, "do you take sleeping pills?"

"To sleep," Dad cut in. The look he gave Officer Dowle made her look away.

She cleared her throat and raised her eyes back to Dad. "Yes, well, I assume I know the reason why."

"Then you should also know that she wasn't charged. It was self-defense."

"Was *this* self-defense?" Officer Dowle asked, but she was still looking at Dad.

"I didn't do it," I said.

They stared each other down. Officer James cleared his throat. "Did you hear anything after that, Mallory?"

"No. Nothing. I was sleeping and when I woke up . . ." The ringing in my ears was back, and Mom gripped my arm.

I could barely hear Officer Dowle over the ringing. She leaned forward and placed her hand on my left leg through the sheet. "Sometimes when people take sleeping pills, they don't really sleep. They think they do, but they don't. They just don't remember. My brother took a sleeping pill once. He got up for work the next morning, packed a lunch, got into a fender-bender on the way. But he didn't remember any of it." Then she placed her other hand on my right leg and said, "Do you think that could've happened to you?"

I thought about it. I thought about what I was capable of. My parents must've been thinking about it too. Because nobody said, *Oh, Mallory wouldn't do that*, or *Mallory's not capable of that*. Instead my father turned to me and said, "Don't answer that."

Officer Dowle squeezed my legs and grinned. They both turned to leave, and then Officer Dowle turned back. "Oh, I almost forgot. The knife. Any idea where it came from?"

The room seemed to hold its breath. I closed my eyes and said, "It's mine."

It was hard to explain why I'd have a knife without going into the reasons why I would want a knife. I told them someone stole it. And then I added, "My old roommate. Brianne Dalton. She knew I had it." Then I repeated, "Brianne Dalton," slowly, hoping someone would write it down. But nobody did. The cops weren't buying it, I could tell. They took my fingerprints and left the room. Dad looked at me in that way where he's asking a question without actually saying anything.

"I was scared," I said, my voice breaking. "I thought I saw . . ." Dad shifted his eyes quickly to Mom.

"You thought you saw *what*?" she asked.

I took a deep breath and closed my eyes. "I thought I saw Brian's mom."

"No. No. That's not possible," she said.

"I know. That's why I said *I thought I saw* instead of *I saw*. It was foggy, but I was—" And then I stopped talking because I wasn't sure exactly what I was.

It sure seemed real. Just like the hand on my shoulder, which was definitely not real.

Dad whipped out his cell, even though there was a sign in the room that said NO CELL PHONES, and I could tell it was the lawyer on the other end. And then Mom started talking to me about absolutely nothing, trying to distract me from the other conversation.

We stayed at the hospital that night, because we had nowhere else to go. And the next day people asked me the same questions over and over, and I said the same thing, over and over, which all amounted to absolutely nothing except me trying to reason out how Jason ended up dead on my floor. By the end of the day, it was clear I was not going to be arrested. But I might be in the future. Something about circumstantial evidence. Something about the knife. Something about my blood. Something about Jason's blood.

Officer James came back and said, "You're free to go, but you'll need to stay in this jurisdiction." And it felt like this weight lodging in my gut. Like I had been waiting for something to happen. Just *something.* But nothing happened. I was stuck in the in-between, which somehow felt worse than being accused or arrested or something.

So we drove back to campus for a meeting. Well, my parents had a meeting. I had a date with the backseat of their car.

We were parked behind the main building, wedged between the back of the bleachers and the Dumpsters behind classes.

There was a shape under the bleachers. Hunched down in a ball. Motionless. I got this sick feeling in my stomach, like I was a magnet for dead bodies.

I pushed my door open, shattering the silence. The shape didn't move. I walked across the pavement and crunched a leaf under my shoe. Fall coming early. Things dying. And then I stepped into the soft grass, and still the shape did not move. Light hair fell across her arms and knees. I cleared my throat and said, "Hello?"

Bree's head shot up. And then she started rocking back and forth a little. "Bree? Are you okay?"

She glanced around at the emptiness. Then she stared at

me and tightened her arms over her knees and said, "This is where Jason kissed me."

"I'm—I didn't know you were together."

"We weren't together," she whispered, like she was saying something important, a secret, which was as important as it got here at Monroe. And then she laughed, loud and sharp, like maybe she was making fun of me. Like maybe she thought I was a prude or something.

And then I didn't feel bad for her anymore. "Did you take the knife, Bree?"

She stopped laughing and recoiled.

"Bree," a voice came from the other side of the bleachers, and I saw Krista and Taryn through the metal slats. Just pieces of them, here and there, as they moved. Like fragments of my imagination when I used to wake up in a half dreamlike state.

She scrambled to her feet and brushed the dirt from her pants. "No, I didn't take the damn knife, you fucking psycho."

She ran to the other side of the bleachers and joined the girls. And as I saw them move together, broken fragments, pieces of each tied up in the other, it seemed like there was an answer there. It was there, just on the other side of the bleachers.

How Bree wasn't acting scared of me because she knew I hadn't done it. And I knew it, right then, standing next to a discarded chip bag under the empty bleachers: one of them did.

My hands were shaking as I pulled at the handle to the car door. And they were shaking still when I pushed down the lock.

"You can't stay here," Dad said as he started the engine. "Not until everything gets cleared up."

"But you can continue your coursework remotely," Mom said.

"We're going home?" I saw Reid in the distance, across the field, just standing there. Alone. I placed my palm against the window, but he didn't see me.

"You can't," Dad said, and I remembered Officer James telling us to stay in town. "I'll set you and Mom up in a hotel nearby."

I thought that this must be what purgatory was like. Can't go forward. Can't go back. Awaiting some official judgment.

Dad said my dorm room was sealed off by the cops, so I didn't have anything. No toothbrush, no clothes, no computer. The only thing the cops returned was my phone, and only because it hadn't been used to make any calls. It was useless. But I gripped onto it like it was worth something while Mom made a visit to the campus store so I'd have stuff to wear.

Great. Looked like I'd be living in Monroe T-shirts and gym pants until I was allowed to leave. Or return. Whichever.

Dad said we were going to a hotel, but there weren't any, not really. Not what he would consider a hotel, anyway. More like an upscale motel, two miles away from school, on the same road past the diner. It was clean, and kind of set up like a suite, but there was no lobby or anything, just doors opening directly to the outside, like the motels that bordered the beach on the party side of the shore.

I checked my cell: no service. This whole place was like one big dead zone. So I powered it down but left it out on the bedroom dresser, like it was a picture frame.

The set-up wasn't too bad: two separate rooms with queen beds sharing one common living room. Dad scribbled the number listed on our phone, told us not to make any calls, and left. Then it got dark, and the walls felt so thin. Not like in the dorm, where I couldn't hear the crickets. Here, the outside sounded so close. And occasionally a car pulled in and the headlights cut through the shades, and I had this fear they could see me, a shadow against the wall.

I didn't know where my sleeping pills were. I guess they were confiscated. And it's not like I trusted myself to ever sleep again, anyway. When the *boom, boom, boom* started that night, part of me wanted to crawl into Mom's bed and watch TV with her—I could hear it through the two walls. But the other part of me wondered whether she had locked the door, and I didn't really want to find out.

Mallory, the room whispered. I rifled through the bedside table and pulled out a penlight. *Wait*, it said. But I didn't. I pulled on a sweatshirt, slid my feet into my sneakers, and snuck out my door. I listened for the television, and when I heard laughter (the television, not Mom), I let myself quietly out the front door.

I didn't turn the flashlight on until I was on the main road, and then I realized how useless it was, with a narrow beam of light. But I figured it would keep me from getting hit by a car, if there were any. I kept on the pavement, the lights from the motel fading into the distance, and when I could only see blackness behind me and blackness in front of me, I started to jog.

I ran away.

And only when I was a good ways past the diner and the gas station did I realize I was running toward something.

No, not something. Someone.

CHAPTER 16

I wanted Reid to know the truth. I wanted him to know I didn't do it. I wanted him to believe me. It mattered. I jogged along the edge of the road, the flashlight beam catching nothing but fragments of trees. Road. Sky. And then that *M* came into focus, darker than the night sky, black on black. And I entered.

I stopped running and skirted around the edge of campus, trying to catch my breath and keep away from the outside lights. When I reached Reid's dorm, I froze. The doors were alarmed at night. He was on the second floor. I shook my head at myself as I picked up a pebble. I used to think it was so ridiculous when people did this in movies. Turned out, it was the best option out there.

I counted windows and knew I had his because there was

a faint glow behind the blinds. Seemed right that he wouldn't be sleeping right now.

Unfortunately, my aim was horrific. It hit the brick next to the glass and the pebble bounced off, landing silently in the grass somewhere. I tried again, and this time connected.

A hand gripped my elbow from behind, and I shrieked.

I spun around and Reid put a finger to his lips. Then he took my hand and pulled me behind the dorm.

In the shadows, gasping in air, I said, "What are you doing out here?"

"Same thing you're doing."

I shook my head. "I was looking for you."

"Yeah, and I was on my way back from looking for you."

"I'm not supposed to be here."

He shifted his lower jaw around.

I clarified, "I'm not *allowed* to be here."

His eyes were unnaturally wide, like he was trying to take in all the light he could. I think I was probably doing the same. I couldn't stop the quiver in my jaw when I said, "I didn't do it."

He took me in his arms and said, "I know, I know."

"I didn't," I said. And then I kept saying it. And Reid kept pushing me farther into his chest, like he was trying to muffle the noise or something, but I just ended up saying it louder.

But then I thought about him saying *I know*, like maybe he knew more than I did. "How? How do you know?" Maybe the cops suspected someone else. Maybe the secrets had made their way to Reid.

"Because I know you," he said.

He said it so simply. So convincingly. I wanted, so badly, for the me he saw in his head to be the real me—a girl who couldn't possibly be capable of that. Of killing Jason Dorchester. So I clutched his sweatshirt, like it was the only thing keeping me on this side of the world.

I tilted my face up and my lips found his and I felt his grief and fear—or maybe that was mine—and, underneath it all, I felt like I was atoning for something. It wasn't for this, but I took it. I took it.

And I tasted salt. Like I had been crying without even realizing it. I took a breath and wiped at my face, and I kissed him again, but I still tasted salt. I put my hand on his cheek and felt his tears. Not mine. His. He looked at my hand, like he was surprised by it too.

Or maybe he was surprised that he was kissing when he should've been grieving, yet again, because he took a step back.

He led me to his car, and we crept out of campus with the headlights off, coasting in neutral until we hit the main road.

I directed him to the hotel, and because I didn't know what to say, I said nothing.

He squinted out into the dark, even though there wasn't really a reason for that. "How did you get there?"

"Where?"

"To me. Campus."

"Oh," I said, looking down the dark road, which looked so much darker and less inviting now that there was nothing waiting at the end of it. I shrugged. "I ran."

"You ran," he said, and he was staring at me, and I could see him perfectly from the outside lights, but nothing else. So it really was like he was the only thing in the world at that moment. And it really looked like he was going to say something I wasn't ready to hear. But it didn't matter anyway because I had basically already said it by admitting I ran to see him.

He didn't say anything. He shook his head, reached out his hand and put it on my face, like he had so long ago. And he was looking at me, like he did back then. But he was seeing *this* me, and not the old me. I could feel it, in the blood running hot under my skin. I closed my eyes, just for a second, and when I opened them, he was focused on something over my shoulder. "Is that—"

I whipped my head around, expecting Brian's mom to come jumping out of the shadows, hair wild and claws bared. But instead I saw my mother, standing in the open doorway, the light behind her, watching me.

"My mom."

"Um, maybe I should come in—"

"No, actually that's a terrible idea." Reid made a grab for his door handle. "Reid." And since I couldn't think of a way for the words not to hurt, I said, "This isn't the best time."

He nodded and moved his hands back to the wheel. "I'll be by tomorrow."

I smiled and closed the door. I waited at the curb for him to back out of the parking lot before walking down the path of closed doors to the one with my mother waiting, half in, half out. His taillights faded away and I stopped smiling.

"Where have you been?" Mom asked as I walked past her into our shared living room. Like the answer wasn't obvious.

We were thirteen when Colleen's dad moved out. Her mom had shrugged it off and went to work the next day like nothing happened. By the time I'd gotten there, Colleen had trashed half the house. I'd walked in the front door, and she was breathing heavily through her nose, like some wild animal. Chairs knocked over, a broken lamp, magazines on the floor. She looked at me, reached her hand out to the side, to the television stand, and sent the picture frames crashing to the floor with a quick swipe of her hand.

I'd walked over to where a frame lay bent but salvageable, and I dug my heel in until the glass shattered into an infinite number of pieces, beyond repair. And that's what we did for the next hour. We ruined things, without speaking.

Her mom came home, and she looked at us standing in the middle of all the debris and said, "Who did this?"

Colleen leaned forward and said, "I did."

And then her mother let out this low sob and Colleen

broke into the kind of crying that sounds like laughter but isn't, and they fell into each other's arms.

They didn't notice when I left.

And now my mother was standing there, like Colleen's mom had done all those years ago, and I wanted to come clean, to feel some forgiveness, something. Anything.

"That's Reid," I said. And in case she couldn't figure it out, I added, "Carlson. Remember?"

"I remember," she said. "I'm just wondering what you were doing with him in his car."

"I'm kind of seeing him and I had to tell him—"

"Are you a fool?" she said, her eyes wide. "You're kind of seeing him? The day after you're accused of murder? Are you out of your freaking mind?"

"I had to tell him—"

She put her hands up. "No more. No. More." I didn't know whether she was talking about my words or me seeing Reid, but either way, it wasn't the reaction I'd hoped for.

My mother was picking up groceries Monday morning when the cops came back. I thought about just standing silently on the opposite side of the peephole, pretending I was out as well, except I hadn't heard a car pull in recently. So I figured they'd been sitting there for a while, waiting for a chance to talk to me alone. Like maybe they knew there were things I didn't want my mother hearing about.

"Good morning, Mallory," Officer Dowle said when I opened the door. "We wanted to talk through a few of the events from two nights ago once more. This isn't a questioning—we just want to make sure we have our facts straight." And the fact that they didn't ask if my mom was around confirmed that they knew she wasn't. I also knew that they could get in trouble for this—and I was fairly certain they didn't know I knew it.

Which is why I said, "Come on in."

Officer Dowle sat on the hotel-green sofa, but Officer James stood near the front window, staring out the curtains like Mom did at home, like he was waiting for something. Worried about something.

"Look," said Officer Dowle, "I'm just going to lay out the story that's being painted by the other statements we've gotten. So you can understand our concerns."

"Okay," I said, and I planted my feet firmly on the carpet and crossed my arms over my chest, because this part I was used to.

"You invited Jason Dorchester to your room."

"What? No! I wouldn't ever—"

Officer James cleared his throat. "We're just telling you a *story*."

Officer Dowle grinned. She continued. "You invited Jason

Dorchester to your room late at night. He snuck over. You gave him something—a drink, maybe—with a bunch of your sleeping pills dissolved in it. And you waited for him to fall asleep. Then you took your knife and slit his arms and he bled out, a very slow death. And then you took a sleeping pill yourself, so you could claim you were asleep when it happened."

They were both staring at me, heads cocked slightly to the side. I was blinking rapidly, because I was so irritated. Because it made sense. Because the knife was mine and the sleeping pills were mine and Jason was dead in my room.

"So tell us," Office Dowle said as she crossed her legs and leaned back on the sofa, which definitely wasn't for reasons of comfort. "What part of that story is wrong?"

I shook my head. "All of it. I don't know who took the knife. But I took one sleeping pill, like always. Bree knew I took sleeping pills. She knew because I gave her one. That's it." And then I saw a slight nod to Officer Dowle's head, which seemed really out of character for her. "You should talk to Bree," I said.

"Is Bree your friend, Mallory?"

"No. She doesn't like me. She was supposed to be my roommate but she moved out." I left out the part about why she moved out.

"You know what doesn't make sense? Why you would give her a sleeping pill if she wasn't your friend?"

"She came to my room a few nights ago. Totally freaked

out about something. She asked to move back in . . . but then . . . changed her mind." Again, I left out the why. "And the next day she apologized for freaking out on me and said it was because she hadn't been sleeping much, and I said I hadn't either. And then I gave her a sleeping pill."

"You only gave her one?"

"Yes. Just one."

"Unfortunate for you, because Jason had at least four in his system."

I shook my head, trying to understand. "She could've stolen them," I whispered, though I didn't quite believe it.

"Ah, but you see, she didn't claim to be sleeping in her room that night. And she has an alibi."

I choked on my laughter. "Jason's cousin, I'm sure."

Officer Dowle narrowed her eyes and flipped through her notebook. "Jason's cousin?"

"Yeah," I said. "You know, Krista Simon."

Officer Dowle kept flipping pages and looked up at me, then down again, then at Officer James. "Jason doesn't have a cousin here," she said. "Krista Simon is a ward of the state."

"No, I thought . . . I mean, I heard . . ."

"What did you hear, Mallory?"

Lies, apparently. "Jason called her his cousin once. And people think it. I mean, they look similar enough. I thought she lived with his family . . ."

"Kids being kids, I guess. Probably a fun rumor for them to start."

This was all becoming a case of he said, she said. Or she said, she said. And this particular she now had what the cops in New Jersey referred to as *a history of violence.*

"What about Bree's roommate, Taryn?"

"What about her?" Officer Dowle stood up, like she was done with the conversation, even if I wasn't.

"Does she have an alibi?"

"Does she need one?"

"I didn't do it," I said as Officer James opened the door.

"You've already said that," he said.

They had enough to arrest me. Or at least to hold me. And they weren't. I took a step toward the door. "No, I mean, you don't think I did it," I said.

"Come again?"

I pressed my lips together.

Officer Dowle looked at me. "You think we have enough to arrest you if we wanted to?"

I kept my mouth shut. Again.

"Maybe," she said. "But it would help if there were any prints on the knife." She grinned, or at least I thought it was a grin. "You still need to stay in town."

They were giving me something. A story. And I had to give them a different one.

The lawyer in New Jersey had done the same thing. He gave me a story. But that time I stuck to it.

"You left the party," he'd said, and I did nothing. I didn't nod, I didn't speak, I wasn't doing any of those things at the moment. Just staring at the blood caked under my nails, wondering when they'd let me wash it all off. They'd already scraped samples from underneath, which was unnecessary, really. It was obvious where it came from.

"You walked straight home, and you locked the door behind you. Sometime later, Brian Cole broke into your house, through the living room window. He broke the phone when you tried to call 911. He pushed you into the china cabinet. He chased you into the kitchen. You took a knife to defend yourself."

He repeated it to me, and asked me to say it back. And I did, in this detached, monotone voice. Repeated it over and over to him and anyone that asked. And a lot of people asked that first day. I said it over and over, with my lawyer nodding slightly beside me. I said those words until it was the only thing I remembered at all.

CHAPTER 17

Mom answered the door when Reid knocked the next day. I'd told her he was coming. Told her and held it out like a dare, wondering what she would say, what she would tell me to do. "No, he's not," she'd said.

"Oh, okay, so how about you drive me over there so I can tell him not to come."

She glanced at the phone that we weren't supposed to use, shook her head, and actually smiled to herself. "Never thought I'd miss cell phone towers . . ." And that was the end of the discussion.

And now Reid was introducing himself—reintroducing himself—like he was trying to make a good impression, and it was kind of painful to see. Because Mom didn't care.

Mom said, "Reid, I don't want to seem rude here—"

I choked on a cough. "I have to get out of this room," I said, brushing past Mom. Mom opened her mouth, then tilted her head to the side, like she was realizing, in that instant, that I wasn't about to listen to her. Not after she'd sent me away. Not after the months where she'd done nothing. Not now.

"Just"—Reid said, his hands held out in front of him—"for a walk."

Mom spoke to Reid, like she thought she'd have more luck with him. "Stay where I can see you."

We left. I glanced once behind me and saw her shadow pass back and forth behind the green curtains. I wondered if this is what she always looked like from the outside.

Reid didn't touch me as we walked to the end of the strip of rooms, and I hoped it was because he thought Mom was watching from the window.

"How's everything at school?" I asked.

"Mallory, there's not any school. Not really. We had this meeting yesterday, and there will be classes, but just for show or normalcy or something. For something to do. Half of campus is gone anyway. Parents picked them up. The rest of us are just going through the motions."

Then we reached the end of the strip and there was nowhere really to go but into the woods, so we walked absently, still in view of the hotel, twigs cracking under our steps.

There wasn't anything left to say, really, after that. Except what I was thinking, which was, "I think it was either Taryn or Krista. Maybe Bree, but I don't think so."

Reid looked surprised, like it hadn't occurred to him that someone actually killed Jason, and that Jason didn't just miraculously appear dead with knife wounds. "Why do you think that?"

"Because they're lying. They're all covering for one of them."

Reid sunk onto a gray stone, twice his width, and I sat beside him. He rested his elbows on his legs and put his head in his hands. "It's not Taryn," he said.

I felt this pang—jealousy, I guess. Because he was defending his ex or something. And then I worried that maybe he knew for certain it wasn't Taryn, and I got this double pang. "How do you know?" I whispered, wanting and not wanting the answer.

"It's kind of a secret. So you can't tell."

"Jesus, Reid. Seriously? Enough with the secrets already. I think we're past that."

"I guess we are," he said slowly. He took a deep breath and said, "Remember how I said that before me and Taryn had a . . . thing, she was with Jason?"

"Yes."

"They were together a while. Over a year, maybe."

And now Jason hardly glanced at her, but they still hung out in the same circle. Awkward with a capital A.

"Anyway," he said, "last year, when Jason was my roommate. I got back from dinner and heard Taryn in the room, and I was going to leave because, well, that's what you do when your roommate has a girl in the room."

I shifted uncomfortably, because I didn't really want to hear about all of this. Of Reid and girls in his room and that there was this whole system because it happened so frequently, and Reid must've sensed it because he rested his hand on the small of my back. He continued, "But they were fighting. Jason was yelling. And I heard something. You know how you hear something and you know exactly what it is? Jason hit her. I'm sure of it. But when I got in the room, she was on the floor next to the desk, holding her chin, and she was bleeding. And Jason kept saying she fell, she fell, and Taryn was crying, but she wouldn't look at me."

He found me looking at him. "I know what you're thinking. Weird that I dated the girl my roommate hit, right? Hard to explain. It was like we had this connection. Because I knew, and she knew I knew, and she didn't have to pretend around me. It was like we could skip all the small stuff, all the bullshit. It was all wrong, obviously. All the wrong reasons . . ." He trailed off. That was something I could definitely relate to.

"She wouldn't tell, though. I guess because of who Jason's dad is. He said, she said, right? And then she and Krista were best friends all of a sudden and Taryn stopped hanging out with me, like she wasn't allowed to or something."

"Reid," I said. "What you're saying is that Taryn had motive."

"No," he said, taking my hand. "What I'm saying is that Taryn is weak." He squeezed his hand around mine, and I knew that he meant that I wasn't, and I hated it. I stood up and started pacing in front of the big rock.

"So it had to be Krista."

"I don't know, Mallory. I don't get that. It doesn't make any sense. She's nothing without him."

"Reid," I said, "she's not even *related* to him."

"What? Of course she is."

"Where does she go in the summer? Does she stay with the Dorchesters?"

"No, I think she goes to camp or something."

"Does she go there for holidays?"

"I don't know. I guess so. Maybe not. It's not like we *talk*. Jason said she was his cousin."

And then I saw Jason as something else. Someone holding all the truths, all the secrets, that Krista had. If secrets were currency, Jason was the richest one of all. Turns out, the richer you are, the more people want you dead.

Then I thought of Krista taking care of the Taryn situation for Jason, convincing her not to tell, because he held the secrets over her. And Krista having to pretend to befriend this preppy girl with a preppy name and a preppy satellite phone. And Bree coming along with the same preppy kind of name and attitude. And Bree telling me that Jason had kissed her under the bleachers, but she'd been trying to tell me something else. Krista had to fix that too. I remembered Jason holding Krista around the neck outside the bathroom, threatening her.

Krista hated him.

Krista hated them all.

I didn't tell Reid. Secrets weren't a currency. They were a burden. A heavy, dangerous burden.

"Okay," I said. "But Reid, *someone* did it."

"I know, I know." He stood up and walked toward me, like he was looking for a way to forget and I looked like the perfect way to do it.

He kissed me like he wanted something from me, but not like how Brian wanted something from me, not that thing at all. But something. Definitely something. And I didn't know what it was. But I didn't stop him either because I felt myself sinking into him, wanting to be more than a way to forget.

His hands were in my hair and then they were on my hips, and I flashed back to that day on the beach with Brian. And I knew Colleen had been right—he hadn't been right for me, not even a little.

I pulled away, glanced down the strip toward the hotel room, and cleared my throat.

"They're interviewing us all," he said. And then he was whispering. "About that night. I can say something."

"Like what?"

"I don't know. Like I snuck over to see you but you were already asleep. So they'd know there was no way you could've done it."

"You mean you could lie."

"But I could have. So easily. It doesn't have to be a lie. I've snuck over to your place before. God, I should've done it."

"Don't," I said.

"I don't even have to lie. I can just start a rumor. About me and you that night. It'll make its way around and this will all be done."

"It'll make it worse," I whispered.

"It won't," he said, and now he was getting agitated.

But I knew it would. It had happened before.

Colleen had lied. Before she found me. The cops showed up at Brian's house, looking for next of kin. Looking for his parents. But nobody knew that. They saw the cops show and they ran. Except Colleen. She never ran away. Besides, they all knew her by then.

She could tell, I guess, that they weren't there to break up the party, once they started asking for Brian's parents. Once they took their hats off. And when it was obvious that his parents weren't there, they asked if anyone had seen me. So Colleen said, "Yeah. You just missed her."

I had about twenty-seven missed calls from her that night. First she went to my house. Then to her own. And then she found me, under the boardwalk. And I know she meant well, because she did. But the cops wouldn't listen to a word she said after the initial lie. So at first they didn't believe my story—the lawyer's story—either.

But eventually the cops stopped asking, because someone else confirmed the lawyer's story.

I never asked who. And I never found out.

And now Reid was offering to lie for me. "Promise you won't."

"I almost did," he said. "I almost came to see you." He was looking past me, like he was imagining it in his head. Like he was trying to make it real.

Mom's voice traveled down the strip. "Mallory?"

"Right here," I called back. "Promise, Reid."

"Promise," he said. I couldn't tell if he really meant it, but I wanted to trust him. I was choosing to believe him.

"How was your walk?" Mom asked, extra emphasis on the *k*. Translation: I know you were making out with that boy, and that's all he's interested in, by the way. Also, you should know better.

"You could've been nice."

"Oh, I'm sorry. Is that why I'm here? In New Hampshire? To be nice to the boys my daughter—"

"Your daughter what?"

She threw her hands up in the air and waved them around. "This stuff," she said, like there was chaos everywhere, "that you are so fit to ignore, is important. A boy *died*, Mallory. A boy is dead. *Dead*. It's serious stuff. Do you get that?"

I stared at her and she stared back and I waited and she waited and finally I said, "Yes, Mother, I get that. I get that, and I'll never not get that." Then I took shallow, short breaths so I would not cry in front of her. Not now.

"I need to call Colleen," I said. And when Mom cocked her head to the side, I added, "She'll be worried. I was supposed to call."

"You can't. You can't call anyone. They could be recording our conversations."

"I have nothing to hide. And besides, this isn't one of your shows."

"Yes, Mallory, I get that. I don't think I'll ever not get that."

She couldn't look at me. But that's okay—I couldn't look at her either. And while we were busy not looking at each other, she unplugged the phone and brought it to her room.

I went to my room and turned on my cell. And even though there was no service, I sent Colleen a message. It would go through whenever we drove through a place with signal. If I was ever allowed out of here again.

I typed: Something happened. Something bad. Will call when I can.

And then I watched as the phone searched for signal, and searched some more, willing something to happen. But nothing did.

The rain started after dinner. The sky turned dark too early, and we watched old episodes of shows we'd seen five years ago. But neither of us laughed or smiled at the right spots, so I'm pretty sure she wasn't watching, just like me. She was keeping an eye on me.

We stayed up late enough that sleep should've come fast, but the rain wouldn't stop. And it wasn't soothing, not for me. It reminded me of that night, when I ran, with blood on my knuckles, under my nails, on my arms. My chest. Everywhere. When I hid under the boardwalk pier and the rain fell through the cracks but didn't do anything to wash off the blood.

There was too much blood.

The rain didn't stop that night, and it didn't stop this night either. Not until morning. The sky was still dark. Dark and heavy, the humidity filling up the living room. Pushing us tighter and tighter until Mom broke first and said, "Let's get some lunch."

We drove to the diner that Reid had taken me to, just a mile down the road. It was packed. Cars were lined up in rows on the grass, and some were just parked on the side of the road, half on the pavement, half in the weeds. But they all had that red parking permit in the back window, for Monroe.

I didn't get out of the car. Mom seemed to sense something was a little off—or a lot off—and that maybe this wasn't the right time for us to descend upon the diner on wheels. But she also didn't turn around. She just sat, engine idling, chewing the inside of her mouth.

Finally she said, "Stay here. I'll go in." She left without asking for my order.

The inside was packed, but the outside was busy too. People holding candles, even though it wasn't dark, or night. The candles were totally unnecessary. And this wasn't where he had died either. I was guessing half the people here didn't even like him. Maybe even more than half. It was more like everyone was just looking for something to do.

My phone made a tiny chime from my bag, a notice that my text had been sent to Colleen. I wanted to grab my phone and write more, but I couldn't take my eyes off the crowd. I searched for Reid, wondering if he was here. Mourning, maybe, or maybe just participating. Being part of something. Like this was an event to attend off campus. Something to do.

Not the place for me to show up.

I scanned the crowd, but didn't see him. But I did see a finger pointing in my direction.

I gripped the handle, thinking I should get out. Confront them. Defend myself. Say I didn't do it. But the girl, I think her name was April, her teeth were clenched. And the boy holding her was staring as well. Same look. And then someone else looked. So I released my grip on the handle and stared out the front window. Very, very slowly, I moved my hand to the automatic buttons and pressed the Lock button.

The noise seemed to echo.

My heart sped up. I thought about mobs. This could so easily be a mob. One person yelling. One person telling others what to do. One idea, floating through the crowd. One call to action—something they're looking for. They were looking for an outlet for their grief, or their fear maybe, and the candles didn't seem like they were really cutting it.

April and that boy moved closer. The third one did too. Somebody said something, loudly, something like *there* or maybe *her*.

I closed my eyes and counted to one hundred, and I felt the air growing muggy, like it had the night with Brian, like the sky was about to break open.

Which it did.

Some people scattered—into cars, into the building—and the flames from the candles turned to tiny wisps of smoke. But some people stayed put, watching me through the rain. And then Mom was yanking at the handle repeatedly, trying to get inside.

I unlocked the door and she slid into her seat. She passed me the bag of take-out food and pressed the lock on the door again. She acted calm, easing the car out of the spot, but I could see her knuckles were white on the steering wheel. She turned right, heading back toward our hotel, and something hit the back of the trunk with a thud. She jumped and pressed down on the gas, and the tires squealed under the pressure, under the rain.

We ate in silence on the couch across from the dark television. She'd gotten me a grilled cheese, which actually wasn't a bad call, except Reid had warned me the only thing worth getting was a hamburger. No cheese. I took a bite, and the cheese was thick, not gooey thick, fake thick. And anyway, I wasn't really hungry.

Mom picked at her sandwich, but I wasn't sure if it was because of the taste or a lack of appetite. Eventually, she wrapped her food up and put it back in the white bag, then rolled it all up into a ball. She stood and walked to the window. "We need to talk to the administration at Monroe."

So she had sensed it too. The way the atmosphere had felt so charged, the air crackling with potential.

"And say what?"

"I'm not sure," she said. "They're not helping," she said, staring out the closed blinds. Staring out the crack between them, into the rain. "And they need to help." I wondered who was in charge, whether the fact that Jason's dad was part of the administration had something to do with their lack of help. And maybe Mom knew it, too, which is why she picked up her purse. "But lock the door behind me."

I opened my mouth to argue, but nothing came out. It was like something had clasped me around the middle so I couldn't take a breath. I put my hands on top of my head, like I did when I was out of breath, only I tried to do it casually, so she wouldn't be able to tell. I turned around and sucked in a deep breath. I only said one syllable, so she wouldn't hear my voice waver. "Mom."

She gripped her purse with both hands and closed her eyes for a moment. "I'll take care of this," she said.

Then she walked toward me, fumbled around in her bag, and pulled out a small container of pepper spray, just like Colleen used to carry around. Her hands were shaking as she pressed it into mine. She squeezed her hands over mine, and I could feel them shaking still. "Take it," she said.

When she pulled her hands back, mine were shaking too,

and this time I couldn't keep the waver out of my voice when I said, "Mom."

"You will be fine," she said. "I know you will." And then she was gone.

And like she asked, I turned the lock behind her.

Then I perched on the edge of the sofa and stared at the dark television screen, trying to steady my breath again. I heard her car come to life and fade into the distance. I turned the pepper spray over and over in my palm, wondering what Mom meant when she said she knew I'd be fine.

And then I heard another car door. A gentle click, under the sound of the steady falling rain.

I glanced toward the crack in the curtains, wondering if it was Reid coming to see me. I jumped up and faced the door, but then I heard the steps on the sidewalk. Familiar somehow. Not Reid.

No, they were the footsteps following me home the night of the party. The way the heel dragged along the ground a second before the step. *Scuff, step. Scuff, step.* I took a step backward, but the footsteps got closer. I wanted to run to the door to check the lock, but I didn't want to get any closer. And besides, would a lock stop something that wasn't real?

I saw a flash through the gap in the curtains. Blond hair. Lanky build. And the hairs on my arms each stood on end. And then I felt the buzzing in the room, like I used to feel in the kitchen at home.

Not real, I thought. *He's not real.*

Except I held the pepper spray forward and flipped the red switch to the unlocked position. I pointed it at the door. The canister was shaking.

Then the door handle moved gently side to side, like someone was testing the lock. I closed my eyes and thought *not real* again. But I could still hear the jiggling of the handle.

And then I heard something more. Metal inside the handle, scraping along the inside, searching for something. Someone picking the lock.

Then the door swung open. Water splattered onto the carpet, falling from the sky, dripping from his hair.

The realest thing in the world.

Dylan took a step inside.

CHAPTER 18

I backed up, moving deeper into the living room until my back was pressed against the bathroom door. It was so thin, I didn't think it would support my weight. Dylan stared at me, water dripping all around him, and I shook my head. Just shook it, and shook it again. The room was buzzing with that other thing that wasn't real. Like the whole room was about to pop.

And still I held the pepper spray out in front of me. But I was too far away now for it to work. Dylan let the door fall shut behind him. The room was crackling with energy. Even Dylan seemed to sense it. He looked around quickly before his eyes settled on me again.

And I kept shaking my head. Because I couldn't figure out what was real and what wasn't. Because in my head I heard those same footsteps, chasing after me. Dylan's footsteps. And I saw the moon in the upper corner of the night sky—the sky that felt like it could burst open at any moment and—

"Hello, Mallory," Dylan said from across the room, all drawn out, like a rumble of thunder.

I lowered my eyes to the floor. Except for a second I saw pavement instead of beige carpeting. I heard his feet move across the ground. *Scuff, step. Scuff, step.* I put one hand on the doorknob behind me, and I kept my other arm extended in his direction, like a warning.

He stopped moving.

I raised my eyes. "What are you doing here?"

He looked around the room, confused, like Brian had done that night, like he wasn't really sure what he was doing here after all. "I've been waiting for you."

"Waiting?" Nothing was making sense. Not back then, and not right here.

And then I remembered Dylan breaking into the lifeguard supply shed the night on the beach, when I shoved Danielle into the wall, so long ago. The paint on my door, and my shirts, slashed up. And the green car driving past Monroe, always waiting. It had always been Dylan.

"What do you want from me?" I kept the pepper spray aimed in his direction, and I stepped to the side, trying to judge the distance between me and the door. I wondered if I could sneak by him before he could grab me. But the whole room was buzzing, thick, like I might not even be able to break through that energy.

Dylan tilted his head back and laughed, only it came out through a grimace. "What do I want? What do I *want*? I guess that's the question, isn't it?"

I took a deep breath and heard myself wheeze a little, and then I blew it out slowly. Dylan took a step, and then another, toward me. "Are you going to hurt *me*, too?" he asked. "Don't you think you've done enough?" He leaned forward, definitely within range now, and he whispered, "You killed him."

I kept staring at him. Of course I'd killed him. That wasn't a secret. I didn't understand why he was telling me this.

The buzzing in the room grew. My eyes darted around, not looking at Dylan, looking for that other thing, taking form somewhere. I could feel it. I knew it was near, just out of sight.

And then Dylan was in my face and the pepper spray was on the floor, and he had both hands on my upper arms, and he was shaking me. "Look at me. Do you know what you did? Do you?"

Then for the first time since I held that knife, since Brian's blood covered the floor and my clothes and my hands, since Colleen found me and I learned he was dead, I felt my own tears. "Yes, I know what I did. I *know*."

"I don't think you do. Did you know my mom had to be committed to a mental hospital?" he asked as he pushed me into the wall.

"Yes," I whispered.

"I have no home anymore. No family. I had to move in with my *dad.* In fucking *Massachusetts.* Did you know that?" he asked again, shoving me even harder into the wall.

I shook my head. And I heard the thud as my back hit the wall, but I felt nothing, really, at all.

He let go of my arms and ran his hands through his hair, only he was pulling at it. "I don't *understand,*" he said. "I don't get how this happened . . ."

And while he was distracted, I dove for the pepper spray, only he dove for it too. My fingers brushed the key ring at the base, and then Dylan jerked it from my grip. I sat with my back against the wall, and he was on his knees in front of me. He threw the pepper spray across the room, where it hit the opposite wall and landed somewhere behind the couch.

I was still breathing too heavily, trying to figure out why Dylan was here at all, what he had been waiting to do to me. "What do you want? *What?*"

He put one hand around my upper arm, and he looked at the base of my throat, but I didn't think he heard me at all. "Joe and Sammy think I should take something from you." He looked at my throat, and then lower. "That you deserve it." As his eyes drifted down, I understood, with sickening terror, exactly what they thought he should take from me.

But he didn't do anything. If Joe and Sammy were here, I wondered if he would have. His face contorted and he squeezed his eyes shut. Finally, he released me—threw his hands up in the air, like he was surrendering to something.

I turned to the door, before he could change his mind, and started walking slowly. Step. Breathe. Step. Glance to the couch, checking for the pepper spray. Another step. But halfway across the room Dylan was suddenly right behind me again. He put his hand on my shoulder and said, "Wait."

Wait.

I heard it echo around the room in a whisper. Like it did every night.

Brian *had* asked me to wait, he did. But the voice in my room at night hadn't been his.

I staggered backward. Because I remembered.

The footsteps following me down the alley and the hand on my shoulder and the voice in my ear—

It had been Dylan.

"Wait," Dylan had said. I had been running, but he caught up. And his hand was on my shoulder. He wanted me to wait. He wanted me. *I spun around in the alley between the back of the homes. The moon*

was bright, but a cloud moved across it, and Dylan's face darkened. "Please, Mallory," he'd said. "I hate that you're with him. I hate *it. I'm a moron, okay?"*

I leaned closer, because I couldn't really see him. Couldn't tell if he meant it or if those were just words he had rehearsed, but I think he misunderstood because he put his palm on the side of my face, and he ran his thumb across my bottom lip, and he said, "Okay?"

I thought that he meant it. And I felt like saying yes.

And just in case I wasn't okay with it yet, he leaned even closer and brushed his lips across mine, and he smiled. Because it felt like this was what everything had been leading up to. We just got there the wrong way.

"Okay," I said. But then I frowned and glanced down the alley, toward the party. "I think I should . . ."

Dylan shook his head. "Did you see him? Not a good idea. Later."

The sky was about to break open. A fat drop fell between us, and then another—he took my hand, and we started running. We were laughing, racing the storm.

Dylan watched as I dug the key out from under the gutter, and then the sky busted open. I ran up the porch steps, and Dylan was right behind me, pressed up against my back to escape the rain. I slid the key into the lock. And I felt him smiling against my neck.

We slipped inside and I turned the deadbolt behind us.

And then I wasn't sure what to do. The windows were still open, and I thought maybe I should close them. I saw there were drops of water on the display table next to Mom's vase.

But Dylan was still smiling like he won something. Or like he was about to win something. He kissed me in the middle of the living room. Not like when I'd kissed him in chemistry class. Like I was the only one he wanted. Me.

He took a breath and said, "No, really, I was a fucking moron."

"You were," I'd said. "You really were."

And he kissed me again.

That's what we did for seconds, or minutes, or hours. Until the beating started.

Boom, boom, boom.

"Dylan!" a voice called from outside.

Boom, boom, boom.

Not a heart from the grave. Not a heartbeat at all. Brian was pounding on the front door.

And now Dylan was asking me to wait again. The room was buzzing. Vibrating. Even Dylan seemed to sense it, because his eyes darted into the upper corners of the room. I turned around and jabbed my finger at his chest. "You were there," I said.

He stared at me, unblinking.

My brain tried to make sense of it. He was there. But then he wasn't. Brian was there. And now Brian was dead. But the mark on my shoulder was exactly where Dylan had grabbed me that night. Like the memory wanted to make itself known. I was stuck in that back alley with Dylan, with his hand, reaching for me. The moment replaying each night, over and over and over again, until it had become something more than a memory. I just hadn't known it.

"I just want to know," Dylan said. "I want to know why. Because I don't understand." He swallowed and his mouth hung open a little, and he looked so empty.

Don't tell.

It was whispered through the room, with the buzz, riding the vibration, bouncing back and forth across the room, off the walls, the ceiling, the floor. Dylan was watching me, watching the room. "Did you hear that?" I whispered.

"Hear what?"

"Don't tell," I said.

Dylan froze. One hand still on my shoulder, his skin the color of ash. He didn't move.

"I think," I said, "I think he's here." I shook my head. Hard. Because I understood that it wasn't the soul of Brian in the room with me. That I wasn't haunted by *him*. I was haunted by an elusive memory. I was trying to remember, but I couldn't. "I think he told me not to tell."

Dylan shook his head, at least I think he shook his head, but he might have just had a chill instead. "No," he said. And then he pulled his hand away and backed into the wall. "No," he said. "*I* did."

Brian had been shouting in the rain. "Mallory!" he'd screamed. "Open this goddamn door." The door smacked against the frame, but the deadbolt held. "I know he's in there. I saw you guys. I saw you."

Dylan had backed away from me. "Shit," he said. "Shit, shit, shit." He cowered, like maybe Brian could see through the walls or something. "He's drunk," he added.

"So are you," I said, which had nothing to do with the situation at all.

"Yeah, but I'm not . . . like that . . . when I'm drunk."

"Dylan, you little shit, I know you can hear me! You fucking lay a hand on her and you're dead. You hear me? You're dead*."*

Dylan scanned the room quickly, walked back through the kitchen, and silently turned the lock on the back door. He gently pulled the door open, put a finger to his lips, and said, "Don't tell."

He eased the door shut behind him.

And I was alone.

"You left me," I said. "Why did you leave me?"

The whole room was pulsating, like my kitchen used to do. "Everything was *fine*," he said. "When I left, everything was fine."

"No, it wasn't *fine.* Brian climbed in the goddamn window. He was looking for you, and he was yelling at me, and he was *completely* out of control."

"He was drunk!" he yelled. "Couldn't you just leave or something? Why did you have to kill him, Mallory?"

And with that, he raced across the room and got in my face like Brian had done that night. "Why did you do it? Why?"

I remembered racing into the kitchen, racing away from Brian, and looking at the back door. Looking for Dylan. Hoping he would see me and come back, hoping he would help me. And Brian was right behind me, practically breathing down my neck. But all I saw, out in the darkness, was the high gate, swinging open and closed with the wind.

Dylan was gone. And Brian said he wanted to kill him. And I was—

"Scared," I said. "I was scared." Dylan didn't back up, so I added, "I'm still scared."

He walked backward, out of the room, out the door, into the rain. And when I looked up to meet his face, I knew he'd left me alone that night for the very same reason: he was scared.

I ran after him and caught him when he was halfway to his car. "Dylan," I yelled. The rain was so loud, I could barely hear myself even when I was yelling. He spun around, and I gripped the front of his shirt.

I had to say something, had to do something. But all I could do was hold onto his shirt, trying to bridge the gap. Remind him of something.

He peeled my hands from his shirt and held my arms down to my sides. He leaned forward over my shoulder and whispered three words into my ear, which I think I must have been waiting for.

"I hate you," he said.

I felt it in my heart, all the way to my bones. Because he meant it all the way to my soul.

"You didn't always," I said. "I remember. Don't you?"

I had my hands on the sides of his shirt again, like I could will him to remember somehow, and he had his hands gripped around my arms. I couldn't tell whether he was pushing or pulling me, and we stayed like that, like he didn't know what to do with me other than hate me. And I didn't know how to make him remember. He must've felt something at some point that was something other than hate. But not now, because he was shaking.

Then I remembered he left me. He *left* me. And if he'd felt anything back then, really, he wouldn't have done that.

He was just a boy I had liked because he smelled good in chemistry, and he smiled at me when I walked in the room, and I could feel him looking me up and down when I was leaning over the lab bench. And I couldn't have him.

I was just a girl he didn't want until he couldn't have me.

And it was the most tragic thing I could even imagine that someone was dead because of something so cliché. Because of us. Because of me.

"I'm sorry," I said. I was doing something halfway between crying and yelling, so it came out all cracked and angry and sad. "I'm sorry," I said again.

"Don't," he said, prying my fingers off his clothing.

That night was a lot of people's fault. It was Brian's fault, it was Dylan's fault, and it was my fault. I grabbed onto his shirt again. "I'm sorry," I said again. "Please," I added, "please."

Dylan was still shaking, and he took these deliberate steps backward, like it was the hardest thing in the world. He got in the car, and I heard him yelling in rage, I heard him through the metal and the rain. No words, just noise. And then the engine turned over, and all I saw were his taillights.

I stood in the rain, watching him go, feeling this unbearable weight in the pit of my stomach.

"I'm sorry," I said again. "Please, I'm sorry." But I wasn't talking to Dylan anymore.

The only answer was the rain, washing away nothing.

"Mallory?" I turned and saw a figure standing in the rain against a car. Reid, frozen, like he didn't know whether to stay or go, like he was trying to make sure it was really me.

I shook my head at him and stepped back toward the hotel room.

"Are you okay?"

I backed up again. Shook my head again. Imagined what Reid thought he was witnessing. Stepped away.

"What was that about? Who was that?" He was coming closer, now that he was sure it was me.

"Nothing. No one." I watched the empty road, silently begging for something. Then I looked at Reid, who looked like he wanted so badly to understand.

Brian. Dylan. Jason.

"Mallory?" he asked again, like he wanted to give me the benefit of the doubt, like always. Like he wanted to believe.

"It has nothing to do with you," I said, which wasn't true at all.

"It has *everything* to do with me," he said. And he was right. Because over his shoulder, down the road, was his uncomplicated life, and his uncomplicated future, and I was its opposite. I wouldn't be responsible for ruining this life too.

"Reid," I whispered, and I put my hands up, face out. "I can't do this."

Reid stopped walking toward me. "What, exactly, can't you do?"

But I didn't need to say anything at all, because he already knew the answer. I fumbled for the door handle behind me, my hand still shaking.

"Don't," he said. "Wait." I couldn't breathe. And I couldn't look at him as I slipped inside and shut the door behind me. Too much. It was all too much.

I put my head between my knees until I found my breath again. The selfish part of me still wanted him here, unwavering, standing with me against everyone. I stood and faced the door. There were things I knew about Reid. Things I was sure of. If I opened that door, he'd come inside. He'd listen. He'd believe me. If I opened that door, he'd stay.

I wondered whether he heard, through the rain, the metal clicking into place as I turned the lock.

I watched through the curtains as his car drove away, down the same road as Dylan, and then there was nothing. No one. Not Mom, not Dylan, not even that presence anymore. And definitely not Reid.

I guess that, at least, I deserved.

CHAPTER 19

I used half the towels in the bathroom to soak up the water that Dylan had brought inside. I showered. I pushed the couch aside and found Mom's pepper spray. And when she returned, I was sitting in the exact same place I was when she'd left. She let her bag drop on the floor and sat next to me on the couch. "Not much they can do about an off-campus incident," she said, leaning back against the cushions.

I pressed my lips together to keep the tremble from my mouth. I sat on my hands so she wouldn't see they were shaking. And I held my breath so she couldn't hear it catch. She placed her hand tentatively on my shoulder and said, "It's okay. Dad's talking to the lawyer again. We'll figure something out. And then we'll get out of this place."

And that did it. My mother telling me we could go—together. My breath caught and she wrapped her arms around me, hugging me from the side. It was like she was seeing me for the first time since the night she came home and found Brian's blood all over her spotless kitchen floor. It was like she was making up for that. Because she didn't hug me that night.

She couldn't. She was shaking too hard.

Colleen had been begging me to stand up. She told me we had to go. Leave. Get out of there. And she was pulling on my arms, trying to get me to my feet.

"Mallory," she said. And I realized she was choking on the word. I looked at my hands, my shirt, and realized what I must've looked like to her with the tide rising up.

I reached both arms up to her and she locked her hands around my elbows and I locked mine around hers and she dug her feet into the sand and I dug mine in too, and then we were standing.

"Come on," Colleen whispered, like we were supposed to go but stay hidden.

But as she started walking I said, "Colleen." She looked over her shoulder, and I said, "I want to go home."

She didn't argue, though I could tell she wanted to. She stopped and faced me, and we stood that way for a minute at least, with the rain falling between us, and then she closed the gap between us, wrapped her arms around me, held on so tight I stopped shaking. Held on like this was the end of something, like this was good-bye.

But all I could think was that I was getting blood on her shirt. "Please," she whispered, and all I could do was shake my head against hers. Though now I realized that when she said please, *she hadn't been saying it to me.*

We were saying good-bye. To the life we thought we'd have. To the future we thought we'd see. Even if it was just the two of us, and the future was just tomorrow. We wouldn't have it. We walked down the back alley, and there were people outside, some with umbrellas. Some without. They parted as we walked, and Colleen held onto my hand. And as everyone parted for us, I saw a figure at the end. My mother, shaking her head, with a hand over her stomach, and a cop with a hand on her shoulder, and my dad with an arm on her back.

She looked up, I guess to see what the sudden silence was about. And she looked at me, covered in rain and salt water and blood, walking toward her, like I was a ghost. Her knees gave out beneath her.

Dad caught her under the arms before she hit the ground.

"Everything will be okay," Mom said, like she should have that night but didn't. Couldn't, I guess. And then after that, it was too late. Nothing was okay after that.

I wrapped my arms back around her, but I wasn't scared anymore. Mostly I was angry. Angry for Brian. Angry for Dylan. Angry for the thing I'd done and couldn't undo. For the future I'd taken and couldn't replace. For time, so finite and unbendable, that I could not go back. Not now. Not ever.

And, if I was being perfectly honest, I was angry at Mom. My hands tightened into fists around her back.

"I can't believe you *sent* me here."

"It wasn't safe at home," she said. "You know that. I was scared she would hurt you. She wasn't right in the head."

"Is that why you hid the knives from me? Because it wasn't safe *for me*?"

"What? You used to stare at that kitchen, like you were remembering something horrible. You *were* remembering something horrible. I put them away so you wouldn't have to think about it every time you walked in the room." Then her whole body tensed. "Is that what you thought? That we sent you away because we were scared of you?"

When I didn't answer, she said, "We were scared *for* you."

"I don't know why I did it, Mom," I choked out. I thought of the choice again—the knife, the door. Death, life. "I should've picked life," I whispered, though I'm not sure she understood.

She stopped breathing. And with my head on her chest, I could've sworn her heart stopped beating for a second too. "Mallory, don't you see? That's exactly what you did."

I clung to my mother like she was the only thing I had in this world.

Which, I guess, she was.

That night there was no heartbeat. There never had been. There had only been my memory of Brian pounding on the door, trying to force his way in. There was no voice, either. No name whispered throughout the room. No hand reaching for me as I drifted away. There had only been my memory of Dylan, calling my name and then grabbing my shoulder in the alley. I hadn't remembered—didn't want to remember—but I needed to remember. *I needed to.* The memory demanded to be seen.

Like Reid had explained, his mother had been stuck. And sometimes the psychological can manifest into something physical. But that doesn't mean it's not real. My shoulder still ached—the handprint still raw, like a healing burn mark. Real as anything, there it was.

And the dream still came. Just because I finally remembered didn't really change anything. It didn't change the fact that I kept remembering. It didn't make the dream any better. Didn't change the ending.

I was caught in between again, as I was waking up. Hearing Brian's heart as he stood before me. *Boom, boom, boom.* No. Not a heart. It had never been his heart to begin with. It was someone at the door. Again.

I opened my eyes and jumped out of bed, thinking maybe it was the police telling me—telling us—that we were free to go. I raced out of my room, still in my pajamas, but Mom was already in the living room, dressed for the day, pepper spray held behind her back.

We stared at each other across the room. Mom went to the curtains and peeked through without pulling them apart. "It's okay," she said. "It's Reid."

I strode to the door, and as I pulled it open I realized that I knew, with every ounce of my being, what Reid meant when he always said, "I know you." He was right. He knew me. I knew him.

I opened the door all the way, like I should've done the day before. Reid stood back, barely on the walkway, almost in the parking lot. And in front of him was Colleen. She had her arms crossed over her chest, and her eyes were bloodshot, and she had a bag slung over her shoulder. She punched me in the arm. "You are *such* an asshole." Then she flung herself at me and I barely caught her, and I laughed so hard I was almost crying.

"What are you—" I said.

Reid sounded far away when he said, without really looking at me, "She was wandering around campus asking for you. She was talking to Bree when I found her."

"That was Bree?" Colleen asked. "Not. Impressed." She disentangled herself from my hold. "You know what else I'm not impressed by? A scary text message." She punched me in the arm again. "Not hearing from you for days. Calling your house and getting no one. Calling the dorm number and some chick telling me you were gone."

"I know," I said, rubbing at my arm. She actually hit me pretty hard. "I couldn't, um . . ." I glanced behind me at my mother, who was still in the same place, watching Reid very carefully.

"Yeah," Colleen said. "What the hell are you guys doing in this dump, anyway?"

Reid had his heels on the blacktop, his toes on the sidewalk. "Reid," I said, as I willed him to take a step forward.

"What?" he said.

But I didn't know what else to say—he was just *waiting* for me to ask him to stay. With Colleen watching. With my mom watching. "Thanks," I said, hoping that would be enough.

He closed his eyes for a second, turned before I could see his face. Then he walked away.

Mom said, "Colleen Dabner, does your mother know where you are?"

And Colleen said, "Um, I was gonna call her when I got here. But there's no service or anything."

Mom sighed and said, "I'll call her."

"What happened to *no calls*?"

"Her mother will be worried sick," she said, sounding so much like her old self that I truly believed we'd all be okay. She disappeared into her room.

"What?" Colleen asked. "You're looking at me like you want to kiss me or something." Which I probably was, because I was grinning ear to ear. "I mean, I get it. Everyone wants to kiss me. But I really didn't think I was your type."

"You're totally my type," I said.

She grinned at me. "Missed you too." Then she pushed her way farther into the hotel room, dropped her bag, and plopped on the couch. "Now talk."

So I did. I sat next to her and told her in a whisper about that night—about waking up to Jason's body on the floor. And about halfway through the story, Colleen reached out and grabbed onto my hand, but she didn't say anything. So I told her the rest. About the knife and the sleeping pills and Bree lying, and Taryn's history with Jason, and Krista, who I thought was related to Jason, but wasn't. I told her as much as I could about Krista, which, admittedly, was not very much. And at a school like Monroe, that's really saying something.

"Well," Colleen said, clearing her throat and easing back onto the cushions. "Reid's kind of hot."

"And I kind of messed that up too."

She raised an eyebrow at me.

"Later," I said, cutting my eyes to the thin wall that separated us from my mother.

"All right. So are we on lockdown here? Are we free to roam?"

Colleen bounced up and paced the room, and it seemed like this motel room couldn't really contain her. Like she was about to bust out of the walls.

"There's not really anything we can walk to."

"How do you think I got here? I have my car."

I ran to the window and looked out, and, sure enough, parked next to the empty spot where Reid's car had been, Colleen's beat-up purple hatchback sat waiting.

"Mom!" I called. "We're going for a drive."

She came back out of her room. "I'm not so sure—"

"Please," I said. "I can't sit here just . . . waiting for something to happen."

"Colleen," Mom said, "I need you to understand that Mallory is in serious trouble here. We're not allowed to leave the county. So please, *please*, do not get her into any more trouble than she's already in. *Please* use common sense."

"I promise, Mrs. Murphy," she said.

"Your mother isn't amused, by the way," Mom said. "You're going home first thing tomorrow."

"My mother is never amused," Colleen said.

"Be back for lunch. And stay in the car."

When we got outside, Colleen said, "Stay in the car?"

"Oh, yeah, we almost caused a riot at the diner yesterday."

Her hand froze with the car key halfway to the door. "A riot?"

"Mmm," I said. "Pretty sure the mob wanted to stone me."

"Huh," she said, but I couldn't see her face since she was letting the curls fall forward as she unlocked the car door. "Kind of a sucky way to go."

"Yeah."

"All right." She backed out of her spot, shifted the gears too hard, and paused at the entrance to the road. "Show me this place."

First we drove by the diner, now empty, which looked not at all menacing without the people all scowling at me. We passed that gas station with the single pump that Taryn had warned me about the first night I arrived at Monroe. And we drove by the woods. The forest. Stretching up into hills and plateaus and down into valleys, and, in the distance, mountains. We drove down the street in front of Monroe, where I'd first seen Dylan driving by, watching me. Waiting for me.

The street was bare now. I wondered if he was back in Massachusetts with his dad. If he'd gotten what he'd come for. If he'd gotten too much or not enough. If I'd ever see him again, other than in my memories.

I told Colleen about Reid—or enough about him—how I

knew him from before, how our fathers were old friends, old roommates, how he almost kissed me then and did kiss me now. She didn't say anything at all. She gripped the steering wheel with two hands and paid extra close attention to the traffic signs.

Colleen paused in front of the gate with the scarlet *M* and said, "This is where I ran into that Bree chick. She was sitting on that bench, just staring. And when I asked for you, she looked sick. I seriously thought she was gonna hurl all over my shoes or something."

"I don't get it, Colleen. It had to be Krista. She had to be the one. There's some secret that only Jason knew, because he could get Krista to do *anything* for him. It was her. I can feel it. But I can't figure out why Bree and Taryn are letting her get away with it."

"Didn't you say Bree was the one who knew about the knife and the sleeping pills? Maybe she's scared Krista can frame her instead."

"And Taryn?"

"It doesn't have to be complicated, Mallory. I'd lie for you."

She was looking at me, but I couldn't meet her eyes. I knew she would. She had. But I couldn't explain the difference. "They're not me and you, Coll."

"Yeah, well, most people aren't."

The car started moving again, toward the woods.

"Back that way is the old student center," I said. "We're not supposed to go out there, though. Years ago, some kid wandered off into the woods and never came back."

"Creepy."

"Yeah. There's this sign, like a memorial to him or something, except it's all overgrown now and totally forgotten. Kinda sad, really."

Colleen turned off the engine. "Let's see it," she said.

"We're not supposed to—"

"We won't talk to anyone. And anyway, I'll kick anyone's ass who comes near you. Cross my heart."

I opened the door. The rain had stopped, but the moisture still clung to the trees and the grass. I heard crickets everywhere. And some bird kept fluttering its wings directly overhead. Colleen followed in my footsteps, down the path to the old student center, where the walls were still half standing.

"What happened here?" she asked.

"Don't know. Some history I don't know about."

"So that kid who wandered off—he's dead?"

"Yeah," I said. "I mean, I guess. There's no body, but it happened a while ago."

I led her to the path that narrowed as we walked, and I kept glancing behind me to make sure I could still see the clearing.

Colleen said, "Don't worry, nobody's following us."

"It's easy to get lost," I said.

I stooped down next to where the memorial should be and brushed the weeds aside. "See?" I said, pointing to the letters on the front. Then I flipped it over for her to see the other side. FORGOTTEN BUT NOT GONE.

"The irony," Colleen said, "is that somebody had to remember about this to write that he was forgotten. You know? You can't know you've forgotten something until you remember it." Then she scrunched up her mouth and said, "That was either really profound or really dumb. I can't decide which."

"Profound, of course," I said, which it was, actually. I hadn't remembered that Dylan was at my house—I hadn't remembered Dylan's role in Brian's death. I hadn't remembered the events between the party and Brian coming in through the window. And I had been so focused on the events I *did* know, I didn't even know I was missing something.

I had been so preoccupied not remembering that the memory became something else. Something more. I guess that's why hysteria was called conversion disorder—it converts. Mind to body. Internal to external. The memory of someone touching my shoulder to a handprint seared onto my skin.

"Maybe it's him," Colleen said.

"What?"

She ran her fingers through the grooved letters. "The killer. It's this kid. Danvers Jack."

"Jack Danvers," I said.

"Whichever."

I shook my head, sick of thinking about ghosts. About what they could and could not do. About what a memory could and could not do. I tried to play it lightly. "I don't think ghosts carry switchblades."

"No. I mean, I bet it's him. The real him. I bet he left because, hello, have you seen this place? Who would want to stay here?"

"So, what, he'd rather hunt his food than be served in the cafeteria? That's not the rich-kid way."

"Okay, so I'm not rich, I get that. But from what you've told me, I'd choose the forest."

I stood up and she followed. "Your choice of boys would be severely limited," I said.

"Ha," she said. "Ha-ha." She turned to head back down the path toward the old student center, but there were voices carried in the breeze.

Colleen froze first, obviously taking to heart what my mother had told her. And what I had told her about our encounter at the diner. She pushed me behind the nearest tree and slouched behind the tree next to mine.

"What are we doing here, Taryn?" Oh God, it was Reid. With Taryn. In private. I looked at Colleen and hoped she understood I didn't actually want to hear this. Not even a little. Colleen gave a tiny nod of her head, like she was reassuring me. Like she had everything under control. Like she wasn't about to let me get hurt again. She had no idea how much this was going to hurt.

"Someone's spreading lies about me," Taryn said. "The kind of lies that could get me in real trouble, you know?"

"Who's spreading lies?"

"Your girlfriend," she said. "Mallory. I don't know what she said, exactly, but the police came by to talk. My dad's lawyer isn't here yet, though, so they have to wait."

But all Reid said was, "She's not my girlfriend."

"Oh. Okay, so maybe you can say I was in your room that night?"

"But you weren't in my room that night. You want me to get detention so you can have an alibi?"

"It's not so far from the truth, really. I used to be in your room all the time. You didn't seem to have a problem with it then."

"That was a long time ago. And then what? Krista decided I wasn't good enough for you?"

"It wasn't like that, Reid. It's just, you know, I was going through a lot of stuff then. And she helped me see I should probably be alone then."

"Krista doesn't help people."

"She does. She cares about me. A lot."

"Then get *Krista* to vouch for you."

"She can't. She already told the cops that she and Bree were working in her room on some history project. So stupid. She wasn't thinking. She should've remembered me."

"Taryn," Reid said, so quiet and careful I had to strain to hear it. "If you didn't do it, you shouldn't need an alibi."

"Damn it, Reid. You know I didn't do . . . that. I couldn't have. But there's my history with Jason—it's going to come out, I can feel it. I need someone to vouch for me, and I was alone in my room. So please," she said. "You know me."

There was silence, followed by footsteps, and I imagined them walking arm-in-arm together. But then I heard Taryn say, "Reid?"

And Reid sounded far away when he said, "No. Actually, I don't know you at all."

Colleen craned her neck around the tree trunk and shook her head. Taryn was still there. We heard bricks scattering. A few smashing sounds. Taryn grunting. It sounded like she was building a fort. Only when I heard her breath, laced with tears, did I realize she must have been throwing bricks at the half-standing walls.

Watching everything crumble around her.

CHAPTER 20

We waited for ten, maybe fifteen minutes, before we finally heard her footsteps stomp back toward campus. Colleen stepped out of our hiding spot first.

"You were right," she said. "We should've stayed in the car." She stared down the path, narrowing her eyes, like she was making sure the coast was clear. "On the plus side, the cops must know she was involved."

"Doesn't matter," I said. "They've got nothing on her. No prints. Nothing. They've got a hell of a lot more on me. And she's about to get her rich-girl lawyer. Bet they won't even let her open her mouth. I know mine didn't."

"That was different."

"Not really."

She spun around in the path until she was facing me. "Yes

it was, Mallory. It was different. You didn't drug him and slit his wrists and leave him to die." She threw her hands up and said, "Argh," like she was so irritated with me, and then she kept walking.

I followed her, but kept my distance, because she was wrong. I did leave Brian to die. That's *exactly* what I did.

"Why did you go to the funeral?" I asked, and every muscle in her body appeared to go rigid.

She spun around and pointed her finger at me. "Why didn't you ever tell me about Reid? Why didn't you tell me you were *leaving* for this place? You didn't think about me. You just . . . left. I snuck out to see you and you were just *gone*."

I didn't know. I didn't know why there were things I kept from her, that I thought belonged to me and nobody else. Or why I didn't call her before I left for Monroe or why I kept Reid to myself back then. "I asked you first."

"I can't do this, I can't. I'm going to be sick, Mallory." And for a second I thought she *was* actually going to be sick. Her face turned pale, and she had her hand on her stomach. And then she started marching down the path, swiping at the low-hanging leaves in her path. I had to jog to keep up.

But she was right. We kept things from each other. The fragile things. The intangible things. We always kept them to ourselves. I caught up to Colleen, fell into stride right behind her. It wasn't that I didn't want to tell her—it's just that I didn't know how.

We drove around some more after that but didn't really speak.

"I'm coming back home after this is over," I said. "If it's ever over."

Colleen nodded. "You should see Marci Schafer. She went all goth."

"Marci? But she's too . . . light. And pretty."

"And now she's dark. And hot."

"What about you, Coll?" Because it had always been just me and her.

She shrugged. "I'm in a few classes with The Ls." The Ls being Lindsey, Laura, and Lainey. The type of girls that giggled and whispered and seemed to share one brain. The type of girls we used to make fun of.

"Coll, really? The Ls?"

"Really, Mallory? You're not there."

She pressed her lips together, which is what she always did to keep from crying. It was the only thing she ever tried to hold in. She never bit her tongue, and she never held back a smile. And I realized that when I left home, I left her too.

"I don't know who I'm supposed to be now that you're gone," she said. But I always thought it was the other way around. Funny how you can be so tied up in another person and not even know it until she's gone. I wanted to say something to her—tell her something true. But I still didn't really know how. The words were lodged inside, so instead I said something that I hoped would make her understand.

"I want to go home," I whispered. But she didn't understand what I meant. She swung a U-turn in the middle of the street and pulled back into the hotel parking lot a few minutes later. I couldn't find the words to tell her that this wasn't what I meant by home.

Colleen was helping Mom clean up the boxes of leftover Chinese food. She was tying up a giant garbage bag to bring outside, but I was frozen on the couch, which is where we'd all eaten.

"Do you want me to make up the sofa bed, Colleen? Or will you be bunking with Mallory tonight?"

Colleen mouthed the word "*bunking*" to me, and smiled like it was the funniest thing she'd ever heard. "I choose bunking," she said, all chipper. "Are there bunk beds? I call top."

"Ha-ha. It's a queen bed. I call right side."

"Get a good rest," Mom said. "You need to get on the road early."

Colleen groaned and Mom took the trash bag from her to bring out to the Dumpster.

We watched a few shows with Mom while the sky turned dark, but I'm pretty sure none of us were paying attention. Just passing the time until night.

Colleen stood and stretched and said, "I'm ready to get my bunk on."

After I finished getting ready in the bathroom, I found her on my side of the bed. "I know you called right and all, but I'm the guest." And I guess this was her way of saying we were done with the previous discussion, done with the accusations.

"Hope you don't have to get up to pee in the middle of the night." I slid under the sheets on the left side and turned out the light. The outside street lamp cut through the blinds, leaving a streak across the center of our bed.

"Okay," Colleen said. "What's the rest?"

"What?"

"The *later* stuff. It's later. I'm leaving tomorrow. So let's hear it."

I took a deep breath. "Dylan was here yesterday."

Colleen bolted upright in bed. "Dylan? *Your* Dylan?"

Not my Dylan. But I sat up and nodded anyway.

"Crap, I didn't know. I mean, he moved. You knew that, right? His mom, she's . . . sick. And he lives with his dad. I don't know where. I was going to tell you . . . eventually. I didn't know he was up here."

Really, it wasn't her job to know. It seemed ridiculous that she would know. But I told her the rest, about how he blamed me, how he hated me. And then I told her the truth, the one I'd just discovered. "He came home with me that night, Colleen."

"What?"

"After the party. He came home with me. We were . . . well, Brian found out. And that's why he broke in. Dylan left. He ran away. And Brian broke in. And I . . ."

She made that *argh* noise again, like she was beyond frustrated. Then she added, "I am so, so sorry."

And I said, annoyed, like always, "Not your fault."

"Stop it. Please. Stop saying that." She was pressing her lips together again, trying not to cry. And finally, I got it.

She snuck out of her house, even though she was grounded. She went to that party so I could see Brian, even though she didn't think I should be with Brian. She went because she knew I wouldn't go without her. Because I didn't do anything without her.

Which she knew.

And she still knew.

And that was why Colleen felt guilty about that night. It wasn't that she thought she left me. It wasn't that she went off with Cody. It was that she went at all.

Colleen thought it was all her fault. Colleen, who found

me under the boardwalk that night. Colleen, who was willing to run away with me. Colleen, who packed up a bag and came here. For me. And this feeling started in my chest, like something rising up inside of me.

I needed to say something: I needed to make sure she understood. I needed to make sure she knew. It was mostly dark in the room, and she was almost crying, and she was *here* in the middle of nowhere, with an overnight bag and a toothbrush. So before I could lose my nerve I said, "You know I love you, Colleen Dabner."

She poked my leg with her big toe and said, "Yeah, I know it."

The slant of light from the gap in the curtains cut between us on the bed until Colleen leaned forward and pushed her face into the light beam. And then she whispered, "Now tell me again about this Krista chick."

So I did. I lay back on the pillow and spoke to the ceiling. "Jason is—was—the only one who knew about her, really. And she did whatever he wanted. Is that bribery?"

"Blackmail?"

"Either way, it's messed up. For one thing, I know she convinced Taryn not to tell that Jason hit her. And I guess she must've convinced Bree not to report something too. But I don't know what. And I don't know why. Jason must've had something big on her. And I seriously don't get why they pretended to be cousins." All I knew for certain was that Krista wanted him dead. And now that he was, the secret was dead too.

Colleen listened and didn't say a word until I ran out of things to say, and there was nothing but breathing. The last thing I remembered was her left leg laying on top of my right leg. Her left hand in my hair.

And in the morning, when I woke, I rolled over to the right side of the bed, and it was empty.

Her bag was gone, the oversized purse that she also used as luggage. The spot next to my shoes was empty, where hers had been. I pulled the curtains apart and my heart dropped as I saw the empty parking spot. No purple hatchback.

I barged out into the common room and ignored Mom's greeting as she ate a bowl of cereal on the couch. I checked the bathroom and let out a sigh of relief—her toothbrush was still sitting on the side of the sink.

"Where'd Colleen go?"

She paused with the spoon halfway to her mouth. "What do you mean?"

I felt this weird buzz in the room, like when you know something's off—kind of like when I knew, but didn't know, that Dylan had been in my dorm room. "Colleen. Her car is gone." She probably went to get some real breakfast. She'd probably walk through the door in a few minutes with a tray of coffee in one hand and a box of donuts balanced on her other hip.

Mom slurped the milk off her spoon. "She must've left for home."

"No, her toothbrush is here."

Mom put her spoon in the bowl and placed them all on the coffee table. "I'm sure she just forgot it. Mallory, honey, I've been up for the last hour. She hasn't been here. I'm sure she wanted to get an early start and didn't want to wake us."

"No," I said, feeling frantic. "She wouldn't leave without telling me. She wouldn't."

"It's after ten. She probably left first thing. She wouldn't necessarily wake you up."

"She would."

"How could you possibly be sure of that?"

Because Colleen wouldn't just leave.

Because she felt guilty, even though she shouldn't have.

Because she knew I had nobody else.

Because she loved me.

I opened my mouth and said, "Because I know her."

Because some things don't ever die, not even with death. Like my grandma, putting my hand on her chest. Not her bones, not her heart, not her soul. Just reminding me of the connection between us. It had consequence. It mattered.

Mom stood and rocked back and forth on her heels for a bit. "All right, honey. Go ahead and call her."

I raced for the phone and punched in the number for her cell. Then frantically hung up, dialed 9 to get out of the hotel, and tried again.

"Straight to voice mail."

"She probably didn't turn it on. Or she's in another no-service zone. The mountains are like that. I'll call her mother tonight to make sure she got in. Okay?"

I shook my head. It was not okay. Not at all. I went to my room and stared at the unmade bed, at my dirty clothes in a pile on the floor. I pulled back the sheets, looking for a note or maybe a clue. Anything. But there was nothing. I checked the dresser, the drawers she'd never opened, the empty spot where her shoes had been. Nothing. I checked the bathroom, felt the dry bristles of her toothbrush, and guessed it hadn't been used this morning.

And suddenly my room filled up with the lack of her. Like I could feel the absence of her as much as I could feel her presence. Like Dad, unable to bear the absence of Reid's father. Or Brian's mom, standing at the edge of my kitchen, feeling something in the emptiness.

Real as anything.

It looked like it was going to rain again, but it didn't. But the clouds sat, gray and thick and ominous. Time ticked by painstakingly slowly. I picked up the phone at eleven and called again. Straight to her voice mail. I called again at noon. And that time I waited for the tone and said, "Call this number, damn it," and hung up.

Mom watched me each time, and I could tell she was starting to get worried as well. Only she was worried there had been some sort of car accident in the woods on the way home. I felt like I was going through the motions, making these phone calls, every hour on the hour, until Mom would call Colleen's mom or the police or something. By two, I started to get anxious. I really hoped she was driving, had been a jerk, and left without telling me. I wanted to believe she'd do it.

I needed to believe she'd do it.

"I need to go look for her."

"She took her car, Mallory. She could be anywhere."

So I sat in front of the window, rocking back and forth, watching the empty road. Leaning a little closer every time I'd hear a car approaching. But it was never Colleen.

Mom finally called the Dabner house at five, but she shook her head at me. "She probably doesn't even get off work until now." Then she turned her mouth back to the phone and said, "This is Lori. We're just calling to check that Colleen made it home. Please call this number when you get in."

"She should be back by now," I said. "Colleen would've picked up the phone at home."

Mom looked at her watch. "Only if she didn't make any stops. I'm sure she stopped for food. And she's bound to hit rush-hour traffic . . ."

"Mom . . ."

The sky started to shift, from light gray to dark gray. Mom looked out the window. "I'm going to pick up some dinner." But before she left, she called Dad. She cleared her throat and said, "Would you please swing by the Dabner house on the way back from work and make sure Colleen made it home?" Which is how I knew she was seriously worried.

The second she left, I threw on my sneakers.

I knew what I'd be doing to Mom. I knew it. I knew the way she looked at me now, remembering how I came to her that night, covered in blood. How she came home to an empty house with a dead body. I knew what it had done to her. The weeks when she couldn't keep the tremor from her hand, when she couldn't focus enough to remember which windows were locked and which weren't. What doors should be locked and which shouldn't. When she couldn't even focus on me.

I knew what this—coming home to an empty hotel room—could do to her. But this was a thing worth risking it for.

The only question I'd been thinking about since I woke up and Colleen was gone was this: where the hell did she go?

She took her car.

She took her bag. Well, she'd need that, since it had her wallet.

And she'd left sometime before I woke.

She could've been anywhere, it's true. But it also wasn't.

Because she hadn't meant to leave me for good. Which meant there was only one place she could've gone.

Monroe.

CHAPTER 21

I left a note for Mom. Told her to call someone—Colleen's mom, the cops, the school, just someone. I told her I was going to find Colleen.

I started off down the road at a brisk walk. And then I started to jog. And then, picturing Colleen waiting at the end, I ran.

At first I could see the road just fine. The cracks at the edge of the pavement, the way it ended abruptly, like a cliff, where the weeds and grass and trees grew. I looked down at the pavement as I ran, watched it blur beneath my feet, same as when I ran to see Reid.

But then the sun must've dropped, or the clouds grew thicker, or maybe just darker. I could still see, but I couldn't make out the details, the contrast. Just the shapes. I was halfway there, I had to be. I was breathing heavily, but I didn't feel out of breath. Just desperate. Because if Colleen hadn't come back, there must've been a reason. And I was guessing it wasn't because she ran into some hot guy.

My foot slipped off the edge of the pavement, and my ankle rolled, and I came down hard on my hands and knees. My right hand landed on something sharp—a piece of glass, I thought. But when I pulled my hand up, I saw a split rock—an edge like someone had taken a knife to it. The corner was dark with blood. My blood.

I held my palm to my face and saw the gash along my palm. Blood dripped from the wound down my wrist. Not too much, I'd be fine. But my heart sped up. I imagined my hands that night. Covered in Brian's blood.

I pounded my fist into the pavement, then flattened my hands to push myself up off the ground. And as I rose, I saw my handprint. A dark stain on the pavement. I couldn't move. Because I remembered something else.

Brian slid to the floor, barely making a sound. Like the way people say that life slips away. He just . . . slipped. And at first there was just a little blood on my hands, warm, but just a little. Like the knife had only scratched him, maybe. Except he was on the floor, and his mouth was gasping.

I fell beside him and stared at the knife. His chest should have been moving, but it wasn't. "Oh God," I said. "Brian." His eyes were open, but he wasn't looking, or maybe he was. Maybe he was looking for something else. "Brian!" I screamed. But he still didn't look at me.

The spot on the front of his shirt was spreading. I put both hands on the knife and tugged. It came free, as effortlessly as it had gone in. And then the blood started, even more than before. Flowing, pouring out. "No!" I cried. "No, no, no."

Stop the blood, *I thought. So I put both hands over the wound in his chest and pressed down, but the blood kept coming, covering my hands, sliding over them and down onto the floor. "Stop," I said. But that didn't help. So I put my whole weight behind it, pressing down on top of him with my hands, my chest, with all of my weight. But the blood kept coming. I could feel it soaking through. Soaking through him, to me, everywhere. I let out a sob and screamed, "Brian!" again.*

The phone was shattered in the hall. My cell was somewhere upstairs. The door was the closest thing. "Just hold on," I whispered in his ear, though he made no indication that he'd heard me. "I'm sorry," I said. Which were, quite possibly, the most inadequate words to ever leave a person's mouth in the history of the world.

And then I ran. Pushed through the back door, into the rain, into the night. Pushed through the swinging gate, leaving a trail of red behind me. I ran into the alley and screamed, "Help! Somebody help!" Then I ran into the neighbor's gate and pounded on the back door, screaming for help. Then through the next gate. And the next. I painted the whole street red with his blood. People came out and I screamed, "Help!" But they looked at me like I was the one needing help.

I pointed a single finger toward my backyard. "He's bleeding!" I cried. And they started to run.

But what I'd really meant to say was he's dying.

It hadn't been enough. Not nearly. They couldn't stop the blood either. Or else there was no blood left to stop by then. I never asked.

I wiped my hands on my jeans and started running faster, toward Monroe.

In the distance, the *M* rose from the horizon, like a dark sun, dripping ivy. Campus was dead. Everyone must've been at dinner. I felt exposed walking across campus, like there were eyes watching me from the dorm windows, secrets spreading like a virus.

I pushed the door open to my old dorm, and the lounge was empty. Stiflingly empty. Then I remembered that Reid had said half of campus was deserted, anyway. I walked down the silent hall, toward my old room, still marked off with crime-scene tape. I wondered if Colleen had been there. Been here.

A door slammed somewhere upstairs, and the echo

carried all the way down the steps, through the hall, to me. I paused in front of Bree and Taryn's door. Bree, at least, knew who Colleen was. Or, if not her name, at least she'd know who I was talking about. I knocked on her door.

Bree opened the door quickly, and opened her mouth like she had been ready to say something, like she was expecting someone, but definitely not me. When our eyes met, she froze, her eyes wider than I thought humanly possible. She took a step back into her room, her arm preparing to swing the door closed on me.

"Wait," I said, diving toward her room. I wedged my foot between the door and the frame so she couldn't shut me out. I had a grip on her sleeve, and she was staring at my hand, her nostrils flared. "I need to talk to you."

"Don't touch me," she hissed. "Are you out of your freaking mind?"

I removed my hand but took a step closer, my entire body now standing in her entryway. "I'm looking for my friend. Colleen. I think she was here, and she's . . . missing."

Her eyes grew wide again and she stuck her head out into the hall, peering out toward the stairs in the corner. "You better leave. They'll come for you, you know."

"Who? Who'll come for me? Krista? Taryn?"

She shook her head. "Get out of here."

"I know you set me up, Bree. And I'm not leaving until I find Colleen."

"So stupid," she mumbled. "She was taken," she whispered, just as I heard footsteps echoing down the stairwell. "And you'll get taken too."

Bree grabbed onto my arm and pushed us both into the hallway. I thought because she was scared or nervous or something.

But then Krista rounded the corner out of the stairwell and raised her eyebrows. Bree dug her fingers into my arm even harder and said, "Look what I found."

"What—" I started, and then I realized who took Colleen, who Bree was talking about. She meant all of them. Including her.

Krista jerked her head toward Bree's open door, but I wedged my foot against the corner of the wall and wouldn't budge. Krista didn't smile, but I could've sworn she wanted to. "So much like that friend of yours."

I lunged for Krista, and her mouth dropped open in surprise. I had her pushed into the wall, Bree looking on in surprise. "Where is she? What did you do?"

She swatted at my arms, which were pinning her to the wall, but something coursed through my veins, making me stronger than I thought I was.

"Bree," she said. "Do something."

"Yeah, Bree," I said. "Like always. Do what Krista tells you to do."

Bree gripped me around the waist and started to pull, so I said, "Tell her why you killed Jason, Krista."

Bree's arms went slack. Krista grimaced. "*I* didn't kill Jason," she said.

I opened my mouth to argue, then saw her grin. She must've convinced Bree or Taryn to do it. Maybe she even watched. She definitely planned the whole thing. But I guess she took that English class lecture to heart: it's nearly impossible to convict a mob. Where does the blame lie? With her? Or the ones that listened?

"Bree," I said, still holding Krista against the wall. "I heard Jason threaten Krista to keep you from telling what happened with him under the bleachers. What happened to you?"

"Nothing," Bree said, getting closer. "Thanks to Krista. She showed up . . . before. She helped me."

She tugged at my shoulders, trying to pull me off Krista, but her arms were so weak. I remembered Bree showing up in my room, terrified. Was Krista planning this all back then? Had she scared Bree off? She must have. Bree went back to her. But Bree was not solid, not like Taryn. She was the link that could be broken. She was the thread barely holding everything together.

So I pulled.

"And Krista convinced you not to tell anyone, right? You know it happened with Taryn too. Krista convinced her not to tell anyone. She wasn't on your side, Bree. She was on Jason's side. She did everything for Jason. She had to. Otherwise he'd tell about her."

"Tell what?" Bree asked.

"Yes, Mallory," Krista said. "Tell what?" She knew I didn't know everything. But she didn't know that I did know something.

"She's not his cousin, you know."

Krista tensed under my weight. But then she relaxed a little, and she laughed. "No, that's right. He's not my cousin." She laughed again, shaking her head. "He was my brother."

I lost my grip on her from surprise, and she wiggled free. We stood across from each other, three points of a triangle, the whole hall tense, waiting to pop. Waiting for one of us to make a move. Waiting for Bree to pick a side.

"Yeah, so that's the truth. He's my *brother*. Only nobody could know. Because my own father doesn't want me. *Nobody* wants me, Bree. I had nobody until Taryn and you." Bree looked between me and Krista, but Krista didn't give her time to think. "The state took me from my mom, which definitely was not the worst thing in the world—but you know what *is* kind of shitty? Foster care. And you know what's even shittier? Tracking down your dad and finding out he's fucking rich. And you've been poor. Know what's even worse? Finding out he already had a family, and nobody's supposed to know about you. He's not evil, though, and he wasn't about to send me away. He just wanted me to keep it a secret. From Jason and his wife. If I kept it a secret, I got to stay. He's not evil. He's just an asshole. You know who was evil, though? Jason. And he overheard the whole damn thing."

Krista took a step toward me, blocking me in. She looked to Bree, but Bree stayed against the wall. "You know what Jason would've done to you? Did you want to end up like Taryn? She's drugged and sleeping upstairs until her daddy shows up. You want to be like her? Everything I've done is because I care about you guys. Jason was a predator. He's a fucking psychopath. You know that, right? I hated him, it's true. I had to do what he said—always. You can imagine what that was like. But I did it for you guys."

"I thought you said you didn't do it," I said.

She cut her eyes to Bree and said, "I didn't do it *alone*."

Bree let out a moan and Krista stretched an arm toward her, but she couldn't reach. So she said, "Listen to me, Bree. We're going to be *fine*. Again. But you have to listen to me."

But Bree wasn't listening. I knew Krista was losing her, and Krista could sense it too.

"Bree," she said again. "I *love* you." And Bree lifted her head up.

But I thought of the things Krista was doing for Bree and Taryn, and I thought of the things Colleen had done for me, and I knew it wasn't even close to the same.

"No, Bree," I said. "If she cared about you at all, she

would've warned you about him. She would've kept you away from Jason to begin with. She *hates* you. She hates you all."

Then I took a risk. I ran for Bree, grabbed her around the waist, and dragged us both into her room. I slammed the door and locked it.

Bree stared at the locked door and started to shake. "She has a master key," she whispered.

Of course she did. Jason must have too. Easy to get when his father was the dean of students. Somehow, I wasn't surprised. Someone had to break into my room to take the sleeping pills. Someone had to break into my room to kill him there.

So I walked to her dresser, bent over, and put my weight behind it. "Help me," I said, and Bree pushed against the side with me until it was in front of the door.

"Where's Colleen, Bree? What happened?"

She shook her head and her face went even more pale than normal. She moaned and started pacing the room. "Oh God," she said.

Bree crumpled to the floor and put her head in her hands. Then she looked up, higher than where I was and choked out, "I'm sorry. I'm so sorry."

I almost cut her off, told her it was too late for that. That those words meant nothing. That there was no going back now. That she'd made her choices and now she had to live with them. But instead I crouched down in front of her and said, "I know you are." Then I put my hands on her shoulders and said, "You can help. This doesn't have to be all of you, you know?"

She broke in my arms, as the realization of everything crashed down on her. And I held her. Until we heard the lock turn and the door push against the furniture. The dresser held, but I wanted to shake Bree. Make her talk. I guess she sensed my urgency because she gritted her teeth and then the words came tumbling out. "She was looking for me, I guess. Because she found me on the way to breakfast. We walked toward that old student center, I guess for privacy, I don't know. But she just kept heading that way. She didn't know that Krista and Taryn were watching. Following. And she kept *talking*. It was so obvious she knew something. So Krista . . ." She stopped talking. Krista was pounding on the door, calling Bree's name, and Bree was staring at the dresser, like the whole situation was just some curious thing happening to some other person.

"Krista what?" I said louder.

Bree looked anywhere but at me. "Hit her with a brick." Then she dropped her voice even lower. "She had to hit her twice." Everything inside of me went dark. I felt like that day in the lifeguard shed when Danielle called Colleen a slut and I wanted to hurt her. Only this was a thousand times stronger. And the only one in the room was Bree.

I made myself back up toward the window. "Where is she?"

"We took her down the path past the old student center. There's a dropoff. It's pretty far, though."

No, I thought.

"Like a ravine really." *No,* I thought again. "We—" Bree took a big breath and said, "She's at the bottom of the ravine. So it would look like an accident."

No.

I pushed her window open just as Krista wedged the door open a few inches. "Bree," I said. "I'm going to find her. Get help. Now."

She glanced at the door, then went to her desk and pulled out her pink lighter. Then she climbed on top of the desk, flicked the top, and held the flame directly under the smoke detector.

I opened the window and straddled the sill. And before I dropped out into the night, I said, "Remember that you did this too."

And then I ran.

God, how I ran.

CHAPTER 22

I was vaguely aware of the tree, of the half-standing walls, now just dark shapes, as I sprinted by the old student center. A few bricks dislodged and scattered under my steps, and I almost tripped twice, but I caught my footing and found the path. I ran until the path narrowed and I couldn't tell where to move next. I froze.

"Colleen!" I shouted, expecting to hear an echo. But the noise fell flat. Swallowed up by the trees or the dirt or the heavy air. "Colleen!" I screamed even louder, and then I listened to the sounds of the forest for any trace of her.

Bree had said there was a dropoff past here—some sort of ravine—but I couldn't see far enough ahead of me. The ground sloped upward, since Monroe was situated in a valley, so I figured I'd keep heading up until I hit it. I kept moving. Every once in a while I felt the ground shift, like I was heading down again, and I readjusted until I was moving up. Not exactly a precise navigation system, but it was better than doing nothing.

"Colleen!" I kept calling, hearing nothing in reply.

Then I tripped over a root and face-planted. I heard the rocks I'd kicked up echoing somewhere below. I crawled forward to the edge and saw blackness. The ravine. A gaping splice through the hillside. Problem was, it stretched side to side in front of me as far as I could see. "Colleen?" Only my voice echoed back to me, and the panic I'd been avoiding crept up into my stomach. Too late. I was too late.

I crawled along the edge until I found a lower spot with a gentler slope, and I half walked, half skidded my way into the ravine. Which was pitch-black. Looking up, the sky looked unnaturally light compared to where I was. I put my left hand on the side of the ravine, and I started walking. It rose and dipped, the sky getting nearer and farther. And I kept saying her name. At first in a whisper, because everything felt so enclosed here. And then, with a panicked ferocity, with tears and anger, with rage. My hand tore at the side of the ravine as I ran.

I almost didn't hear it at first, over the sound of my panicked breathing.

But I thought I heard my name.

I listened again. A gasp of air from somewhere ahead. And then a hoarse word. "Mallory."

I ran forward and nearly tripped over the dark shape on the floor of the ravine. I was laughing because I found her, but then I pulled her into my lap and I stopped laughing. Her hair was damp with a thick liquid. Blood. I knew that feeling. And she barely had a voice. But I held onto her and I started laughing again.

"I found you," I said.

And she said, "My fucking legs."

I looked down, trying to see in the darkness, and immediately recoiled from the way her right leg twisted out at an unnatural angle. Then I took a breath and looked again. Her left looked okay to me, but obviously it wasn't since she said *legs*. Plural.

"I can't get out," she said. "I tried. But I can't."

"I can. It's not too steep." I crouched beside her and said, "Okay. Ready?"

She pushed herself onto her elbows, then a sob escaped her from the shift of weight. "Ready for what?"

"It's probably going to hurt. When I pick you up."

Colleen collapsed back onto the ravine floor. "You can't. I'm too heavy. And you're—you can't. Go get help and come back."

"No," I said. I didn't have the heart to tell her I didn't know how to go get help, or how to come back after. She had no idea how far into the woods we were, and how much of a miracle it was that I'd found her in the first place. But all I told her was, "I won't leave you."

"Mallory. You can't."

I leaned forward and felt the words before I said them, needing to believe they'd become true. "I can." I took her arms and wrapped them around my neck, and I put an arm under her horribly twisted limbs, and another around her back.

And I stood up.

She cried out, and my legs were shaky, and my back was pulling, and my grip was unnatural and awkward. But I stood up. I told myself to start walking. And I did.

"Hey," she said, her face pressed up against my shoulder. "Remember that time you kicked Danielle's ass?" Maybe she noticed I was shaking and was trying to distract me. Or maybe she didn't notice anything at all. I didn't respond—couldn't really. I was concentrating on each step. "God, that was so awesome." I found another slope farther up the ravine that weaved into the side of the hill, a little less steep, like a creek used to run down it, and I took it.

My feet kept slipping on the dirt, and we were getting absolutely nowhere. I tried backing up the slope instead, but I lost traction and we landed together in a heap at the bottom. Colleen was screaming from the pain.

"I'm sorry," I said. But she was in too much pain to acknowledge me. "And I'm really sorry for this," I said. I gripped her under the shoulders, and I dragged her behind me, up the ravine.

She screamed the whole way. And it took me a while to realize I was crying with her. But then she went silent and all I could hear was myself. Colleen's body went limp as I heaved her over the side.

I fell beside her in a panic. She was breathing, but unconscious. Which was probably for the best, since I still had to drag her some more.

We kept going up. It was the only thing I could think to do. I saw a crest up ahead—something above the treeline, and I had to get there. I had to get up there to find a way back out.

When I finally reached the top, I set her down. And I gasped. Because from the top I could see multiple paths snaking down behind me, in front of me, to the side. A thousand ways out.

"You were right, Colleen," I whispered to myself. Because I realized right then, that boy who wandered off, he probably didn't die out here. There were a thousand different paths out of the woods—maybe he just chose a different one.

Far away in the distance, I could see light. Past the dark trees, the dark forest, there were signs of life. Towns. Communities. Cities. And closer still, flashes of red lighting up in the sky. Fire trucks maybe. Or ambulances. Police. Either way, I knew it was Monroe.

I gripped Colleen under the shoulders and started moving toward the flashes of red lighting up the sky.

The woods were dark, but the world was light.

Colleen just hung there, so I tried to think of something else. Something to distract myself from each torturous step.

We were so close. I could tell by the way the ground leveled out and the space between trees grew wider. And then the red lights went out. I had taken too long. I panicked again, but I couldn't stop moving. So I kept heading in that direction, or what I thought was that direction. I would hit something—if not Monroe itself, then at least a road—if we just kept moving.

And then I saw a light in the distance. Just a flash, coming through in split frames. Here and not here. Like the way I used to wake up from a dream.

There. Blink. *Closer.*

Blink. *Closer.*

Flashlights.

"I'm here!" I screamed, easing Colleen to the forest floor. "We're over here!"

The footsteps approaching grew more frantic, and suddenly I worried that it was Krista, or all three of them—Krista, Bree, and Taryn—and I crouched down beside Colleen and held my breath.

Then I heard the crackle of a walkie-talkie. I stood up and waved my arms and said, "We're here," and I was nearly blinded by the beam of the flashlight, aimed directly at my face.

So I looked at Colleen, illuminated by light, who was perfectly still. Too still. Too pale. Too much blood. "Colleen," I cried. "Wake up."

CHAPTER 23

Mallory," Mom called from the kitchen. "Lunch is ready."

I joined her at the kitchen table, eating grilled cheese and drinking soda. We ate in silence, not really looking at each other. She didn't start clearing the dishes when she finished, just sat with her hands folded on top of the table. "Are you sure?" she asked.

I put down my sandwich. "I'm sure."

Dad came into the kitchen and said, "Smells good." He grabbed his grilled cheese off the pan on the stovetop and backed out of the kitchen. "I've got some phone calls to make."

"He's happy," I said.

Truth was, Dad had been smiling for days. Ever since I asked him if he knew anything about what happened to a boy named Jack Danvers.

"Never heard of him," he'd said at first.

"He was a boy who disappeared in the woods and . . ." I thought of the makeshift cross. "Danvers Jack, maybe?"

His pen froze an inch from the paper he'd been writing on. "What do *you* know about Danvers Jack?" he'd asked.

"He wandered off during initiation," I said. "So they say. And they never found his body. Some people say he haunts the woods." I thought of Reid telling me how he thought he could feel something out there. "They say they can feel him."

Dad's face cracked—first down, then up. And then he was laughing. "Haunting the woods, huh? Is that what he's been up to?" He pressed his fingers to the bridge of his nose, and laughed some more.

"Dad?"

"Danvers Jack wandered off, that's for sure. Couldn't stand the idea of being trapped anywhere. Of anyone telling him what to do. We'd been marched into this ravine and left there for the night. Tradition, as I'm sure you know." He grinned at me. I guess he didn't realize how well I knew that ravine. "Anyway, about an hour in, someone noticed he was missing. Everyone panicked. He didn't show up back at the dorm or anything, but when we walked into first period, he was sitting at his desk, smiling at us. Became a bit of an urban legend, I guess. Or, like you said, a warning." He smirked.

"Stay with the group," I said. And Dad smiled, like we shared a secret. I leaned forward and said, "I didn't."

And then he was laughing again. "Of course you didn't."

"Maybe in twenty years, someone will name a dorm after me too."

"Name a dorm after you? Oh, *Danvers*. Other way around, Mallory. Danvers Jack isn't his name. He was named after the *dorm*. We had several Jacks that year. He was the Jack who lived in the Danvers dorm. So when they were trying to find out who went missing, someone said 'Danvers Jack.' And it stuck. He was my roommate." And then he started laughing again.

And then so was I, because all this time Reid didn't realize he'd been learning about his own father. Didn't realize how close he'd always been to him. Didn't realize it was him he felt standing at the edge of the woods. Dad said, "And here I thought he was gone for good."

Jack Carlson, gone but not forgotten.

"You don't have to do this," Mom said. "This isn't about Dad. Or me."

"I know." I picked up our plates and took them to the sink. "It's for me," I said. Then I slid on a pair of flip-flops and said, "I'll be back soon."

Then I let myself out the back door and the high gate, walked down the alley and across the road, where no green car waited, and I let myself into Colleen's backyard. Her window was closed this time. And anyway, it's not like she could've gotten up to open it herself.

I knocked on the back door. Her mom opened it and let me in, though she didn't look even remotely pleased to see me. I wasn't sure if that was a new thing or not. I never saw her after Brian died, since Colleen had been grounded and our parents weren't exactly friends, so I wasn't sure if the new anti-Mallory attitude had started back then or if it wasn't until after her daughter left home and almost got killed for me. Either way, I didn't blame her.

She ignored the fact that I was standing in the kitchen with her. It looked like she was fixing a tray to bring to Colleen's room. "Can I take it to her?" I asked.

She waved her hands at it, which I guess was as much civility as she could muster at the moment. I picked up the tray and walked to Colleen's room.

Colleen smiled when she saw me and turned off the television across from her bed. "Room service. What's the occasion?"

"Ha freaking ha," I said, and set it on the dresser so I could put the lap table over her legs. She still had a bandage on her head, but that would heal soon. Her left ankle was in a short cast, and she wiggled her blue toenails at me. "My mom did it for me. It's kinda nice having everyone waiting on me. Except when I have to pee. Then it sucks."

Her right leg was in a full cast. She'd had surgery. She'd walk fine after physical therapy, the doctors promised. But there would be scars. I was there with her in the hospital when they'd told her. I saw her face drop for a minute, and then she flipped her hair over her shoulder. "Bad-ass chicks have scars. Right, doc?"

That poor doctor, who looked like he was barely out of med school, never stood a chance. He blushed and looked away. "Yeah, scars are cool," he'd said. And that's when I knew that Colleen would be fine.

I placed her lunch on the table and said, "So, I need to tell you something."

She took a monstrous bite out of an apple and said, "Go on."

I took a deep breath. "I'm going back to Monroe."

Colleen swallowed the chunk of apple and pounded on her chest, like it wasn't going down on its own.

"You're what?"

"On Monday. I'm going back."

"You don't have to," she said. "Dylan's gone, you know. His mom is gone."

"I know," I said. Which was all there was to say, really. I didn't try to explain that I wanted to move forward—that I didn't want to see the house where he had lived, or the streets that he had walked on. I wanted to focus on the future, whatever comes next, like Reid did.

Colleen took another bite and watched me from the corner of her eye. "You better not be ditching me for some *boy*," she said.

I rolled my eyes and grinned. Like that was even a possibility. "I'm not," I said. "I promise I'm not."

And I wasn't. That day, two weeks earlier, when I stood on the ridge and saw all the paths out of the woods, all the paths I could choose, I saw Colleen in every one.

"I'm mad at you," she said.

"I know," I said. And then I sat beside her while she ate. Colleen and me, we were forever. Moving away wouldn't change that. "Thanksgiving break is only a month away," I said.

"By the way," she said as she chewed, "I like Reid for you."

"Maybe in the next life, huh?"

Colleen passed me the apple. I took a bite and she said, "I'm pretty sure we only get the one."

I rested my head on her shoulder as she ate. And I thought of Krista and Taryn and Bree, who were God knows where. Detention center, or homebound, awaiting trial. Awaiting their fates. I used to think Bree was pathetic for wanting to be part of something, no matter what the cost. But with my head on Colleen's shoulder, I thought I understood.

Mom helped me pack the next day. I dragged my suitcase down the hall and paused in front of my grandma's old room. "Do you ever sense her?" I asked.

Mom jerked her head, like she was unprepared for the question, then shrugged. "Sometimes," she said. "Like if I'm thinking of something we did together. I think the memory keeps her alive."

I nodded and brushed my hand over my shoulder, where the handprint used to be. It had scabbed over. Faded to a faint pink. I could only see the marks if I looked closely. It would be gone soon.

"I'm ready," I said.

This time, my parents drove me all the way up to Monroe. They helped me unload the car and move into Bree's old room, which felt odd, like her presence was left behind. She had left that feeling in my old room, though, too. My old room had been converted to storage, full of things that would soon be forgotten.

Dad patted me on the shoulder and Mom said, "We're staying at the hotel overnight, and heading back really early." Then she pulled me into a hug and said, "Good-bye, Mallory love. Be good."

It was the same thing she'd said to me when she left me at the train station. But this time I wasn't mad. This time I hugged her back, because it felt possible.

I waited until after lights out. People knew I was back. It was the latest secret up for distribution. Though it wasn't a very good one. Nearly everyone knew. Reid had to have known I was back. I didn't know what it meant that he ignored it.

I snuck out my window—Bree's window—and ran across the quad. I knocked on a window on the first floor, and some guy from the soccer team opened the window and flinched. "Let me in?" I said. "I need to see someone."

He looked confused, still half asleep, but he reached a hand down and helped me into his room. "Thanks," I said. And as I left his room, I could imagine all the rumors running through school the next day. The whispers, the secrets. None of them important.

I tiptoed up the flight of stairs and stood outside Reid's door. And I froze.

For some reason, I was thinking of that night on the beach with Colleen, after the fight with Danielle, after we slept on the cold sand. I was thinking of the next morning, of her shaking me awake and the sky looking pink behind her. "Come on," she'd said.

"What?" I'd asked, squinting against the new light.

"Let's go swimming."

And then I was awake. "This is when sharks eat," I'd said. "No thanks."

"There aren't sharks here. Get up!"

"Ever see *Jaws*? There are so sharks here." Then I'd rolled back onto my side.

"Fine. There are sharks. Two. Maybe three. In that whole goddamn ocean. What are the chances?" She'd tilted her head to the side and pulled on my arm, and I knew she knew she'd won.

I looked at the scratch Danielle had left on my arm. "This'll sting."

"Only for a second," she'd said, and I knew she was right. "Unless the sharks smell your blood," she added. "But don't worry. I'll protect you." Then she smiled and showed me her nonexistent arm muscles.

"Well, in that case . . ." I let her pull me up and we ran for the ocean.

And I thought that this moment, in front of Reid's door, felt exactly like that, except I was facing it on my own. Like racing toward uncertainty. Like anything could happen. Anything at all.

I raised my closed fist and knocked gently.

Nothing.

I was about to knock again when the door creaked open. Reid rested against the door frame, the door still mostly closed, blinking back against the light from the hall. He stared at me, his mouth slightly open, his hair god-awful perfect, and shifted his weight to the other foot.

I stared back. And I reminded myself that I was capable of absolutely anything. That I was capable of this. I looked right into his eyes and I said, “I’m sorry.”

He let out a long breath, and he opened the door.

I took a step inside.

I thought again of swimming in the ocean that summer morning. We dove under the first wave, and Colleen had been right. It stung. But just for a moment. And then my head was above water again and I sucked in air and I looked around for Colleen. She was swimming toward me, laughing. The swell from a wave moved around us, and she reached out a hand for me.

And I thought forgiveness felt exactly like that. Like salt water and a moving current and a hand, reaching out for me.

Reid’s fingers brushed mine.

I closed my fingers around his hand and held onto him. For this moment. And the next.

ACKNOWLEDGMENTS

I am especially grateful for the following people who helped turn this idea into a story—and this story into a book:

My agent, Sarah Davies, who sees the big and small of everything—from an idea to a book to a career—and whose guidance I rely on for all of the above.

My brilliant editor, Emily Easton, and the entire team at Walker/Bloomsbury, including Mary Kate Castellani, Laura Whitaker, Katy Hershberger, Kate Lied, Kim Burns, Rachel Stark, Beth Eller, Linette Kim, Nicole Gastonguay, Donna Mark, Emma Bradshaw, and the folks at Bloomsbury UK and Bloomsbury Australia. It's such a pleasure working with you all.

The greatest critique partners a girl could ask for, who are also, coincidentally, great friends: Jill Hathaway, who listens to every idea and reads every sentence, and whose opinion I trust without question; Marilee Haynes, who is willing to read everything I write—always; and Elle Cosimano, whose brilliant insight saved my revision. This book would not be what it is today without their support. And Shelli Johannes-Wells, who reminded me, early on, what kind of book I was writing.

My mother, who talks characters like she knows them and plot points like she's lived them. And my father, who is always willing to babysit so that I am able to write.

Mark Gartner, who answered every hypothetical question (and surprisingly didn't end up blocking my e-mail address), and who also watched over me for the five years I was at his school—and never quite stopped.

Finally, thank you to my family and friends. I am reminded each day of how lucky I am to have you all in my life.

By the time Delaney was pulled from a lake's icy waters by her best friend, her heart had stopped beating. Despite being underwater for eleven minutes, she survives. But at what cost?

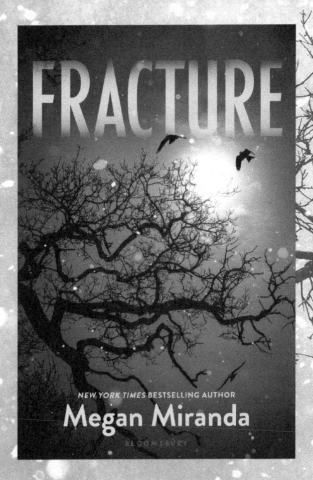

Read on for a glimpse at *New York Times* bestselling author Megan Miranda's thrilling debut.

The first time I died, I didn't see God.

No light at the end of the tunnel. No haloed angels. No dead grandparents.

To be fair, I probably wasn't a solid shoo-in for heaven. But, honestly, I kind of assumed I'd make the cut.

I didn't see any fire or brimstone, either.

Not even an endless darkness. Nothing.

One moment I was clawing at the ice above, skin numb, lungs burning. Then everything—the ice, the pain, the brightness filtering through the surface of the lake—just vanished.

And then I saw the light.

A man in white who was decidedly not God stuck a penlight into each eye, once, twice, and pulled a tube the size of a garden hose from my throat. He spoke like I'd always imagined God would sound, smooth and commanding. But I knew he wasn't God because we were in a room the color of

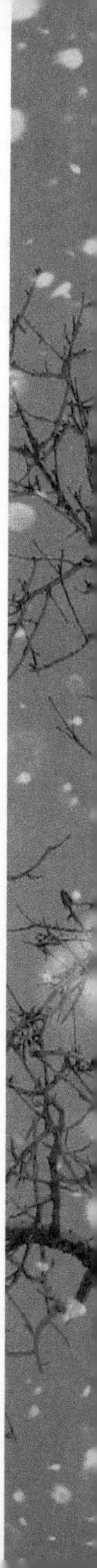

custard, and I hate custard. Also, I counted no less than five tubes running through me. I didn't think there'd be that much plastic in heaven.

Move, I thought, but the only movement was the blur of white as the man passed back and forth across my immobile body. *Speak,* I thought, but the only sound came from his mouth, which spewed numbers and letters and foreign words. Sound and fury, signifying nothing.

I was still trapped. Only now, instead of staring through the surface of a frozen lake, I was staring through the surface of a frozen body. But the feelings were the same: useless, heavy, terrified.

I was a prisoner in my own body, lacking all control.

"Patient history, please," said the man who was not God. He lifted my arm and let it drop. Someone yawned loudly in the background.

Tinny voices echoed in the distance, coming from all angles.

"Seventeen-year-old female."

"Severe anoxic brain injury."

"Nonresponsive."

"Coma, day six."

Day six? I latched onto the words, clawed my way to the surface, repeated the phrase until it became more than just a cluster of consonants and vowels. *Day six, day six, day six.* Six days. Almost a full week. Gone. A stethoscope hung from the neck of the man in white, swinging into focus an inch in front of my nose, ticking down the time.

* * *

Rewind six days. Decker Phillips, longtime best friend and longer-time neighbor, yelled up from the bottom of the stairs, "Get your butt down here, Delaney! We're late!"

Crap. I slammed my English homework closed and searched through my bottom drawer, looking for my snow gear.

"Just a sec," I said as I struggled with my thermal pants. They must have shrunk since last winter. I hitched them up over my hips and attempted to stretch out the waistband, which cut uncomfortably into my stomach. No matter how far I stretched the elastic band, it snapped instantly back into place again. Finally, I gripped the elastic on both sides of the seam and pulled until I heard the tear of fabric. Victory.

I topped everything with a pair of white snow pants and my jacket, then stuffed my hat and gloves into my pockets. All my layers doubled my normal width, but it was winter. Maine winter, at that. I ran down the steps, taking the last three in one jump.

"Ready," I said.

"Are you insane?" Decker looked me over.

"What?" I asked, hands on hips.

"You're not serious."

We were on our way to play manhunt. Most kids played in the dark, wearing black. We played in the snow, wearing white. Unfortunately, Mom had gotten rid of last year's jacket and replaced it with a bright red parka.

"Well, I'd rather not freeze to death," I said.

"I don't know why I bother teaming up with you. You're slow. You're loud. And now you're target practice."

"You team up with me because you love me," I said.

Decker shook his head and squinted. "It's blinding."

I looked down. He had a point. My jacket was red to the extreme. "I'll turn it inside-out once we get there. The lining is much less . . . severe." He turned toward the door, but I swear I saw a grin. "Besides, you don't hear me complaining about your hair. Mine at least blends in." I messed his shaggy black hair with both hands, but he flicked me off the same way he swatted at mosquitoes in the summer. Like I was a nuisance, at best.

Decker grabbed my wrist and tugged me out the door. I stumbled down the front steps after him. We cut through my yard and Decker's next door and climbed over a snow drift on the side of the road. We ran down the middle of the plowed road since the sidewalks were covered in a fresh layer of snow. Correction: Decker ran. I jogged anytime he turned around to check on me, but mostly I walked. Regardless, I was fairly winded by the time we rounded the corner of our street.

When we reached the turnoff, Decker flew down the hill in six quick strides. I sidestepped my way down the embankment until I reached him, standing at the edge of Falcon Lake. I bent over, put my hands on my knees, and gulped in the thin air.

"Give me a minute," I said.

"You've got to be kidding me."

My breath escaped in puffs of white fog, each one fading as it sunk toward the ground. When I stood back up, I followed Decker's gaze directly across the center of the lake. I could just barely make out the movement of white on white. Decker was right. Even if I reversed my jacket, we'd be hopeless.

Under the thick coating of white, a long dirt trail wove through the snow-topped evergreens along the shoreline. Decker traced the path with his eyes, then turned his attention to the activity on the far side. "Let's cut across." He grabbed my elbow and pulled me toward the lake.

"I'll fall." My soles had traction, like all snow boots, but not enough to make up for my total lack of coordination.

"Don't," he said. He stepped onto the snow-covered ice, waited a second for me to follow, and took off.

In January, we skated across this lake. In August, we sat barefoot on the pebbled shore and let the water lap our toes. Even in the peak of summer, the water never warmed up enough for swimming. It was the first week of December. A little soon for skating, but the local ice-fishermen said the lakes had frozen early. They were already planning a trip up north.

Decker, athletic and graceful, walked across the lake like he had solid ground beneath his feet. I, on the other hand, stumbled and skidded, arms out at my sides like I was walking a tightrope.

Halfway across the lake, I slipped and collided into Decker. He grabbed me around the waist. "Watch yourself," he said, his arm still holding me against his side.

"I want to go back," I said. I was just close enough to make out the faces of eight kids from school gathered on the opposite shore. The same eight kids I'd known my entire life—for better or worse.

Carson Levine, blond curls spilling out from the bottom of his hat, cupped his hands around his mouth and yelled, "Solid?"

Decker dropped his arm and started walking again. "I'm not dead yet," he called back. He turned around and said, "Your boyfriend's waiting," through clenched teeth.

"He's not my . . . ," I started, but Decker wasn't listening.

He kept walking, and I kept not walking, until he was on land and I was alone on the center of Falcon Lake. Carson slapped Decker's back, and Decker didn't flick *him* off. What a double standard. It had been two days since I broke Best Friend Commandment Number One: Thou shalt not hook up with best friend's other friend on said best friend's couch. I slowly turned myself in a circle, trying to judge the closest distance to land—backward or forward. I was just barely closer to our destination.

"Come on, D," Decker called. "We don't have all day."

"I'm coming, I'm coming," I mumbled, and walked faster than I should have. And then I slipped. I reached out for Decker even though I knew he was way out of reach and took a hard fall onto my left side. I landed flat on my arm and felt something snap. It wasn't my bone. It was the ice. *No.*

My ear was pressed against the surface, so I heard the fracture branch out, slowly at first, then with more speed. Faint crackles turned to snaps and crunches, and then silence. I didn't move. Maybe it would hold if I just stayed still. I saw Decker's legs sprinting back toward me. And then the ice gave way.

"Decker!" I screamed. I felt the water, thick and heavy,

right before I went under—and then I panicked and panicked and panicked.

I didn't have the presence of mind to think, *Please God, don't let me die.* I wasn't brave enough to think, *I hope Decker stayed back.* My only thought, playing on a repetitive loop, was *No, no, no, no, no.*

First came the pain. Needles piercing my skin, my insides contracting, everything folding in on itself, trying to escape the cold. Next, the noise. Water rushing in and out, and the pain of my eardrums freezing. Pain had a sound; it was a high-pitched static. I sunk quickly, my giant parka weighing me down, and I struggled to orient myself.

Black water churned all around me, but up above, getting farther and farther away, there were footprints—small areas of bright light where Decker and I had left tracks. I struggled to get there. My brain told my legs to kick harder, but they only fluttered in response. I eventually managed to reach the surface again, but I couldn't find the hole where I had fallen through. I pounded and pounded, but the water felt thick, the consistency of molasses, and the ice was strong, like steel. In my panic I sucked in a giant gulp of water the temperature of ice. My lungs burned. I coughed and gulped and coughed and gulped until the weight in my chest felt like lead and my limbs went still.

But in the instant before everything vanished, I heard a voice. A whisper. Like a mouth pressed to my ear. *Rage,* it said. *Rage against the dying of the light.*

* * *

Blink.

The commanding voice spoke. "And today, she's breathing without the aid of the ventilator. Prognosis?"

"At best, persistent vegetative state."

The voices in the background sharpened. "She'd be better off dead. Why'd they intubate her if they knew she was brain dead?"

"She's a minor," the doctor in charge said, leaning across me to check the tubes. "You always keep a child alive until the parents arrive."

The doctor stepped back, revealing a chorus of angels. White-robed men and women hugged the walls, their mouths hanging open like they were singing to the heavens.

"Dr. Logan, I think she's awake." They all watched me, watching them.

The doctor—Dr. Logan—chuckled. "You'll learn, Dr. Klein, that many comatose patients open their eyes. It doesn't mean they see."

Move. Speak. The voice, again, whispered in my ear. It demanded, *Rage*. And I raged. I slapped at the doctor's arms, I tore at his white coat, I sunk my nails into the flesh of his fingers as he tried to fight me off. I jerked my legs, violently trying to free myself from the white sheets.

I raged because I recognized the voice in my ear. It was my own.

"Name! Her name!" cried the doctor. He leaned across my bed and held me back with his forearm against my chest, his weight behind it. And all the while I thrashed.

A voice behind him called out, "Delaney. It's Delaney Maxwell."

With his other hand, the doctor gripped my chin and yanked my head forward. He brought his face close to mine, too close, until I could smell the peppermint on his breath and see the map of lines around the corners of his mouth. He didn't speak until I locked eyes with him, and then he flinched. "Delaney. Delaney Maxwell. I'm Dr. Logan. You've had an accident. You're in the hospital. And you're okay."

The panic subsided. I was free. Free from the ice, free from the prison inside. I moved my mouth to speak, but his arm on my chest and his hand on my jaw strangled my question. Dr. Logan slowly released me.

"Where," I began. My voice came out all hoarse and raspy, like a smoker's. I cleared my throat and said, "Where is—" I couldn't finish. The ice cracked. I fell. And he wasn't here.

"Your parents?" Dr. Logan finished the question for me. "Don't worry, they're here." He turned around to the chorus of angels and barked, "Find them."

But that wasn't what I meant to ask. It wasn't who I meant at all.

Dr. Logan prodded the others out of the room, though they didn't go far. They clumped around the doorway, mumbling to each other. He stood in the corner, arms crossed over his chest, watching me. His gaze wandered over my body like he was undressing me with his eyes. Only in his case, I was pretty sure he was dissecting rather than undressing, peeling back my skin with every shift of his gaze, slicing through muscle and bone with his glare. I tried to turn away from him, but everything felt too heavy.

Mom elbowed her way through the crowd outside and gripped the sides of the doorway. She brought both hands to her chest and cried, "Oh, my baby," then ran across the room. She grabbed my hand in her own and brought it to her face. Then she rested her head on my shoulder and cried.

Her hot tears trickled down my neck, and her brown curls smelled of stale hair spray. I turned my head away and breathed through my mouth. "Mom," I said, but she just shook her head, scratching my chin with her curls. Dad followed her in, smiling. Smiling and laughing and shaking the doctor's hand. The doctor who hadn't even known my first name, who'd thought I would never wake up. Dad shook his hand like it was all his doing.

I worked up the nerve to say what I had meant before. "Where's Decker?" My voice was rough and unfamiliar.

Mom didn't answer, but she stopped crying. She sat up and wiped the tears from her face with the edge of her sleeve.

"Dad, where's Decker?" I asked, with a tinge of panic in my voice.

Dad came to the other side of my bed and rested his hand on my cheek. "He's around here somewhere."

I closed my eyes and relaxed. Decker was okay. I was okay. We were fine. Dr. Logan spoke again. "Delaney, you were without oxygen for quite some time and there was some . . .

damage. Don't be alarmed if words or thoughts escape you. You need time to heal."

Apparently, I was not fine.

And then I heard him. Long strides running down the hall, boots scuffing around the corner, the squeal on the linoleum as he skidded into the room. "What's wrong? What happened?" He panted as he scanned the faces in the room.

"See for yourself, Decker," Dad said, stepping back from the bed.

Decker's dark hair hung in his gray eyes, and purple circles stretched down toward his cheekbones. I'd never seen him so pale, so hollow. His gaze finally landed on me.

"You look like crap," I said, trying to smile.

He didn't smile back. He collapsed on the other side of my bed and sobbed. Big, body-shaking sobs. His bandaged fingers clutched at my sheets with every sharp intake of breath.

Decker was not a crier. In fact, the only time I'd seen him cry since it became socially unacceptable for a boy to be seen crying was when he broke his arm sliding into home plate freshman year. And that was borderline acceptable. He did, after all, have a bone jutting out of his skin. And he did, after all, score the winning run, which canceled out the crying.

"Decker," I said. I lifted my hand to comfort him, but then I remembered the last time I tried to touch his hair, how he swatted me away. Six days ago, that's what they said. It seemed like only minutes.

"I'm sorry," he managed to croak between sobs.

"For what?"

"For all of it. It's all my fault."

"Son," Dad cut in. But Decker kept on talking through his tears.

"I was in such a goddamn rush. It was my idea to go. I made you cross the lake. And I left you. I can't believe I left you. . . ." He sat up and wiped his eyes. "I should've jumped in right after you. I shouldn't have let them pull me back." He put his face in his hands and I thought he'd break down again, but he took a few deep breaths and pulled himself together. Then he fixed his eyes on all my bandages and grimaced. "D, I broke your ribs."

"What?" That was something I would've remembered.

"Honey," Mom said, "he was giving you CPR. He saved your life."

Decker shook his head but didn't say anything else. Dad put his hands on Decker's shoulders. "Nothing to be sorry for, son."

In the fog of drugs that were undoubtedly circulating through my system, I pictured Decker performing CPR on the dead version of me. In health class sophomore year, I teamed up with Tara Spano for CPR demonstrations. Mr. Gersham told us where to place our hands and counted out loud as we simulated the motion without actually putting any force into it.

Afterward, Tara made a show of readjusting her D-cup bra and said, "Man, Delaney, that's more action than I've had all week." It was more action than I'd had my entire life, but I kept that information to myself. Rumors about me and Tara being lesbians circulated for a few days until Tara took it upon herself to prove that she was not, in fact, a lesbian. She proved it with Jim Harding, captain of the football team.

I brought my hand to my lips and closed my eyes. Decker's mouth had been on my own. His breath in my lungs. His hands on my chest. The doctor, my parents, his friends, they all knew it. It was too intimate. Too private, and now, too public. I made sure I wasn't looking at him when I opened my eyes again.

"I'm sorry," Dr. Logan said, saving me from my embarrassment, "but I need to conduct a full examination."

"Go home, Decker," Dad said. "Get some rest. She'll be here when you wake up." And Mom, Dad, and Decker all smiled these face-splitting smiles, like they shared a secret history I'd never know about.

The other doctors filed back in, scribbling on notepads, hovering over the bed, no longer lingering near the walls.

"What happened?" I asked nobody in particular, feeling my throat close up.

"You were dead." Dr. Klein smiled when he said it. "I was here when they brought you in. You were dead."

"And now you're not," said a younger, female doctor.

Dr. Logan poked at my skin and twisted my limbs but it didn't hurt. I couldn't feel much. I hoped he'd start the de-tubing process soon.

"A miracle," said Dr. Klein, making the word sound light and breathy. I shut my eyes.

I didn't feel light and breathy. I felt dense and full. Grounded to the earth. Not like a miracle at all. I was something with a little more weight. A fluke. Or an anomaly. Something with a little less awe.

My throat was swollen and irritated, and I had difficulty speaking. Not that it mattered—there was too much noise to get a word in anyway. I had a lot of visitors after the initial examination. Nurses checked and rechecked my vitals. Doctors checked and rechecked my charts. Dad hurried in and out of the room, prying information from the staff and relaying it back to us.

"They'll move you out of the trauma wing tomorrow," he said, which made me happy since I hated my room, claustrophobia personified in a hideous color.

"They'll run tests tomorrow and start rehab after that," he said, which made me even happier because, as it turns out, I was really good at tests.

Mom tapped her foot when the doctors spoke and nodded when Dad talked, but she didn't say anything herself. She got swallowed up in the chaos. But she was the only constant in the room, so I held on to her, and she never let go of my hand. She gripped my palm with her fingers and rested her thumb on the inside of my wrist. Every few minutes she'd close her eyes and concentrate. And then I realized she was methodically checking and rechecking my pulse.

By the end of the day, several tubes still remained. A nurse named Melinda tucked the blanket up to my chin and smoothed back my hair. "We're gonna take you down real slow, darling."

Her voice was deep and soothing. Melinda hooked up a new IV bag and checked the tubes. "You're gonna feel again. Just a little bit at a time, though."

She placed a pill in my mouth and held a paper cup to my lips. I sipped and swallowed. "To help you sleep, darling. You need to heal." And I drifted away to the sound of the beeping monitor and the whirring equipment and the steady *drip, drip, drip* of the fluid from the IV bag.

A rough hand caressed my cheek. I opened my eyes to darkness and, to my left, an even darker shape. It leaned closer. "Do you suffer?" it whispered.

My eyelids closed. I felt heavy, water-logged, drugged. Far, far away. I opened my mouth to say no, but the only thing that came out was a low-pitched moan.

"Don't worry," it whispered. "It won't be long now."

There was a rummaging sound in the drawers behind me. Callous hands traced the line from my shoulder down to my wrist, twisted my arm around, and peeled back the tape at the inside of my elbow. This wasn't right. I knew it wasn't right, but I was too far away. I felt pressure in the crook of my arm as the IV slid from my vein.

And then I felt cold metal. A quick jab as it pierced the skin below my elbow. And as the metal sliced downward, I found myself. I jerked back and scratched at the dark shape with my free arm. The voice hissed in pain and the hands pulled back and the metal clanked to the floor somewhere under my bed.

Feet shuffled quickly toward the door. And as it opened,

letting in light, I saw his back. A man. In scrubs like a nurse, a hooded sweatshirt over the top.

My eyelids grew heavy and I drifted again. I drifted to the sound of the beeping monitor and the whirring equipment and the steady *drip, drip, drip* of my blood hitting the floor.

MEGAN MIRANDA is the *New York Times* bestselling author of *Fracture, Vengeance, Hysteria, Soulprint, The Safest Lies,* and *Fragments of the Lost,* as well as the adult thrillers *The Perfect Stranger* and *All the Missing Girls.* She spends a great deal of time thinking about the "why" and "how" of things, which leads her to get carried away day-dreaming about the "what-ifs." She lives in North Carolina with her husband and two children.

www.meganmiranda.com
@MeganLMiranda